The Hunters and the Hunted

MARK HOUSTON

Published by MARK HOUSTON, 2020.

THE HUNTERS AND THE HUNTED

First edition. October 30, 2020.

Copyright © 2020 MARK HOUSTON.

ISBN: 978-0995760257

Written by MARK HOUSTON.

ONE

Alexei slammed the door of the apartment the gang used for the honeytraps, trapping the queer inside. On the outside he made sure he came across as his usual confident self; on the inside he sighed with relief that his part was over. He felt the queer's eyes burning into him, accusing him of this betrayal. Avoiding him, Alexei pushed through the crowd of men crammed inside the small room. A few gave him half-hearted claps on the back for delivering yet another successful trap. Most of them didn't. It irked that despite being the honeytrap and key to trapping queers, he wasn't the most popular guy in the gang: too close to the leader for the men's liking; too distant from them for their choosing.

The apartment's windows were closed, to keep the din inside and the gang's activities private. Not that anyone really cared. The closed conditions made it hot and the place reeked of sweat. No one lived here. The paint had long since peeled from the walls, and all it contained was a battered old sofa and a rusty tin bath. Alexei made his way to the sofa and sat down next to the only female in the gang, his sister, the leader. Next to Svetlana was her boyfriend, Maxim, a typical alpha male, brimming with testosterone that forever threatened to spill over, on to friend or foe alike. Alexei leaned back and risked a look at his honeytrap victim. Leo's eyes were blazing with confusion and fright; gone was the thrill of a secret meeting.

Alexei recognised Leo from their Internet chats and sat down next to him by the fountain. The guy acted twitchy. His eyes flitted about, checking out the people in the park, including Alexei. This was the first time they'd met in person. Despite the hours Alexei had spent gaining Leo's trust, he remained cautious. Queers in Russia could trust no one, not their closest friends, not even their family. In finding partners, queers played a dangerous game. People often pretended to be someone else. Alexei was one of those people.

He acted the part of a would be boyfriend and pretended to look around too, as if searching for a quiet place the two of them could be alone. The cool spray from the fountain was welcome under the blazing Moscow summer sun but noisy. Alexei leaned in on Leo so that they could talk privately. He didn't want anyone with big ears getting the wrong idea and denouncing him as gay. 'There's too many people here. Have you anywhere we can go?'

Leo shook his head. 'I live with my family. It wouldn't be possible to take you home.'

'They don't know about you?'

'They wouldn't understand. I have to be careful to keep hidden who I am.' He gave Alexei a searching look. 'We all do, don't we?'

Alexei looked away. 'Have you done this before?'

'Sometimes. Not very often. Too risky.'

'Where do you go?'

'Usually to their place.'

'Is that safe?'

'I never go on the first meeting. Only when I get to know them better.'

'Shame,' Alexei said, breaking the body contact between them. 'I have a place to go. A friend's place. He's away now but will be back tomorrow night. Then the chance will have been lost.'

A toddler lost control of his ball, which Leo caught. He smiled as the boy came over on unsteady legs to retrieve it, handing it back to him and ruffling his hair. Alexei caught sight of Dmitri and Vadim in the distance, glowering and spitting. A number of gang members were spread around the park, hemming in Alexei and Leo. Now physical contact had been made with the prey, he wouldn't be allowed to get away. He would have to go with them, the hard way or the easy way. Alexei ran his fingers through his hair, then smoothed down the front of his jeans. Aware of Leo's eyes following his every move. Showing him what was on offer.

'I can't,' Leo said. 'I just can't.'

'Too bad.' Alexei slowly got to his feet, giving Leo a dejected little smile.

Leo put a hand out. 'Wait. Are you sure you can trust your friend? Will it be safe?'

Alexei sat back down. Leo was hooked. All he now had to do was reel him in. 'My friend doesn't know anything. I've used his apartment before, and he was none the wiser. But if you don't feel safe going there, let's stay here.' Alexei shaded his eyes from the sun and took a squint around the park. With people milling around in every direction, there was no place they could go for a quick fumble.

'No, you're right. It would be safer to go to your friend's place. If you're sure?'

'I'm sure,' Alexei said, meeting Leo's nervous eyes with a steady expression.

Those same nervous eyes were now desperately searching for a way out of the mess he'd got himself into. But there was no way out. The windows were closed to his cries for help, and more than a couple of dozen men, tanked up on beer and hate, stood between him and the door to freedom. Sweat poured out of Leo. He mounted a desperate scramble, trying to force his way through his captors. The men battered him down and ripped the clothes off his back, ignoring his screams. Naked and cowering on the floor, he raised a hand and pleaded for them to stop. They grabbed him and threw him into the tin bath. The men surrounding the tub took out their cocks and pissed on him. The urine got everywhere, in his hair, in his mouth.

When they'd finished, Maxim pushed them out of the way to reach the queer. He punched Leo in the face and screamed at him. 'This is what we do to filthy child molesters.'

'You've got it wrong,' Leo cried. 'I'm not a child molester.'

'We were watching you in the park. How you looked at that little boy. How you touched—'

'I gave him his ball back, nothing more.'

'Is that how it starts? How you get friendly with the innocent, draw them in and then pounce on them to satisfy your sick perversions?'

'I've never touched a child. Never even thought—'

'Liar!' Maxim screamed, spit flying from his lips. 'You queers can't have kids of your own. So you recruit ours. Normal kids. You turn them queer and make them sick.'

Leo opened his mouth to reply but never got the chance. Maxim dragged him from the tub and flung him at the feet of the men crowding around. His body was lost beneath the barrage of fists and feet flying in to punish him.

Svetlana's laughter cut through the male bellowing. 'Don't be so hard on the lady man,' she chided them. 'He's not used to such rough men. You'll upset him.'

The apartment shook with laughter at the slur to the homosexual for not being a real man. Maxim gave him one last kick before heading back to Svetlana on the sofa. He wrapped a beefy arm around her, grinning and kissing her at the same time. His handiwork was left sobbing on the floor, bloodied and beaten. Maxim always pounded along a fine line in punishing the queers. One day he'd go too far.

'Get it out of here,' Svetlana said.

Leo was dragged to the door and thrown naked into the corridor. A trail of his blood was left behind on the floor, like a trophy. His wallet and valuables were taken before his ripped clothes were tossed after him. The other residents wouldn't say anything. They wouldn't want to get involved. They never did. Everyone despised homosexuals. Even soft hearts wouldn't dare risk being seen as sympathetic to their sick cause. The homosexuals themselves dared not risk reporting the gang. Outing themselves to the authorities would only gain them further State-sponsored persecution. The gay hunting was only possible because the police turned a blind eye.

Alexei grabbed a beer and took a big swallow. With the queer gone, the men changed. One minute, savage hunters and the next, like big kids, fooling around with their mates, cracking open beers, joking and play fighting. Considering that the gang only existed to punish queers, it was funny that they spent most of their time in an all-male world. Few of them had girlfriends. The only sex most of these warriors had was in their tiny minds.

Svetlana called for the men to gather round. She checked they were ready for the upcoming journey—tickets, passports, money ... She'd decided she wanted a change of scenery from Moscow and had settled on London, where they could mingle with the considerable expat community and where the large gay scene would provide a limitless supply of victims for the gang to hunt, trap, punish and rob.

Alexei couldn't care less where they went. Here, there or somewhere else were all the same to him. One shit place was much like any other. He did his job, delivered the victims, made his money and kept his mouth shut. Afraid to do otherwise. That was his life. Nothing could change it.

TWO

Travelling in London was like being assaulted, bodies everywhere, people in your face and the non-stop din of voices and traffic. Even the wind from the incoming tube train almost blew Arran away. It was like he'd been sleepwalking through life back in Northampton. In London you either went with the flow or got out of the way. The people that flocked here were on a mission, to do something and to be someone. They were in a hurry and took no prisoners.

A great surge at his back catapulted him on to the tube train at Victoria. He grabbed hold of a side bar to avoid going down. A rowdy crowd of men had caused havoc by forcing their way forward as the train doors opened. They didn't seem to care who they hurt.

Despite their booming voices, Arran couldn't make out what they were saying. They had the look of Eastern Europeans. One of their number with white blond hair and stunning blue eyes was a good looking guy. He was on the outskirts of the group, pressed up against the train doors and looking towards where the other men were pointing, at an ad for a gay dating agency. Arran couldn't read his expression but had no trouble understanding what the other men felt about it. They were mocking the image of two men together, putting their arms around each other, making kissing noises, then roughly pushing each other away and seeming to find the idea absurd. Arran itched to say something but didn't think it would do much good, even if they could understand him. On the way out of the station he noticed the blond guy again, behind him on the escalator. A dark haired girl at his side gave Arran a hostile glare. He turned away.

Arran left the gloom of Vauxhall underground station for bright sunshine. He pulled out the London A-Z guide his mum had given him and checked how to get to his new lodgings. It looked to be only a handful of streets away. He shoved the guide in his pocket and set off walking. A bike swerved around him, the rider shouting for him to *Watch his fucking step*. He grinned, reminded of his mum's warning that London could be a dangerous place and to have his wits about him at all times. Her vision of London was a black hole, where money and people disappeared without trace. He'd smiled

5

away her concern, confident he could look after himself. He crossed the busy main road, went under the bridge and along the street, taking in his new home. Rainbow flags fluttered in the light breeze over many of the shops and bars. A few guys, pressed into tight t-shirts and short shorts, gave him the eye. Gays were more obvious here; blatant, some of them with the eye contact. Finding a boyfriend would be a doddle.

The turn off leading to Boy Lane was marked by a newsagent's shop on one corner and a fancy café on the next. A few customers were sat out under a green canopy, sipping drinks. The back streets had a different vibe, quieter. Tall terraced houses, black railings and black lantern street lighting gave it an old fashioned feel. Farther along, Arran's eyes were drawn to a patch of green, a little park or community garden, somewhere to exercise. He carried on for a couple more streets, then came to Boy Lane. At number 19, he rang the doorbell. Footsteps approached. The door opened on an older lady, curly brown hair and soft brown eyes. She introduced herself as Miss Givens. Dressed in a pinny and slippers, she was a younger version of his late nan, except for the deeper voice. Arran had never met a man that dressed as a woman before. Not in real life, anyway. He wasn't sure how he should react, mention that he'd sussed or just ignore it. He ignored it, for now. The lady led him on a tour of the house before coming to a standstill outside one of the bedrooms. 'This is yours. Over there is Jez's room, and Gregor has the attic. The boys are out, but you'll get to meet them soon enough.'

Arran was relieved that other regular guys would be around that he could get to know. Hopefully, they'd be into the same things as him.

'Welcome to the family,' Miss Givens whispered, on leaving him to his unpacking.

Arran moved around his new bedroom, large, comfortable and neat, like the rest of the house, quickly finding homes for his possessions in his eagerness to put on his running gear so that he could get out to explore the neighbourhood.

He found his way to Kennington Park, according to the sign at the entrance and headed in. At a spot off to one side he found an empty bench and stopped to loosen up with some stretches. He read the gold plate fixed to the bench: In Memory Of Artie Leonard 1930 to 2017. Nice name. And a nice idea, having somewhere to come and chat to a lost loved one. Pity they hadn't thought of that with dad. The sunny park weather had people out in numbers. An old Oriental guy was practising Tai Chi, which looked interesting and was on Arran's list to try. As he set off running, a football came to rest at his feet. He kicked it back to the group of lads having a kickabout, just missing the head of a sunbather, who shot up and gave him a dirty look. He raised an apologetic hand to her before starting laps around the park path. On his second lap, he clocked two guys slipping into the undergrowth. The gasps and moans told him how they were getting on each time he lapped by. Several laps later, one of the guys emerged from the bushes and gave him a cheeky wink. The guy didn't have a blush in him.

Back home, Arran took his usual cold-hot-cold shower, towelled off and wrapped the towel around him. On opening the bathroom door, a face appeared around the doorframe. Arran jumped back, startled to realise it was the same face he'd seen emerging from the park bushes.

'I see we've already met,' the guy said, grinning. 'You must be Arran Rush, our new housemate from Norwich. I'm Jez Truman.'

'It's Northampton,' Arran said, shaking Jez's outstretched hand, 'where I'm from.'

'Right,' Jez said.

Arran headed back to his room. Jez followed, invited himself in and lay down on the bed. Not wanting to appear too uptight, Arran picked up an extra towel and finished drying himself. Jez watched. The guy never seemed to blink. Arran slipped on a pair of undies before dropping the towel from his waist.

'Spoil sport,' Jez said, actually looking sad.

'You must be the local bad boy.'

'That's for me to know and you to find out. Hurry up and get dressed, we're going out. Someone has to take the new boy in hand, take you out, show you off and point out the sights. And that's me, if you have no objections?'

Jez gave Arran the guided tour of Vauxhall, steering him along the narrow pavements by an arm draped over his shoulder. Arran enjoyed the closeness, the heat of Jez's body, the matey feel of their heads drawn together and the stories about gay landmarks. He'd never heard of the supposedly famous Royal Vauxhall Tavern, and the underground gay clubs that had sprung up back in the Nineties were before his time. He did take in all the gay bars, cafes, saunas and shops they breezed by, with the intention of going back to them over the next few days to see if they were hiring. Jez knew the place, seemed to belong here and made Arran want to plant his own roots alongside him in the gay village of Voho.

'I think that now you and I are both here,' Jez said, 'it can be said that Voho has finally arrived and is the premier gay scene in London.'

One look at Jez's face told Arran he was playing with him. He couldn't help laughing anyway. Jez was infectious, picked up quickly and, with any luck, slow to go away. The tour ended when Jez came to an abrupt halt and pointed to the bar sign above them. 'Welcome to the Sanctum.'

Jez led the way in and headed to the bar for drinks. Not one of the poseur glass and mirror bars, Arran liked it, the rough wood flooring, dark green faux leather booths down one side, steps leading to an upstairs bar at the far end and not too loud music playing from a jukebox on the back wall. A dozen or so men were dotted about the bar. He could feel their eyes on him as he made his way to a corner booth. Arran checked out Jez. His unruly hair and cheeky smile were enough to summon the barman from his perch. The follow up routine—leaning in, whispered comments, eye play—tipped the barman's hands into spilling the drinks and he had to top them up. It seemed that Jez acted matey with everyone. The special feeling that had built up in Arran slipped away. Stupid, anyway. They'd only known each other for two minutes flat.

Jez came across with the beers. He slipped into the booth and sat with one leg resting on the seat. The crotch on his jeans was well worn.

'Looks like you're a hit with the barman,' Arran said, his eyes moving above Jez's waist.

'Donny? We flirt all the time. It's a game. Though I suspect he has a secret crush on me.'

Jez struck Arran like London had. Another assault. The lie of his face and lips, the way he moved ... pure sex. His eyes stripped a body naked. 'Jez is an unusual name.'

Jez spread out his arms. 'Do you see a Jeremy here? Jez is me.'

Jez was right, his birth name didn't do him justice. He was different to anyone Arran had ever met. They just didn't make men like Jez in Northampton. Or, Miss Givens, come to that. 'Miss Givens is an unusual, er, woman.'

Jez laughed. 'Where is it you come from? The moon? Have you never met a cross-dresser before?'

Arran felt himself blushing and wished he'd never opened his mouth.

'You haven't, have you? Look, it's no big deal. Miss Givens is a brave woman. She lives the way she wants to live, and you won't meet a kinder, more generous soul. You'll see.' Jez took a swig of beer before asking Arran who he'd insulted to get kicked out of Norwich. 'And don't spare your blushes.'

Arran didn't correct Jez about his home town; too busy racking his brains for some morsel to make a better impression. Only, he didn't have much material to work with. Scout camping trips, where nothing out of the ordinary had happened. Lusting after unattainable straight mates, where nothing at all had happened. Jez yawned and closed his eyes.

'Am I boring you?' Arran said.

'Not at all.'

'You were only pretending to nod off, then?'

'I was en*tranc*ed.'

'I noticed what you did with that word.'

Jez grinned. 'It's just ... well ... did nothing bad ever happen to you?'

'Bad in what way?'

'Oh, I don't know ... like ... you got expelled for seducing your games teacher or your mum found you in bed with Tricky Dicky from next door or you got a big boner in your speedos on the starting blocks at the swimming gala. Anything like that?'

'I never wore speedos.'

'You were naked?'

Jez was taking the piss. Arran sank back into the faux leather. So much for making a big impression. He was boring the pants off Jez. If only ...

'What are you now, seventeen, eighteen?' Jez said.

'I've just turned eighteen.'

'Well, just remember that London is not Norwich and—'

'Northampton.'

'Northampton, then. And not everyone is like you and me. There's some crazy stuff goes on here and some crazy guys doing it. So don't go throwing yourself under the nearest guy just for the thrill of it.'

Arran couldn't decide whether Jez was being serious or not after what he'd heard coming from the park bushes. He smirked as he looked around at the regular looking guys in the bar and then back to Jez. 'You're the nearest guy. Are you trying to tell me something?'

'Not about me.'

'People like you, then?'

'No, I'm not crazy, but I've met plenty who are. Wait until you've been here for a while, you'll see for yourself.'

Great! Jez looked on him as a kid. A wet behind the ears innocent, to be protected. Not a hot stud, to get it on with.

'What do your old ones think about your move to London?' Jez said.

'Dad died, a few years ago.'

'That's tough.'

Arran nodded. He missed his dad. 'Mum re-married not so long ago.'

'Wicked step-dad?'

'Another old story—student falls for teacher. Mum met John on a car maintenance course.'

'So with your mum settled, you thought you'd strike out on your own. And now you're here.'

'And now I'm here, with you.' Arran sought out Jez's eyes and held them for a spell. It was Jez who broke it, asking what Arran had lined up. That's what Jez was like, close one minute, far away the next. Arran shrugged. 'Nothing yet. Though I should be all right. I have enough money to get by until I have a wage coming in.'

'What do you want to do?'

'Pretty much anything—'

'Like the sound of that,' Jez said, leaning into him. Close again.

'To get started,' Arran continued, laughing. 'The plan is to save up enough money for a fitness instructor course. Are you fixed up?'

'Well, you've got the body for it,' Jez said, eyeing Arran's chest. 'Miss Givens texted me and described you as *Chipped from nature*. I see what she means, but to answer your question, I've been at Flesh, another gay bar around the corner, for several years now, assistant manager. It really suits my talents, even if I do say so myself.'

'Insulting people?'

'Making people feel good about themselves and seeing they have a good time, cheeky.'

'Maybe I could get a job at one of the bars.'

'I'll put my feelers out, seeing it's you. Fresh, hunky looking, willing ... There must be something out there with your name on it. Go-go boy, maybe?'

'No chance.'

'You could wear your speedos.'

'I don't wear speedos.'

'Naked, then.'

THREE

Arran slumped back in the chair, dismayed. His CV was young, like him. Even with size 14 font, there was more white space than black ink. Jez's CV was probably jet black, even though he was only two years older than Arran. He would have asked for Jez's help, if not for the certain ridicule he would receive for his Scout badges and achievements. But without them, the page would be nearly blank. Moving from one extreme to the other, he considered his two A-levels in physical education and biology and hoped they didn't make him over-qualified. He was only looking for bar or shop work, to pay the bills and get a foothold on the job ladder. Not that he was jumping the gun. Even though the exam results weren't out until the end of summer, he was sure he would pass. Nevertheless, at his age, the CV shouldn't be overly important. It was only a way of getting a toe in the door. Face to face, he felt confident he could win over employers with his energy and enthusiasm.

He added Tai Chi to his list of hobbies. The old oriental guy he'd seen in the park on his first day in Vauxhall had turned out to be Mr Cheung. One day he'd stood observing Arran's stretching routine, shaking his head, looking troubled and making Arran feel uncomfortable. 'Can I help you?'

'No, but I can help you,' Mr Cheung said.

'What's wrong with what I'm doing?'

'You're doing it all wrong, too quick, too impatient. Let me show you a better way.'

The two began to meet up in the park on a daily basis. Mr Cheung introduced Arran to Tai Chi, teaching him how to breathe and move in a controlled way. Balance in all things was the virtue Mr Cheung extolled to him above all others. Within a few sessions, Arran's running style improved. His core hardened and he lost the side to side sway. He felt really connected to what was happening inside him, as if he could feel all the moving parts. He was hooked. Mr Cheung promised more. With practice, Arran would become the master of his mind as well as his body. Arran was drawn by the mysticism of the martial art, learning techniques thousands of years old, handed down from generation to generation and now to him. Everything he was learning he would channel into his future career in fitness and maybe even make his mark by coming up with a new form of exercise, fusing Eastern and Western techniques. One day he'd be running his own gym and teaching others.

Working from a Rainbow Flag listing of gay bars and businesses in the Vauxhall area, Arran made the rounds, enquiring about job vacancies and dropping off his CV. If he had a job for every time the managers hit on him, he would be working around the clock. But he didn't and was still looking. It was Jez who came through for him. 'I've heard there's a job going at Sydnee's that could be right up your street. Have you done shop work before?'

'Some shelf stacking at the local supermarket through school.'

'There you are then, you're experienced, go for it,' Jez advised. 'In fact why don't you go there this afternoon and strike while the iron's hot?'

Arran stepped smartly down Kennington Lane in a pressed white shirt and black trousers. It struck him how easily the pieces of his new life in Vauxhall were falling into place. He had good digs, new friends and was now closing in on a job. He sighted Sydnee's Big Girls Boutique and read the bold signage, advertising a gilded treasure trove for Cross-dressers, Transsexuals and Transgenders, and the pieces were tossed back up into the sky. He closed his eyes, cursing Jez. When he opened them, he was face to face with a woman like no other. She was another Miss Givens but came from a far more exotic branch of the family. Her hair was bright red, the same colour as the clingy catsuit she was showing off. Her perfume made him cough. She must bathe in it.

'Don't be shy, sweetie. Come on in and be fabulous.' Her voice was rich and husky.

She took Arran's arm and led him into the shop. Pressing the door firmly shut with her back, the look she gave him made his Adam's apple bob about. 'W-e-l-l,' she drew out, 'what can Sydnee do for you today? Don't tell me! Let me guess. Now let me see ... that hard, hard body needs softening. What you need is a bodyformer to give you curves and big breasts.' She escorted him to a big display, where she pulled off a large bodyformer and shoved it into his arms. 'Now for some sexy lingerie to show off that devilishly young flesh. Red or black? Red it is,' she decided, not waiting for his reply. Silky brassieres and knickers were loaded into his outstretched arms and topped off with a red lacy dress and matching bag. She looked down at his feet. 'Size 12?'

Arran, unable to speak, just nodded. With great satisfaction showing on Sydnee's face, she added patent leather high heel boots onto his growing pile. The door bell rang and two burly men entered the shop. Mortified, Arran dropped the mountain of female garments and underthings onto the floor, ran past the open-mouthed men and fled. Sydnee shrieked with laughter and called out for him to come back soon. Her laughter tormented him all the way down the street to Flesh.

Arran was breathing heavily when he entered the bar. The afternoon drinkers stared at him, striding around the bar in search of Jez. He was fuming at the way Jez had made a fool of him. No sign of the joker. Arran collared the barman. 'Where's Jez hiding?'

'No hello or how do you do?' the barman said.

Arran wasn't best pleased to find out Jez was visiting a supplier and wouldn't be back until later. 'Tell him he's dead!' he ordered the barman and then stalked out, ignoring the applause of the punters.

Arran headed back to Boy Lane and told Miss Givens what had happened and how Jez had set him up.

'Oh, that's wicked!' she exclaimed. 'Did you buy anything?'

'No I did not!' What was she implying? Was cross-dressing bloody compulsory in this part of London?

'Well, it's always the quiet ones, so people say.'

Arran went out for a hard run. After taking a cool shower, he went back to Flesh and apologised to the barman. Martin pulled him a beer and nodded his head in the direction of Jez. Someone was with him. A big lady, in red. Strong perfume. She turned and he found himself confronting Sydnee, his tormentor from Big Girls. The penny dropped. 'You two set me up!'

'Sydnee has been giving me the low-down on your taste in ...' Jez coughed. 'I had no idea you were into red lace in such a big way. At least now I'll know what to buy you for Christmas.'

'Enough,' Arran ordered, sitting down at their table.

Sydnee leaned forward, tapping her cheek with her finger. 'Come, give Sydnee a big kiss, just to show there are no hard feelings.'

Arran spent a red-faced couple of hours at their hands. The end came when Sydnee told him the interview had gone well and he was hired.

'Must be your winning personality,' Jez teased.

'We're just kidding,' Sydnee said. 'But, seriously, there is a real job going at Bananas.'

'And Bananas is what?' Arran snorted.

'Well, it's not a fruit dildo company, so don't make a puddle,' Jez said. 'It's a gay bar, a bit off the beaten track, down in the industrial bit.'

'Go down there tomorrow afternoon around three, when it's quiet, and ask for Jason, the manager,' Sydnee instructed Arran. 'Tell him I sent you.'

Jez grinned. 'Wear your red dress for the interview. You'll look a knockout in it.'

'We do hire out,' Sydnee informed him.

'I thought he was bad enough on his own,' Arran groaned. 'Now there's two of you, I'm mincemeat.'

FOUR

From behind the bar, Arran checked out the packed dance floor. How so many guys found their way to Bananas was a mystery. On his first visit for interview, he'd walked up and down Back Street several times before finding the little passage that led to the bar. The wall outside showed only a picture of a yellow banana on a black background, not unlike the Velvet Underground album cover stacked in Denny the DJ's booth. Arran guessed Denny was in his early forties, which explained the retro music he favoured and which the punters revelled in. Each step down into the expansive cellar bar was like stepping back in time—retro music, matt black walls and furniture, even the manager himself. Jason liked to fashion himself in black combat gear complete with a handlebar moustache, like a 70s clone. The interview with him had been a formality. Thank you, Sydnee. Even in this technological age, it was still who you knew that counted. He'd already updated his CV, to make it look more respectable in showing a proper full-time job.

Arran was teamed behind the bar with Serge, who showed him the ropes. He wasn't sure if Serge was shy or standoffish, and it wasn't until Arran had intervened when a punter was giving him grief that the barriers started to come down.

'Thanks,' Serge said, in his Russian accented English. 'English words go out of my head when someone gets in my face like that.'

Once Serge had taught Arran the basics—pulling pints, changing the optic bottles and beer barrels, working the till and glass washer machine—they found time to have a little fun. A game they enjoyed playing was spot the married men. That they all seemed to be called Tony, Steve or Kev was a dead giveaway. One or two of them came on strong, but neither Arran nor Serge wanted to be someone's dirty little secret. Those guys did have a lot of success coming on to the younger ones who came in the bar, new to the gay scene and nervous, by taking them in hand, buying their drinks and flattering them with little comments about their looks.

Bananas attracted people with secrets, up for the anonymous sex and one-night stands on offer. If they had nowhere else to go, they sometimes had sex on the premises, in dark corners or other less pleasant places. That is until Jason went on patrol and kicked them out for lewd behaviour and risking his bar licence.

The Bananas crowd formed a mixed picture. Ethnic groups were well represented—Asians, Orientals, Eastern Europeans. Arran felt for them, born into communities that outright rejected homosexuals. Talk of honour killings of homosexuals to protect the family name circulated. Live openly gay and completely sever ties with family and friends, or live a secret gay life, risk being found out and die. That was their life choices. Arran was glad he wasn't in their shoes. Serge was wary of the Eastern European guys, not trusting all of them to be gay. Suspecting that some might be a bit twisted and looking to bash or rob gay guys, who they saw as easy prey. 'Happens all the time in Russia. Why do you think I'm living here?'

Arran thought Serge a little paranoid. 'This is London, not Moscow. What's the worst that can happen here, a bit of name calling or a slap? Over here some guys pay for that kind of thing.' Laughing at his own joke, he sensed that Serge wasn't convinced.

One night Arran noticed Serge seemed more jittery than usual. Several glasses slipped out of his hands to great cheers from the punters, which caused Jason to stick his head out of the office and threaten to take the breakages out of his wages. During a lull at the bar, Arran asked Serge what was going on with him.

He acted all hush-hush. 'Don't look now, but there's a guy over there who's had his eyes glued to the bar ever since he came in. Hasn't spoken to anyone, except to knock back a few admirers. His accent's like mine. I don't know what he wants or even what he's doing here. It's weird. He's freaking me out.'

Arran took his time to discreetly look over to where a blond guy was peering out of the shadows. His eyes were piercing and locked on Arran, who turned away and moved off to the glass washer machine. He had the strangest feeling he'd seen the guy somewhere before ... But for the life of him he couldn't recall where or when that was. These days every face was a new face. He was meeting new people all the time and couldn't keep track of them all. Now Arran was aware of him, it seemed that every time he looked up the guy's eyes were on him.

Serge noticed it too. 'He's checking you out.'

'It's a gay bar.'

'Exactly! That's what gay guys do. But he's only interested in you and no one else. That's odd.'

'Cheers, mate.'

'He's marked you out. I've got a bad feeling about him.'

'Marked me out for what?'

'Look,' Serge said, indicating with his eyes towards the blond. 'He's on his phone. He'll be on to the ones he works with, telling them he has someone in his sights. They'll be on their way down here. You need to be very careful when you leave here. They could be waiting for you outside.'

'To do what?'

'These villains are up for anything, beat you up, take your money, abduct you or even kill you.'

'You're being a little fanciful, don't you think?'

A big guy, pushing his way through to the bar and yelling for their attention, interrupted their conversation. 'You're not paid to stand around gossiping. Get me a beer and be quick about it.'

Arran held his stare. 'You're not our boss and we are working, damned hard.'

The guy looked none too pleased at being answered back. 'Just do your job and hold the Smart Alec remarks.'

Arran pulled the beer and placed it in front of the man, who slapped money down on the bar and left without waiting for his change. Arran gave Serge a look that commented on how rude some customers could be as he rang up the sale. He threw the change into the tips jar and got on with stacking the clean glasses. When he looked up, the blond guy had disappeared.

The clean up at the end of the night seemed never-ending. When finally they finished and went to leave the bar, Serge held Arran back with his arm before leaning forward and checking up and down the dimly lit passageway. Only then did he allow him to continue. Nobody was about, and the only sound was their footsteps echoing down the old cobbled streets. On both sides they were overshadowed by huge warehouses and manufacturing sweatboxes. The area was a warren of narrow roads that modern delivery wagons struggled to negotiate. Arran had flattened himself against a wall more than a few times to let one pass and had the tricky job of directing the beer wagon to the rear of Bananas on delivery days. Now, in the dead of night, they could walk safely down the middle of the deserted streets. Arran was amused by Serge's paranoid antics and chatted away to soothe his frayed nerves, asking him about his life back in Russia. Only minutes into the telling and Arran understood much of Serge's nervous concerns. A sudden rush from a nearby alleyway slammed into them. Arran was knocked to the ground, taking Serge with him. Before Arran could roll away, a ten ton weight landed on him, driving the air from his lungs. Rocking from side to side, he dodged the sluggish punches aimed at his head. Stale beer blasted his face as the fat man on top laboured to keep him down. Serge grabbed the guy's head and wrestled with it. The shift in weight allowed Arran to shove the man off. He got to his feet and targeted the fat guy's gut. A series of punches put him down. Rolling him over onto his back, they saw it was the angry punter from the bar. He found his voice and started yelling at Arran, calling him an arrogant, lazy fuck. But he was a spent force.

Arran bent over to ease the pain in his ribs and sucked in much needed air. The guy was floundering on the floor like an overturned beetle. Off to the side, the shadows moved.

Someone was watching.

Arran grabbed hold of Serge and staggered off down the street before they attracted further trouble.

FIVE

Alexei left Nikolay and Pavel to continue setting up the computers for the online honeytrap and joined the others in the living room. The gang had managed to find a large enough place to house them all, more than a couple of dozen men. The rent worked out cheap since there were only two tenants named on the rent book. Alexei plucked a beer from the booze mountain in the corner and took a swig, screwing up his face as he swallowed the beer to mask his irritation at the nature of the conversation going on. The never-ending tirade against homosexuals. The men never seemed to tire of it. They loved nothing better than thinking up new ways to punish and humiliate queers, the ways becoming ever sicker and more depraved.

Svetlana joined in the rant. 'Sissy guys are disgusting and against nature.' She shuddered. 'They need putting in their place. I hate them. I can't believe this soft country allows these filth rights and privileges as if they were normal people. Foreigners can say what they like about Russia, but at least we do not allow perverts to flourish. Russia knows exactly what to do with their kind. Crush them!'

The sound of beer cans being crushed and flung at the bin in the corner filled the room.

'How are Nikolay and Pavel getting on?' Svetlana asked Alexei, who nodded his head until he'd emptied his mouth of beer. 'They nearly have the computers set up. Then they'll work on putting the precautions in place and ensure nothing can be traced back to us.'

'They know what they're doing and won't take any chances. The West takes homosexuals more seriously than Russia. The last thing we need is for some sissy to go complaining to the authorities, be taken seriously and an investigation started. We can have a good time in London, hunting perverts and bleeding them dry.'

A big roar erupted when Maxim dived on Pyotr and the nightly wrestling contests began. The men formed a circle around the two, clapping and cheering them on. The young Pyotr was wiry and agile and kept slipping out of Maxim's grasp. Maxim baited him, saying, 'Come nearer, boy. You're not frightened, are you?' His arm muscles rippled as he readied himself to pounce. With their eyes locked on each other, they circled, feinting moves and drawing back, trying to engineer an opening. Pyotr's only chance was to keep on the move. Maxim's permanent grin and Pyotr's twitchy eyes made for a cat playing with a helpless mouse spectacle. Then, in a flash, it ended with Pyotr caught in a bear hug. Once more the victor, the smiling Maxim let him go and sent him off with a ruffle of his hair.

The winner was the champion and could pick his next opponent. Maxim picked Alexei, who lost a breath at the sound of his name being called out. The contests were opportunities for the alpha male to show his dominance, test the underlings and suss out their weaknesses. While Maxim waited for Alexei to make up his mind, he stripped off his t-shirt. The catcalls and jeers from the men only stopped when Alexei took off his own top and threw it on Maxim's. Across the circle, Maxim was all rippling muscle and near naked. Alexei hoped his body wouldn't betray him.

Maxim crouched low, dancing about, searching for a weakness in Alexei's defence. Taking the initiative, Alexei dived in with a legsweep to take Maxim down. Then pounced on his back. Maxim bucked and rolled, trying to shake him off, his skin smooth and cool to the touch. Already Alexei's skin was hot from riding the three hundred horsepower body. Maxim rolled and grabbed Alexei from behind, pressing into him. The feel of Maxim's groin grinding into his butt disturbed Alexei's concentration. Reacting to calls of *pussy* and *limp dick*, he twisted around and used a knee to heave Maxim over, his body slapping onto the ground, to the cheers of the men crowding in. Then Alexei dove on top of Maxim and wrestled to pin him down. Rolling around the carpet, their bodies melded together, skin on skin. Maxim's hands were all over Alexei's body. He could have sworn that Maxim was turned on. He wasn't the only one. Alexei was struggling to keep control himself. They slithered over each other's sweat oiled skin, trying to find purchase for a winning move. Maxim's hot breath was in Alexei's ear. 'You've grown stronger.'

Through gritted teeth, Alexei said, 'That's right. Careful I don't take you down this time.'

Maxim roared and Alexei immediately regretted baiting him. A hand between Alexei's legs levered him over, landing on his back with a thud. Before he could roll away, Maxim slammed down, driving all the breath from his body. Alexei's attempt to slither away was halted, caught in a headscissors. With his head gripped by Maxim's powerful thighs, Alexei was done. He slapped the carpet in surrender.

Maxim climbed to his feet with his arms raised in triumph, like a Russian warrior of old he thought he was, acknowledging the cheers of the men. Alexei lay panting on the ground, Maxim's overpowering scent all over him.

*

His name was Kenny. Probably not his real name. Alexei introduced himself as Alex while examining Kenny's pale face. Hungry little eyes peered back at him. It was down to Alexei to make sure the guy fitted the gang's target profile. Only then would he lure him into a honeytrap.

First and foremost, the gang were gay hunters. Their mission, to punish homosexuals. They liked young guys. Young guys took risks, believing they were invincible. Only too late did they come to realise they weren't. Alexei had heard many of their stories. How they moved to the city to escape dull lives in the towns and villages or to escape the bullies making their lives a misery. How they moved around to pick up work. This nomad existence made them isolated and easy to befriend. The targets were in work, bringing in a wage and maybe had savings in the bank. The money was an additional perk. Seldom scooping outrageous amounts at any one time, they still had made a good living from all the queers trapped over the last few years. The queers and the money just kept rolling on and would continue to do so in London. All Alexei had to do was pick the right victim.

'What do you do Kenny?'

'Admin by day and a barman at night. A gay bar—'

'Really? Which one, maybe I'll know it?'

'You won't. It's not on the beaten track.'

'Try me.'

'Maybe when we get to know each other better.'

Alexei understood the need to be cagey. He could bide his time; they all talked to him in the end. He would take his time to build up a picture of the target and to check and re-check his story. They almost always lied about themselves. It seemed that entry into the virtual world of the Internet gave them a passport for telling lies. Alexei was now eighteen and had been setting honeytraps since he was fifteen. He knew all the little tricks to trip up the liars and determine the truth.

'You like to hold back, don't you, Kenny? Tease me a little, keep me keen?'

'No, it's not like that.'

'Sure it is,' Alexei said. 'Don't be coy, I like it. Really, I do.' He gave Kenny a reassuring smile to settle him down and then kicked back in his chair. 'Now you've got me interested, I want to know all about you.'

SIX

Arran, high on the sweet smell of burning pumpkin, tripped back to childhood Northampton, collecting firewood for Guy Fawkes' night with his mates, and making plot toffee and Parkin gingerbread cake with his mum. Those times seemed a long way away.

A thunderous bang and a shower of colour in the blackened sky snatched his attention. The night was perfect for Miss Givens's Halloween dinner party. He left the porch and found her in the living room, shivering. Wearing an old floaty dress and pale haunting makeup, she looked perfectly in keeping with the dark decorations surrounding her. 'Are you cold?'

Miss Givens looked up from where she was setting out cutlery on the dining table. 'No, it's the living room transformed into a satanic salon that gave me the chills.'

Darker than Arran was used to, the only light came from candles and the fire, the flamelight licking at demonic looking witches, ghosts and ghouls lurking in the shadows. He picked up a knife from the black tablecloth covering the dining table and turned it over in his hand. Cold to the touch, it had a mother of pearl skeleton inlaid into the handle. A small army of skeletons were lined up around the table. A pair of silver candelabra stood on guard at either end, with red candles dripping molten wax. The hairs on the back of Arran's neck were prickling nicely. Strange how a familiar place made unfamiliar had the power to unnerve a body. 'You've done a great job. It looks hellish.'

'My mother was one for superstitions. She'd watch like a hawk to make sure no one went from the dining table leaving their knife and fork crossed. And putting shoes, even new ones in a box, on the table wasn't allowed. When we were out, she'd always salute a magpie, which earned her some funny looks. I mocked her then, but I must have inherited her superstitious nature because to this day I never have my hair cut on Friday the thirteenth. Now I find myself hoping I haven't set up the house to receive negative vibes with all this dark paraphernalia.'

'Don't worry, I think it only works if you believe in them. I heard that in a movie.' Did her Halloween disguise also come from a movie? Arran was careful to compliment her before asking who she was meant to be.

'Don't tell me you've never heard of Miss Haversham?'

He had the feeling he should have.

'She's from Great Expectations, a book by Charles Dickens. There are lots of film versions.'

He shook his head.

'Well, I suppose you're more the outdoor type. Is that why you've come as Robinson Crusoe?'

Arran opened out his arms to present a tattered jean jacket and jeans, ginger tufts sprouting from his ears and pointy plastic canine teeth. 'I'm Teen Wolf.'

Miss Givens shook her head.

'I felt sure you'd recognise me. It's a character in an old comedy horror movie from way back.'

Miss Givens gave him a withering look before gliding off into the kitchen, from where came the clash of pots and pans. Arran hoped he hadn't upset her.

A knock at the door preceded the entrance of Harry Potter, aka Serge, who had captured the young Potter perfectly by spiking his hair and wearing the familiar little round glasses. The zigzag on his forehead was a dead giveaway. When Dumbledore arrived, he and Harry Potter stood gaping at each other.

'Russians must think alike,' Arran said. 'Gregor, meet Serge.'

Arran played waiter while the two countrymen got to know each other. Dumbledore suited Gregor's studious nature down to the end of his wispy beard. Chatting and sipping at their drinks, Arran saw them slipping him the odd quizzical look and was afraid he'd made a mistake with this old movie character. He'd just happened to catch the movie on TV late one night recently and thought it would be easy to copy, as dressing up wasn't really his thing. Sydnee didn't help matters, breezing in after her trademark perfumed entrance and bluntly asking him who he was supposed to be.

'Teen Wolf,' Arran groaned through his pointed teeth, thoroughly dispirited now.

Mercifully, Sydnee's attention had shifted. She was embracing Miss Givens like an old friend. Then they chatted and complimented each other's costume. There was no mistaking this black and white version of Sydnee. The stuffed Dalmatian dog squashed under her arm clinched it. She was the image of Cruella de Vil, complete with the imperious demeanour. Arran continued to play waiter and served her up a Transylvanian red wine in a black goblet. The rising murmur of conversation was deadhalted by the arrival of Jez, fashionably late. Arran's mouth dropped open at the sight of him wearing next to nothing. He had horns sprouting from his head, sparkly trunks barely covering his necessities, leather lace up boots, a silky cape and was holding a devil's pitchfork. All in red. He made the perfect sexy Red Devil.

With everyone present, Miss Givens called for them to take their places around the satanic table and served up tomato soup with floating bread eyeballs. Arran had been intrigued by how she and Sydnee had greeted each other. 'How do you know each other?'

'From way back in the Nineties,' Miss Givens said.

Arran burned red, like the soup.

'I'd just set up shop,' Sydnee said, 'because back then it was difficult for cross-dressers to find the outsize garments and lingerie they needed. I fancied myself as a designer and needed someone with a sewing machine to run up the designs for me. A friend told me about a wonderful seamstress she knew, who turned out to be Miss Givens. We teamed up and Big Girls blossomed.' Sydnee reached over to Miss Givens and squeezed her hand. 'We had such fun in those early years, when Miss Givens did her sewing in the shop. We used to roar laughing at the faces passers-by would pull in trying to make sense of Big Girls. We saw them all, from the disbelieving housewife, the snarling little punk and the outraged vicar to the dawdling take a sly peek labourer. We were saved and prospered on the backs of the brave souls who dared to venture in. Even if the gamble had failed, we could have got jobs as window cleaners, the number of mornings we had to scrub the windows of the messages left for us overnight. Really original insults, like *Sod off back to Gomorrah, cocksuckers* and *You're going to Hell*. Nothing we didn't do or suspect already.'

'Speak for yourself,' Miss Givens said, laughing.

'I had no idea you knew each other,' Arran said. 'It's a small world.'

'More like the United Nations around this table,' Jez said, with a nod to Gregor and Serge. 'What did you do for Halloween back in Russia?'

'It was never a Russian custom,' Gregor said. 'Even now it's frowned upon as a sign of Westernisation.'

'Apart from the dressing up, do you know what Halloween is all about?' Miss Givens said, bringing out to the table ribs and coffin-shaped baked vegetables covered in a dark sauce.

Gregor and Serge shook their heads.

'Halloween is the night of All Hallows Eve when, so tradition tells, the souls of the dead pass over to the Other Side and ghosts, fairies and demons mingle with the living. The ghastly get-ups frighten off these evil spirits let loose from Hell, and humour is used to mock the Bringer of Death.'

Arran wasn't feeling particularly humorous when it was his turn to greet more of the trick or treaters that kept knocking at the door. One of them asked him who he was meant to be and almost had the treats wrenched back out of his hands.

Miss Givens revealed again her superstitious nature by resisting to put their names on the shortbread gravestones that went with the graveyard cake for dessert—chocolate sponge covered in hot chocolate sauce. Not wanting to tempt Fate, she had settled for RIP in chocolate piping. 'I know we're all either too young or too good to die, but I didn't want to take any chances.'

After that the party really got started. Arran put on a music compilation Denny the DJ had made up for him that he promised was pure evil. The retro sounds—*Somebody's Watching Me*, *Psycho Killer*, *Nightmare On My Street*—got them on their feet. The drinking and dancing continued for hours until one by one they flagged. When the clock on the mantelpiece chimed midnight, Jez had an idea ...

SEVEN

KEEP OUT, ordered the sign on the huge wooden gate. Kenny didn't have Alexei down as a rule breaker. Neither was he. 'Are you sure we should be here?'

Alex was straining to hold the gate open and gestured for Kenny to hurry through into the building site. He hesitated for only a second before heading inside. Alex joined Kenny, taking his arm and guiding him towards a big black crow looming in the distance. Closer up, Kenny made out a half-built building shrouded in scaffolding. The attached heavy plastic curtains were flapping around in the swirling wind. Alex led them to a dark metal door. Kenny couldn't hear anything coming from inside the building, no conversation, no music ... Nothing. 'Wait a minute.'

Alex paused, his hand gripping the handle.

'The party's in there?' Kenny said, dubiously.

'It's Halloween. Didn't I promise you something different? You've got to trust me.'

Alex pulled on the handle and slid open the door. Kenny searched Alex's face for signs of something amiss and found nothing. He couldn't believe badly of Alex. Not when they'd spent so much time getting to know each other. He did trust him. He stepped inside. Behind him, the door careered along its tracks and closed with a crash.

Alex slipped on a Halloween mask as the music was turned up. Kenny let out the breath he hadn't realised he'd been holding. The party must have been going on for some time, judging by the heavy odours of beer, smoke and sweat souring the air. Alex hadn't lied. This party was really Halloween—shooting flames, pulsing tribal rock, men in masks. They should get a beer. He looked for Alex. He'd disappeared. Probably had the same idea and gone to find the bar.

Kenny set off to find Alex, moving towards where the bulk of the men were congregated, weaving his way through the crowd and ducking the flailing arms of the dancers. It struck him that something was wrong when the arms started connecting with him. Bewildered, he thrust out his arms to defend himself against striking fists. Shouts and screams bounced off the walls, the words distorted by the grotesque masks the men wore. Big ugly words ... *COCKSUCKER* ... *FAGGOT* ... *QUEER* ... He must be wrong. What they were saying didn't make sense. Alex had said they were coming to a gay Halloween party.

Liar! What was going on?

Kenny had to get out of here and lashed out at the men attacking him. His feeble strikes were no match for the battery of fists that sent him crashing down among a horde of legs. He thrashed about on the beer soaked ground, trying to avoid the kicks and stamps to his head and body. He searched for a way out of the darkness. There was no escape. At every turn boots blocked his way, landing on his ribs and back, crushing his fingers, making him scream. Pain exploded all over his body. He made himself small and prayed he would make it out alive.

After what seemed like a lifetime, the attack died down, the boots shuffled away and light entered. Kenny raised his head and was surprised to see a woman in a witch mask, lounging on a pile of sacks. A man in a wolf mask lay beside her. He was glaring at Kenny, his eyes painful to look at. The Witch got up and slunk towards Kenny. She sank down on one knee and softly stroked his cheek with the back of her hand. Hope rose in Kenny that everything was going to be all right. He'd just been the victim of some stupid joke.

'Don't be afraid,' the Witch said to him. 'Just tell us what we want to know and then you can go. Okay?'

Kenny nodded, willing to do anything to escape this nightmare.

'Are you a homosexual?'

Fear clogged his throat and he couldn't speak.

'We don't have anything against them. We just want to know about you. Are you a homosexual?'

Kenny nodded.

'Say it!'

He started at the harsh rise to the Witch's voice. 'I'm a homosexual,' he whispered.

'Louder.'

'I'm a homosexual.' Louder this time, his voice cracking with the strain.

'Stand up.'

Sore from the beating, Kenny moved slowly. The Wolf flew off the makeshift sofa and laid into him. Kenny cried out, pleading with the vicious animal to stop.

'Don't kill him,' the Witch said, gently, as if the man was rubbing too hard at a stain on delicate fabric.

The Wolf punched Kenny one last time before stepping away. Kenny struggled up, pleading with the Witch to let him go. She slapped him across his face. 'Stop your whining and strip.'

Kenny couldn't believe what he'd heard and gave her a quizzical look.

'Strip,' she yelled, pulling at his clothes. 'Strip.'

The Wolf made a move towards him, so Kenny started to take off his clothes. Soiled and stinking of beer and stuck to him, he whimpered with pain when peeling them from his trampled flesh. He felt foolish taking off his clothes in front of all the hostile men, glaring at him, like he was filth.

'Dance while you strip,' the Witch told him.

The music was cranked up. Too fearful to disobey, Kenny jerked his arms and feet to the strange beat. Laughter rang in his ears as he removed his shirt and trousers. A bottle hit him on the temple, opening up a cut. Blood trickled down into his eyes. He hoped he'd done enough for them to let him go.

'Take off everything,' the Witch said.

Too frightened to be embarrassed, Kenny stepped out of his underwear and stood naked before the crowd. The men laughed and pointed at his shrunken cock. The Wolf called him a cocksucker and ordered him down onto his knees. Kenny did as he was told and knelt on the cold concrete floor, looking up into the Wolf's eyes and seeing an evil glint. The Wolf raised a bottle of vodka to his lips, took a long swig and then poured the rest over Kenny's head. The alcohol stung Kenny's cuts and set his eyes on fire. He whimpered and rubbed at them, which only made the burning worse. He spat into his hands and bathed his eyes. The men laughed at his suffering, calling him a filthy pervert and a paedophile, and saying he deserved to die.

'We're going to make you into a Gay Fawkes,' the Wolf said, 'and burn you on a bonfire.'

He struck a match.

EIGHT

The clock struck midnight. The witching hour. Jez suggested they each tell a ghost story.

By the time it came to Gregor's turn, the fire had died down and the shadows lengthened. 'In a land far from here, everyone is equal but some are less equal than others. Citizenship and freedom, tolerance and support can be given. They can also be taken away. This is a true story, a human story and you should pray it never happens here ...'

The whistling of a rocket, sounding perilously near, silenced Gregor. On and on went the whistling ... Getting ever closer ... Almost on them ... Everyone looked over their shoulder, waiting for the explosion ... When it came—elsewhere—audible relief sounded in the room.

'I love Halloween,' Miss Givens sighed, 'but I don't want my windows putting through.'

With the threat over, Gregor cleared his throat. All eyes turned back on him. 'Every year at midnight, on the anniversary of his own death, a ghost appears and stands at the foot of his lover's bed. The ghost wears death makeup and a stained, ragged nightgown. His lover knows why he's here. Their story is one he can never forget ...'

I was given the name Denis at birth, the youngest of three brothers. Somehow I was perceived of as different—a little quieter or more sensitive, maybe—and picked on by my brothers and the other kids in the neighbourhood, and pushed further into my shell. Bullying became a way of life. I found solace in books and music, which only served to alienate me further from the other kids. When I did venture outside, I always ran the risk of a beating and a bloody nose.

After yet another beating, a youth, only a year older than me but more experienced, offered a tissue to clean off the blood. That was the start of our friendship. Stephan took me to the local gym and taught me how to take care of myself. He showed me how to build up my strength by lifting weights and taught me a few defence moves. I never would be a fighter, but I changed from being quiet to quietly confident and stood up for myself against my tormentors. Life became bearable.

I worshipped Stephan. When he confessed his feelings for me, I was both overjoyed and terrified, knowing the trouble that being different in any way could bring. Despite the risk, we became lovers, talked of running away to the West, listened to a little transistor radio to improve our English and made plans for the future. Life was the best it had ever been for both of us. But dark days lay ahead.

Unbeknown to me, Stephan had been involved with an older man for some time. This man had got careless and his sexuality had been discovered. He was reported to his employer, who dismissed him. His home was vandalised. Ruined, financially and socially, he took his own life. His abusers took the opportunity to ransack his apartment and steal his possessions. Recklessly, Stephan had allowed the man to take a couple of nude photos of him. They were found and he was recognised. Confronted by a mob of hate filled youths and chased down the streets where we lived, Stephan ran for his life and was hit by a tram. He died two days later.

I was left alone. Distraught. Stephan was the love of my life. I finished school one year on and then fled to the West. Just as we'd planned.

'Denis shrank beneath the bedclothes as the ghost of his dead lover, Stephan, picked up his ragged gown and revealed the horrors beneath. A body crushed and mangled by a speeding tram. Ugly black stitching was straining to hold back a bulging abdomen. Foul stenching dark liquid oozed from the ragged wound. What was left of his manhood was dangling by a thread of bloodless skin. Denis screamed into the cruel night.'

At his final words, Gregor bolted upright, startling everyone and drawing a gasp from Miss Givens. 'Don't worry, I'm sure all of us are safe here,' he said as a single tear cut a path down his cheek like a scar.

NINE

On hearing the match struck, Kenny scrambled to his feet in a panic. Half-blinded by vodka, he stumbled about ... Running into hands, pushing him back ... Tearing off in a different direction ... And finding more hands, slapping him down ... Hands everywhere ... And laughter, at his feeble efforts to escape.

Lots of matches were struck, the stink of sulphur filling the air. The men flighted the lighted matches at Kenny like darts. They flew in from all sides, landing on his body and hair, singeing him. Kenny shrieked and flapped about, swatting away the matches before they could set the vodka on fire. Frightened out of his wits, he jerked about like a lunatic. All around him, the men were collapsing from laughing so hard.

The Wolf grabbed Kenny's hair and forced him to kneel in the middle of the room. He ordered Kenny to repeat what he said:

I am a dirty filthy animal not fit to live alongside decent men
I am a dirty filthy animal not fit to live alongside decent men
I am a dirty filthy animal not fit to live alongside decent men ...

Kenny chanted the ugly mantra while the men partied around him, knocking back vodka and beer, smoking and dancing. Those needing a piss took out their cocks and pissed on him. When the piss ran down Kenny's face and entered his mouth, they pissed themselves again, barking with laughter. Zipping up, they spat on him and called him disgusting.

London had always felt safe. Where had these monsters come from? Kenny cursed his own stupidity for letting this happen to him. After always playing safe, he'd risked everything with one lapse in judgement that had put him in this situation—he had trusted Alex. Nice, genuine, tempting Alex. But Alex had only been pretending to be gay. The face of a gang that ensnared gay men to ... Kenny stared at the men with rising terror. With their masks now removed to drink and smoke, he could see their faces. They didn't seem to care if he saw them. They didn't care because they were never going to let him leave.

They meant to kill him.

Kenny was going to die in this filthy hole. His mum and dad might never know what had happened to him. They'd be so worried. Tears burned from his eyes and streaked down his face. Something hit him. He flinched. Looking down, he saw a bundle of clothes. His clothes. He looked up into the face of the man who'd thrown them. Pure hatred glared back.

'Get dressed, you piece of filth.'

Kenny rose on shaky legs and hastily dressed. Were they really going to let him walk? Or was this another one of their sick jokes?

They took Kenny to a bank cashpoint, where he gave up his bank card and PIN number. He didn't care about the money. All he wanted was to be free of these madmen. A few of them disappeared, returning with bagloads of stuff from the shops. They drove the car to a deserted spot and bundled Kenny out. Left him with threats ringing in his ears about what they'd do if he went to the police. They knew all about him, his name and where he lived. He lay at the side of the road, sobbing. Grateful to be alive.

*

Several days later, when Kenny felt strong enough to leave his flat, he went to the police and told them how he'd been trapped, beaten and robbed. They asked how he'd managed to end up in that situation. He gave them a description of Alex, the man he'd met online and told them of the arrangement to meet up for a Halloween party. He couldn't tell them where the party had been held, as he'd been blindfolded, to make it a surprise. He could tell from the way the officers dealt with him that they thought he was stupid for trusting a man he knew next to nothing about. He should have known the police wouldn't help him. It was clear they thought he'd brought the whole mess on himself. He left the police station feeling completely alone.

He wanted to go home and see his mum and dad but couldn't let them see him in this state. Anxious and vulnerable, he went to see his doctor, who listened for several minutes before dismissing him with anti-depressant pills to help him sleep. Even as the physical signs of his ordeal subsided, the nightmares continued. His weight dropped; he had no appetite. He kept the curtains to the outside world closed and avoided leaving his flat. His employers were unsympathetic, pushing him to return to work. No one cared. The whole rotten business left him feeling suicidal.

He prayed that no one else would fall victim to the gang and be put through the same hell. A forlorn hope. Those depraved monsters were free to carry on their vicious homophobic activities because no one was concerned enough to stop them.

TEN

Vast swathes of glistening white marble, rays of light filtering down from a high glass dome, and men huddled together and speaking in hushed tones, the cavernous chamber seemed more like a church than a Russian Baths in the East End of London. And not the kind of place Arran would have associated with Jez. It seemed almost disrespectful that they were near naked, dressed only in flimsy white towels. Jez's invitation for Arran to spend the day with him had come out of the blue, and he'd given nothing away of the agenda: 'It's a surprise.'

Jez nudged Arran. A grizzled looking old man in the middle of the chamber was beckoning Arran to come forward. The man sat him on a worn wooden stool on a raised circular platform, like an altar, and then used a massive mitten worn on his right hand to scrub him down, moving methodically around him, washing his arms and legs, then chest and back, before rinsing him off with water from a battered metal jug. After Jez had been scrubbed and rinsed they headed out of the chamber.

'My skin feels electric,' Arran said. 'What's next?'

'The sweat boxes.'

'Nice. You trying to electrocute me? Water and electrickery shouldn't mix.'

'Ha, bloody, ha,' Jez said. 'Don't worry, you've survived worse shocks to the system.'

'I have?'

'London ... Sydnee ... Me!'

'I have.' Arran's laughter dissolved in the hot mist swirling inside one of the steam rooms that Jez shoved him into. The two edged their way along, bumping into legs and standing on toes and apologising to unseen bodies, until their eyes adjusted to the semi-dark and revealed acres of naked male flesh sweating it out on the shelves in this men only world. They claimed a stretch of free shelf alongside the rock chamber.

'This is hot,' Arran said, flinching from the heat of the marble shelf on his bare skin and tucking the towel under his leg.

'This is the least hot,' Jez said. 'The idea is to work up to the hottest steam room so that you gradually open up the body's pores. It's supposed to be more effective that way.'

Arran patted the blond mat of hair plastered to his head. 'It's working, already.'

'How's Bananas working out?' Jez said.

Arran hadn't seen much of Jez since starting at the bar. 'I've got all the basics down pat, pulling beer, changing barrels and fighting off angry punters upset with the service.'

'You should send them to Flesh. We give excellent service.'

'I'll bet you do.'

Jez grinned. 'It's a bit rough, then?'

'Well, it's not the kind of place to learn big shot cocktail tricks. Even our most sophisticated punters only go in for a Snakebite or a Black Russian. I wouldn't have the time anyway. You wouldn't believe how busy such an out of the way bar gets.'

'Bananas has been going for the last twenty five years or so, which would make it around one hundred years old in gay bar years. Most go bust in next to no time. Word gets around. Its isolation is a plus for a lot of men who don't want to advertise they go into gay bars, pick up men and have gay sex, even in this day and age.'

Arran nodded. 'I feel sorry for them having to hide who they are. Serge is paranoid about the ones from Eastern Europe, convinced they're up to no good.'

Jez threw a ladle of water onto the hot coals, sending sizzles of steam clouds spurting upwards, mistying the view. 'He may be right about some of them. Bananas welcomes people with secrets, and keeping secrets can lead to trouble.'

'Sounds like you're talking from experience.'

'How are you getting on with Jason?'

'Hardly ever see him unless it's mega-busy or trouble kicks off. I spend most of my time with Serge and Denny the DJ. He seems a bit old for a DJ, must be fortyish. But the crowd seem to love the retro stuff he spins.'

'Don't let Miss Givens or Sydnee hear you coming out with those ageist comments. They'd put you over their knee and spank you. Come on, let's make a move while you still have a future.'

Arran trailed Jez across to the far side of the main chamber, up a few steps and into a roomy cubicle containing a man dressed in loose fitting white cotton. Not until the man turned to greet them did Arran realise he was looking at his other housemate and called out to him. Gregor smiled at hearing his name echoing around the chamber.

'Sorry,' Arran whispered, 'I forgot this place was like an echo chamber. I don't even know why I was surprised, when I knew you were a masseur.'

'Gregor's not just any masseur,' Jez said. 'He's the best.'

Gregor drew a heavy rubber curtain across the cubicle to give them some privacy and then gestured for Arran to climb onto the worn wooden massage table. Gregor poured oil onto his hands and rubbed them together before spreading it across his back. Arran melted into the table as Gregor worked his magic, sweeping his hands over his naked skin, hard and firm, then soft and caressing, until nothing else mattered except for the next sweep of the hands. Gregor seemed to intuitively find all the knots of tension on Arran's body, from all the miles run pounding the streets of Vauxhall. The head massage sent Arran spiralling down a bottomless hole of relaxation from which he never wanted to climb out. Jez had to order him off the massage table.

Jez was a moaner. The guy had no shame, purring with contentment. Arran imagined being the one pleasuring him. Nothing had happened between them yet. Was Jez thinking about him in the same way? Arran noticed with a start that he was aroused and mentally poured cold water over his excited fella stood to attention. How did Gregor avoid getting a hard on? Maybe it was a perk of the job.

'Dreaming of me?' Jez said, cutting through Arran's daze.

'Don't flatter yourself.'

Before moving off, they hugged Gregor and arranged to meet up for a drink later in the week. They widened their eyes and nodded towards Gregor's next customer. He smiled and waved them off before disappearing behind the curtain with the swarthy looking guy. A nice little job Gregor had cornered for himself.

The massive poolroom had a series of small circular pools of rising temperature and a cooler rectangular swimming pool. Jez and Arran settled in the warmest pool, sitting on the floor and resting back against the side. The shallow water rose to their upper chests. Only pinpricks of light from the shallow domed roof pierced the mellow gloom and barely a word or a splash broke the solitude. Jez closed his eyes and played lightly on Arran's shoulder with his fingertips. Floating around in Jez's world was Arran's idea of bliss, dreaming of what might be ... He had to be coaxed into leaving and swimming a few lengths before hitting the showers. The shower cubicles were uncurtained. From the opposite cubicle, Arran followed the falling water as it held Jez's body, taming his thick wavy hair and sliding down his back before disappearing down the deep cleft of his butt.

'You checking me out again?'

'I was just wondering whether it was still you. I've never known you to be so quiet for so long.'

Jez smiled. 'There's more to me than meets the eye.'

Just the eyeful Arran had seen of the naked Jez made him long for more.

Jez and Arran emerged from the tangled bowels of the underground network at Tottenham Court Road, headed down Oxford Street and then cut into Charlotte Street. Jez strode into *Tapas* and was greeted like an old friend by the staff. He was just as at home here among the tangerine walls, mahogany furniture, bustling waiters and the sound of Spanish guitar strumming the air as he had been in the magical realm of the Russian Baths. The manager, Goyo—short for Gregorio—joined them for a glass of Rioja wine.

'We've missed you,' Goyo said, stroking the back of Jez's head. 'Where've you been hiding yourself?'

Jez nodded toward Arran. 'In deepest darkest Vauxhall, looking after this one.'

'Well, if it means seeing more of you, immigrate to the West End and come work for me. Bring your friend, too.'

'Arran's still serving his bar apprenticeship. He'd cost you more in damages and lost customers than the business could stand.'

'I don't believe you. He's as fair as an angel.'

'A dark angel in disguise.'

'That would be him, not me,' Arran said.

'Now that I could believe,' Goyo agreed, winking at Arran. As their tapas arrived, he stood up to leave. 'Enjoy, my friends.'

The waiters loaded the table with tapas served on white saucers decorated with swirls of blue and yellow. Arran's hand dithered over them, not knowing where to start; he was used to everything arriving on the same plate. Jez pointed out each unfamiliar dish and described it for him like an expert. Arran lapped up his every word. This was why he'd come to London, to experience a different life. And life with Jez was a journey into the unknown. He never knew what to expect next.

Arran felt giddy as they made their way across Oxford Street and into Soho, joining the early evening revellers milling about the criss-cross of streets and alleyways. He followed Jez down what looked like several dead ends before he cut down a flight of steps and entered a cellar bar with no name. Sharply dressed people stood chatting in clusters in the dimly lit interior, boosted by candles placed on each of the little round tables. Arran felt as though he was on the wrong side of the bar. Jez headed to the bar for drinks and was greeted by the bartender. Jez knew everybody and everybody knew Jez, it seemed. And they were all pleased to see him. 'Jez, my man, where have you been? It's nice to see you.'

'You're looking well, Davy. How about two of your coldest beers?'

'Coming right up.'

Arran noticed that Jez never did answer questions about himself. They took their drinks to a quiet corner table, where a man in his late twenties approached them.

'Looking for Darius?' he said, eyeing Jez.

'Arran, this is Andrew.'

They shook hands. Jez and Andrew chatted until a young guy with a resentful pout beckoned him back to the group. He raised his eyes in mock irritation before striding off to re-join his friends.

'Who's Darius?' Arran said.

'Just some guy I was hooked up with.'

'Tell me about him. I'm interested in what kind of guys you're interested in.' Jez surprised Arran by not going off subject.

'Darius was a rich guy's kid I ran around with a while back. Although he's not a kid, he's late twenties.'

'What does he look like?' Arran said, scratching an itch.

'Everyone always said we looked alike, except that I have wavy hair and his is straight. Andrew always referred to us as the dark twins.'

Arran felt a pang of something. Disappointment? Jealousy? 'Why did he call you that?'

'Darius was a playboy type—lots of money, out to the best restaurants, seen at the *in* nightclubs. We ran around, living it up. It was mad. He was a magnet for attractive people ... The sex was wild ...' Jez's eyes glazed over for a spell. 'After a time, life with Darius lost its appeal. I wanted to move on, and he wanted everything to stay the same. He was used to getting his own way, so he didn't take the split too well. Things turned nasty.'

'Is that why you haven't been around here?'

Jez took a sip of beer and shrugged. 'I've been busy getting on with my own life.'

Arran couldn't help himself. 'Is that why you wanted to come here today, to see Darius? Do you miss him?'

'Darius and I are history, never to be repeated. And that's all there is to tell, so help me God,' Jez said, raising his right hand.

Arran's giddiness deserted him. Darius sounded like a rich good looking thrill seeker. No wonder nothing had happened between himself and Jez. He wasn't his type. He headed off to the bathroom. Andrew was stood at a urinal when Arran entered. They stood pissing side by side and in silence until Arran spoke. 'You're a friend of Jez?'

'We know each other.'

'What's the story with him and Darius?'

'Ask him.'

'I just did.'

Andrew shook his cock dry. 'Let's just say that Darius is Jez's type. He's dangerous.'

Arran didn't know what to make of Andrew's parting words. He did know that no one had ever described him as dangerous. Regular, boyish and chipped from nature sprang to mind.

The tube to Vauxhall was packed, preventing conversation. Jez checked in at Flesh and found everything under control. Next, he called in at a mini-market while Arran waited outside. On their way home, they smiled at a man weaving towards them as if he'd had one tipple too many.

'What are you two queers grinning at?' the drunk said, barging through and elbowing them out of the way.

Jez caught him by the arm and spun him around. 'Don't drink if you're not man enough to handle it.'

The drunk was a good six foot tall, the same as Jez and Arran but much more muscled. He shook Jez off and faced him. Arran thought he was going to strike Jez and pulled him away. 'C'mon, leave it, he's pissed.'

'Listen to your girlfriend.'

Jez and the man eyeballed each other, neither one backing down. Arran kept on tugging on Jez's sleeve until he allowed himself to be led away. The man waved to them.

'Bye-bye, girlies.'

Arran turned to look. He was staring at them with intense unblinking eyes, as if making a photograph.

When they arrived in Arran's room, Jez pulled out a bottle of Rioja from the mini-market bag, poured two glasses and handed one to Arran, who took a sip, then brought up the incident with the drunk. 'He was frightening. I thought he was going to attack you.'

'I thought so too,' Jez said, 'but I couldn't back down. We talk about the problems of gays in homophobic far away places, conveniently forgetting that homophobia still exists in this country, simmering under the surface and waiting for an opportunity to boil over.'

'With that thick accent, he sounded like he came from one of those far off places. But don't let him bother you. People like him are not worth it, and he's probably harmless when sober. Let's talk about something else.' Arran started to talk about their day together.

Jez perked up. 'You've reminded me ...' He delved into the mini-market bag again, emerging with a small bottle of massage oil. 'Get your kit off.'

Arran stripped down to his undies in double quick time and hopped onto the bed. Jez teased him on his eagerness while oiling up his hands for the massage. He was no Gregor, but his touch electrified Arran—taunting, teasing and testing his control by lingering and loitering over the very places Arran wanted his hands. They were going to get together. Tonight was the night. Another reason Arran had come to London was to meet different sorts of guys and Jez was as exciting as he was hot. Being with him would be a dream.

Arran prayed for that to happen and for the massage to go on and on. The slap on his butt signalled that Jez wanted his turn. Arran poured oil onto his hands, rubbed them together to warm it and then laid his hands on the longed-for body. His technique was less massage and more caressing as he traced a path over every inch of Jez, savouring every touch of his smooth skin, the contours of his muscles, the hardness of his legs and the feathery dark line of hair running from his navel to disappear beneath his black briefs. He knew he was doing a good job from all the moans of encouragement that were coming from Jez. All the images of the day flashed through Arran's mind, like a movie, to culminate at this point in time and leaving him feverish for the next frame ...

Jez stayed on when it was time for bed. Arran spent a long time awake, holding him and enjoying their closeness. Noticing as their two bodies synchronised their breathing. The moonlight through the shutters formed bars across Jez's face. Arran had no idea what went on inside that head. Tonight they'd come close to becoming lovers ... It hadn't happened. But it was surely just a matter of time.

When Arran awoke in the morning, Jez was gone. One minute, close; the next, far away.

ELEVEN

Forced to set up another honeytrap put Alexei in a black mood. His name was Phil. One of those gays who kept flicking his hair and touching his lips. Effeminate men made Alexei feel sick.

Alexei had argued it was inviting trouble to go after another target so soon after the last. Because they were in a strange country, with different customs, habits and ways of policing, they should wait to see whether the last gay made a complaint and if anything came of it. But he was a victim of his own success. The first honeytrap on British soil had gone like a dream, making the men push for another. Wanting to keep them sweet, Svetlana had agreed. She also had Maxim whispering in her ear. All the men had jobs, apart from Svetlana, Maxim and Alexei. Whatever their background, it was easy to pick up cash-in-hand jobs on one of the many construction projects going on all around London. The Russian expats looked out for one another. Maxim didn't want to work but did bore easily. The lure of the hunt never seemed far from his mind.

With the decision taken to search for another target, Alexei had no choice but to go ahead. Svetlana had reasoned that no one knew how long the search would take, but it had taken no time at all. British queers didn't have to lead a double life that made them cagey and suspicious of others, afraid of the consequences if someone discovered their sexuality. Unlike in Russia. Finding a target was easier in London because here some queers were often just lonely for company. Their desire made them vulnerable. 'You look like an interesting guy, Phil,' Alexei said. 'Tell me something about yourself.'

Phil looked pleased, as if no one had said this to him before. He droned on about his friends always bagging the best guys and how he could never seem to find that someone special.

'Who would be special to you?' Alexei said, a little smile playing at the corners of his mouth, inviting Phil to confide his secrets in him.

Phil reddened and looked down, seemingly unused to asking for what he wanted. 'Well, I'd like someone handsome ... manly ...'

'You like a man to take charge, don't you, Phil?' When Phil looked up, Alexei could see in his eyes that there was more to it. 'You like it a little rough. Is that it?'

Phil covered his smile with a hand. 'I feel like you know me already, Alex.'

Alexei leaned back. Be careful what you wish for. The little wallflower had no idea what was headed his way. 'I'd like to. So why don't you tell me a little more about yourself.'

Phil told Alexei, with Nikolay and Pavel listening in, everything they needed to know. About his work in a high end men's store in the West End. How he hadn't been going out much because he was saving up for a cosmetic procedure—nothing drastic, just a little reshaping of his nose. He laughed and put his nose down to a Jewish grandmother on his father's side, joking that he got the big nose but not the money. Pavel and Nikolay pulled awful faces on hearing about the Jewish heritage. Homosexual and Jewish added up to double hate. Phil came from a village outside Reading but now lived in Wandsworth. A room in a house share. A bit basic, but it would do until he was ready to move up. With his parents divorced and caught up in new relationships, he didn't hear from them all that often. He was pretty much on his own. Which was why he would really, really like to meet someone special.

Alexei couldn't believe how much these gay guys gave away about themselves, even the quiet ones. With only a little encouragement from a good looking guy, the dam broke and they were off yabbering about their drab little lives. He wished Phil would shut up now. While Alexei was lost in his own thoughts, Phil started to ask him questions. Personal questions. Not going to happen. Alexei closed down the conversation. The look of intense disappointment on Phil's face only lifted when Alexei asked if he would be free to chat the next day.

*

Nikolay gave Alexei a wink and tapped his nose with a finger. 'You really know how to wind in these queers and keep them keen. You're a natural. If I didn't know better, I might think you had insider information.'

Alexei spun around and punched Nikolay, then grabbed his hair and jerked his head back. 'What's that supposed to mean?'

'Nothing, Alexei, I was only joking with you. Relax, I meant nothing by it.'

Alexei let him go. Although Nikolay was more than a match for him physically, he wouldn't dare fight back. He knew his place in the pecking order. Alexei left the room, irritated with Nikolay, himself and life in general.

TWELVE

Arran entered the Sanctum. It was heaving, and it took him a few minutes to find Gregor and Sydnee. 'No Jez, yet?'

Gregor poured Arran a beer from a pitcher. 'Jez's disappeared.'

Arran sank down into a seat, the music and chatter fading into the background. The last time he'd seen Jez, they'd had a heated exchange. After their day out together, they had slept in the same bed and come close to making love. Then zilch. Like what had happened counted for nothing. Later, when he caught Jez heading by his room, he called out to him. He dawdled for a few seconds before entering the bedroom.

'Haven't seen you for a couple of days,' Arran said. 'Avoiding me?'

'Why would I?'

'After we slept together, you just disappeared without a word.'

Jez laughed. 'We didn't sleep together.'

'You know what I mean.'

'I had things to do, no big deal.'

Jez's words smacked Arran in the face. What had happened between them mattered to him. Always believing it was just a matter of time before they got together, he was annoyed that Jez might have led him on. Tired of pussyfooting around, he tackled him head on. 'Why have you never made a move on me? God knows, I've given you enough hints and encouragement.'

'You know I like you, we're great friends.'

'I know we're friends. That's not what I asked. Will we be anything more?'

'Let's not do this now.'

'Do I stand any chance with you?'

'All right,' Jez said, his whole body seeming to sink into itself, 'we both know there's been something between us right from our first meet. But there are things about me you don't know ... Things I have to work through before I can be with anyone.'

'Like what? You know you can trust me.' Arran was used to seeing Jez confident all of the time. It unsettled him to see Jez looking less than that. Struggling to find the words to express himself.

Jez sighed. 'I don't want to get into it right now. I don't know how long it will take, and I wouldn't ask you to wait but you know I will always be here for you.'

Arran hadn't meant to rattle Jez and regretted his outburst. He'd suspected he wasn't ready for a relationship. What puzzled him was why.

'What do you mean he's disappeared?' Arran asked Gregor.

'I just meant he's done his usual disappearing trick.'

'Have you tried him on his phone?'

'Not answering.'

'Which only means he'll be busy somewhere,' Sydnee said.

'Or busy with someone,' Gregor said.

Arran flinched. Knowing they couldn't be together at this time was one thing. Knowing he was out actively chasing other men was a killer.

'We don't know that for sure,' Sydnee said. 'He could be off doing any number of things.'

'Does he go AWOL often?' Arran said, his voice flat.

Gregor nodded. 'Often enough.'

Arran took a swig of beer, his heart rate settling now he knew nothing bad had happened to Jez.

'He'll be back,' Sydnee said, 'with some tall tale about meeting a man who knew a man who had a yacht—'

'Like Darius,' Arran said.

'You know about Darius?'

'I know he was some rich guy who turned Jez's head. He made it sound as if it was nothing special. Was it?'

'Darius was a few years older than Jez and with enough money to turn anyone's head. Jez got caught up in a whirlwind for a time, but it blew itself out.'

'Up West, we met a friend of theirs in a bar they used to go in. He mentioned Darius. Maybe it opened up old memories for Jez. Do you think he could be with him now?'

'You should put Darius out of your mind because I'm sure it's over between them.'

Arran took another swig of beer, swirling it around in his mouth. It tasted bitter.

'When Jez told you about Darius,' Gregor said, 'was that the day you came to the Russian Baths?'

Arran nodded.

'Stunning, aren't they?'

Arran settled back into his seat, feeling again the soothing waters and mellow atmosphere of the baths ... the play of Jez's fingers on his skin. 'Dreamy. You're lucky to work there.'

Gregor's smile lit up his face. 'I love working there. They date back to when Russian immigrants came to London by the thousands in the mid-nineteenth century, seeking work and a better life. They settled in the East End, building shops, places of worship and places to bathe. And—'

Arran sniffed the air. 'You Russians are a bit pongy. You need big baths.'

'I have no idea what pongy means,' Gregor said, punching Arran on the arm, 'but I do know when I'm being insulted.'

Arran laughed. Even though Gregor was only twenty two, he seemed older. He was more studious than the rest of them and could often be found reading in his room, with classical music playing low in the background. 'When we were at the baths, many of the men were speaking in a foreign tongue. Were they all Russian?'

'Pretty much. Around a hundred and fifty thousand Russians make their home in London. The baths is an important centre for the expats to meet up and socialise, make contacts, find work and do deals.'

'I saw a film on TV,' Arran said. 'I think it was called Russian Promises ... no, Eastern Promises, and it was about the Russian mob living in London. Talk about brutal. Those guys loved their tattoos. So come on, Gregor, don't be shy. Let's see yours.'

Gregor laughed. 'Sorry to disappoint you, but I'm no mobster and there are no tattoos on this body.'

'Shame. Get another pitcher of beer and I'll show you mine.'

Gregor leaned forward, his eyes widening. 'Really! You have tattoos?'

'No.'

'Then it's your round, teaser.'

'Get two pitchers,' Sydnee said, 'and you can tattoo on me anywhere you like.'

THIRTEEN

Alexei put on a wistful face for Phil and asked, 'Have you been thinking about me?'

Unlike Alexei, Phil was a bad actor. Although he protested his innocence, his whole manner suggested just the opposite. Alexei pouted, feigning disappointment. 'There's someone else, isn't there?' He'd met Phil online every day since their first meeting, finding out about his life, building up a picture and making sure he fit the gang's victim profile. Tonight he intended to set the honeytrap. Though Phil would walk himself into the trap.

'It's not that,' Phil said, quick to speak. 'It's just that all we talk about is me, so I hardly know anything about you.'

'Only because you're so much more interesting than me,' Alexei said, hoping that Phil wouldn't prove difficult.

When Phil's face lit up, Alexei relaxed. These needy guys always fell victim to flattery; they couldn't help themselves. He continued to talk, to give Phil the impression he was sharing and letting him in while not saying anything of any substance. He finished by putting Phil on the spot. 'I'm right here with you. Don't you like what you see?' The anguish on Phil's face was amusing to see. He was tying himself in knots, trying to find out what he needed to know without seeming to pry and without causing offence. Alexei let him suffer awhile before telling him he was just kidding. 'I'm bang on six feet tall and have to keep myself in reasonable shape for my job. I work as a police community support officer at the moment, though sometime soon I'll be joining the regular police force.'

That took the wind out of Phil's sails. Now he knew Alexei was in law enforcement, any doubts about meeting a stranger online were blown away. He looked and sounded like a different person. The anxiety he'd been feeling for himself switched to concern for Alexei. 'Working for the police, aren't you worried about going into gay chatrooms?'

'Naturally. But I'm careful and very choosy. I only go for the nice guys, and I can see you're a very nice guy. I'm right, aren't I? Or have you a dark side you're not telling me about?'

'No, I don't have a dark side for you to worry about,' Phil said, almost sadly.

'Pity,' Alexei said, pulling his own sad face.

'Except in bed. And then I can be really naughty.'

Alexei straightened up to signal his interest. 'Now you're talking. But you have to prove it when we meet.'

'When will that be?'

The sap was responding exactly as Alexei intended. With Phil's suspicions quelled, the hunger to meet up with Alexei in person was written all over his gullible face. 'Entirely down to you. But you've got me hot, so don't leave me hanging.' Alexei sat back and watched the show. Phil's eyes were darting around, his little mind working overtime. It was pitiful to see.

Finally, Phil came up with a suggestion: 'How about this Friday evening?'

'It's a bit soon. Let me check ...' Alexei looked down and flicked a magazine below the desktop. Out of the corner of his eye, he kept tabs on Phil. He was fidgeting about and no doubt hoping he hadn't pushed for a meet too soon. Desperate not to get knocked back.

Phil, in a small voice: 'Is everything okay?'

'Just checking my work schedule. Won't be a minute.' Alexei left it another whole minute before he spoke again. By this time, Phil was sliding down in his seat. Visibly wilting.

Alexei looked up, beaming. 'It's a date.'

Phil shot up as if he'd won the Lottery. A big smile lit up his face. Alexei gave him the instructions Svetlana had given him, the location and time they should meet, and then pulled the plug on their Internet connection.

With the honeytrap set, Alexei sat back and sighed with relief. Job done.

FOURTEEN

Arran made like a Golden Rooster, standing on his right leg and extending his right arm, then lifting his left knee and bending his left arm, before chancing a look at the low lying dark clouds gathering over the community garden.

A rainstorm was brewing.

The next second, Arran was in a heap on the decking, viewing his sorry reflection in the small ornamental pond. Above the water, trickling into the pond by his ear, Arran heard Mr Cheung tutting and telling him to concentrate. He climbed to his feet and dusted himself down, issuing a *sorry* to Mr Cheung for his clumsiness. A dense curtain of green plants and trees surrounded them, closing them in and increasing the mugginess of the air. Arran wiped the sweat from his brow, then took off his tracksuit top, throwing it onto one of two benches made from a huge tree trunk.

Mr Cheung coughed. Arran looked across and copied his stance—a wide base resting on the balls of the feet, arms out in front, palms facing in. His mentor lowered his body into a low sitting position, perfectly balanced, before slowly gliding up like smoke and down like a feather. The perfect image of grace and control. Arran waited until he timed his movement with Mr Cheung's ... then pushed up and lowered back down into a squat. The slowness of the actions made his thigh muscles burn. He lost sync with Mr Cheung and tried to further slow down. The effort made his thighs shake and his breathing ragged. He had to strain to raise up his body and then couldn't control the drop. He cried out as his legs gave way and he crashed backwards, hitting his head on the bench behind. He rubbed at his sore head while Mr Cheung looked down on him. The expression on his face seemed to ask who this clown was at his feet.

'Sorry,' Arran muttered again, mad at himself for wasting this golden opportunity to learn techniques that could enrich his life. Mr Cheung was giving him his time and expertise for free, and all he asked in return was commitment and concentration. Arran felt embarrassed at being outdone by a man sixty years his senior and seven inches below him.

Mr Cheung adopted a crossed-legged pose on one of the benches. Arran clambered to his feet and copied the pose on the twin bench. What feat would his mentor have them next perform? Arran peered over the side of the bench. There was now an extra eighteen inches to fall. He put out a hand to steady himself before glancing upward at the threatening black sky bearing down on them. The storm was about to hit.

'Remember when I told you about my family back in Hong Kong?' Mr Cheung said. 'And the family stall where we sold food?'

Arran nodded, relieved that the Tai Chi was on hold for one of Mr Cheung's stories. He loved hearing about Mr Cheung's early life, his family and what he'd got up to when he was young.

'The stall barely made enough money to feed and clothe the family. When I was fifteen, I had to find some way to make money and take my burden off them. Few opportunities existed back then for poor boys, barely educated. To improve my chances, I joined a neighbourhood gang. The Triads—'

'You were in a Triad gang?' Arran blurted out, not trusting his ears.

Mr Cheung nodded.

'Unbelievable! What was it like?'

'I thought I was the cat's paw for a while. I was well rewarded for doing very little. Gang members collected the protection money from the casino and shop owners, threw their weight around to ward off rival gangs and strutted around the neighbourhood to intimidate the locals. But it put money in my pocket and allowed me to give my family luxuries they could never otherwise have afforded. Only as time went on did I come to understand the true cost to the little businesses, like my own family's food stall, of making the insurance payments to the gang. Having to put up with squalor, hungry bellies, ragbag clothes and the lack of opportunities while the Triad gangmasters and their families grew rich and fat. But the failure to make payment resulted in severe beatings to the owner or their family.'

'You beat people up?' Arran said, unable to picture it. Mr Cheung was someone who was purposeful and dignified, who exercised every day in the park come rain or shine, who was a fountain of knowledge for Arran and someone who didn't make noise even as London buzzed all around him. He was not someone who hurt others.

'I did what the gang leader asked of me. When asked to teach someone a lesson, then that is what I did.' Mr Cheung shook his head. 'It didn't sit well with me and I wanted out. Impossible. The gang owned me.'

Arran had leaned too far forward on the bench, so engrossed was he in the story. Recognising the danger, he righted himself. 'What did you do?'

'My father told me to leave Hong Kong and never come back. That was the only way to be free of the Triads. My girlfriend left with me. We worked our passage to England on a steamship, disembarking at Southampton and made our way to London. We married and found waiting jobs in Soho's Chinatown. After saving up for the next fifteen years, we moved to Vauxhall and opened our own take-away, serving dishes based on my family's recipes. The shop is in the hands of my eldest son and his family now.'

'Awesome,' Arran said. He hoped that in the years to come he would have some great stories to tell to his students.

'Those were tough times and I had to take some tough decisions,' Mr Cheung said.

Arran had to hand it to Mr Cheung, he was as sharp as a tack. He'd worked out that the reason for Arran's off day was because there was something on his mind.

Mr Cheung asked Arran to focus on the life breath ... to slow his breathing ... quieten his mind ... and let any distracting thoughts or anxious feelings drift away like tiny clouds ... The biggest, darkest cloud in Arran's sky was Jez. He wanted him but couldn't have him and didn't know why. He didn't know if they would ever be together. After Jez's disappearing trick the other night, he'd turned up the next morning with a big grin on his face. Wouldn't say where he'd been. But it was obvious he'd had a good time. The light in the sky dimmed dramatically and the black clouds burst. The thick boughs of the trees overhead kept Arran and Mr Cheung dry. Heavy raindrops drummed on the leaves all around them, releasing heady scents into the air. Arran closed his eyes and slowed his breathing ... moving air in through his nose and out through lightly pursed lips ... in and out ... like he was learning to breathe for the first time ... in and out ... in and out ... until he could no longer sense where he ended and the world around him began ... at one with himself and nature ... In his connected state, everything became clear.

Jez needed space and time to do whatever was needed to release his pain. Arran didn't have to understand the nature of that pain. Jez would tell him in his own time, if he needed to. Arran would let Jez go and trust the future to take care of itself.

FIFTEEN

Phil arrived first at the pick up point. He was glad, wanting to savour every single moment and remember every little detail of his first date with Alex. No one was around, except for one guy talking on his phone at a nearby bus stop. Five minutes later, a fancy black car pulled to the kerb alongside him. Alex had come. It was really happening. This would the best night of his life and the start of who knew what. He only hoped Alex wouldn't be disappointed in him.

Phil had taken the afternoon off work to shop for something new to wear. Dress to impress is what they say, and he wanted to impress Alex like no one else he'd ever known. Who could blame him? Alex could slip onto the pages of *Attitude* and mingle with the other fashion models, no problem. To think he was interested in Phil was unbelievable. After floating up and down Oxford Street, Phil eventually settled on a light blue shirt to match the khaki trousers he planned to wear. The shirt would bring out the blue of his eyes, especially when he'd polished them with *Dazzling Eyes* eye drops. The fantasy they might sleep together that night meant he couldn't resist buying new boxers. Leopard print. He was feeling feisty. Finally life was going well for Phil, out on his own, paying his own way and all he needed to be perfectly happy with his lot in life was a boyfriend. Phil's heart skipped because Alex wasn't just any old boyfriend. He was unreal.

Back in his rented room, Phil forced down a chicken salad sandwich while the bath was running. The new shirt he hung on the rail above the bath for the steam to take out the creases. He slipped into the hot foaming water, breathing in the sweet scent of *Spiced Candy Apple* bubble bath. He closed his eyes and dreamed of the pleasures the coming night might bring …

With a grass sea-sponge, he scrubbed his chest and between his legs until his skin burned. Thoroughly cleaned and smelling good enough to eat, he dragged himself out of the cooling water, dried off and brushed his teeth with whitening toothpaste. He ran product through his hair and swept sections into place before using his fingers to quirk the ends. Having dressed in his new gear, Phil stood in front of a full length mirror to check out the results. Why me? Guys like Alex don't just happen along for guys like me. He set out determined to make the most of his good fortune, even though it might be for one night only.

The first thing Phil noticed was the fluorescent yellow police community support vest on the back seat of the car. Without a care, he hopped in and they pulled away. Alex smiled and complimented him on his look. That smile. Phil was beside himself that Alex had noticed all the effort he'd made and pinched himself to make sure he wasn't still dreaming. Within minutes, Phil had goosebumps. The car turned off the road and headed behind a block of old work units. He shouldn't give in too easily. But one glance at Alex ... and the elastic on his undies felt like it had snapped. 'Have you got an ulterior motive for parking up in the dark?'

The door on Phil's side opened without warning. Two men dragged him out and bundled him onto the floor in the back of the car, sitting either side and blocking his way out. When he tried to get up, they punched him and threatened more of the same if he made a sound. The car set off. Phil couldn't move for fear. Why was Alex allowing this to happen? Who were these men? They'd come out of nowhere, leaving him no time to react. Scared of the unknown, where they were going and what was going to happen to him, he hoped they wouldn't hurt him and resolved to hand over whatever they wanted. When he was freed, he would never ever go back online to meet men.

The car rode over bumpy ground and came to a stop. Phil was hustled into a nearby building, giving him no chance to escape. The room was lit by burning oil drums. The shooting flames popped and made him jump. In the middle, a crowd of men were smoking and drinking. Heavy rock pulsed through the air. Phil's fear level dropped. This was a party. He'd been set up. The abduction and rough treatment were all part of the joke. That was more like the mischievous Alex he knew. He would give him hell when he caught up with him. Phil moved through the sheets of plastic hanging down around the entrance and played along with the men behind, pushing him towards the partygoers. Closer up, they looked strange. Their eyes bore into him with something that looked like ...

Hate.

Phil stopped walking.

This place, these men ... Something was off. Looking around for a way out, his eyes came to rest on a dark haired woman lying on a pile of sandbags. The sight of a female made him breathe a little easier.

She spoke to him. 'Don't worry'—she indicated with her hands at the men surrounding them—'they're all just normal men. But you're not normal, are you? Just tell us that and then you can go.'

Phil wasn't sure he understood. 'What do you want me to say?'

'We want you to admit you're a homosexual, that's all. That isn't so hard to do, is it?'

'I'm a homosexual,' Phil trotted out, wanting away from this strange woman, these strange men and this strange happening.

The woman got up from the sacks and walked towards him—dark haired, dark features, threatening. 'Say it louder.'

'I'm a homosexual.'

'Say you are a dirty ... stinking ... perverted ... animal.'

Phil baulked at this and stared at her. What was this madness? He put himself back in his little room, at a time before this ... whatever it was ... was happening. When he was still free and safe. He should have seen the obvious. Him and Alex were never going to happen. One look at Alex should have told him that. It had all been a delusion, a dream. A stinging slap brought him back to the dark woman. Back to the nightmare. He recited, 'I'm a dirty stinking perverted animal.'

'See, that was easy, wasn't it?' the dark woman said, her voice softer.

As she stalked back to her seat, she flicked her head and the men descended on Phil. Like a pack of wolves, they punched and kicked and stripped him. He was left trembling on the hard concrete, covering his genitals with his hands. Why had Alex done this to him? Picking him out at the back of the mob, Phil pleaded with his eyes for help. When Alex lowered his eyes, Phil knew he was on his own and at the mercy of these crazed homophobes. He would just have to hold on until they got bored. He hoped it would be soon. He didn't know how much more punishment he could take.

A couple of men grabbed Phil and forced him to bend over a stack of beer crates. He yelled for them to stop. This couldn't be happening. What the hell were they going to do to him? His mind went into meltdown. With a strength he didn't know he possessed, he yanked his arms away from his captors and pushed away from the crates. Rushing at the men between him and freedom, he lashed out for all he was worth. His sticklike arms were no match for the heavy punches that drove him down onto the cold ground. Bleeding and dazed, the men dragged him back and threw him over the crates. They held him tightly, pinning him down. He saw large black boots heading his way and lifted his head. Before him stood a beast of a man. In his hand he held a big black whip. 'Oh, God, no. Please don't. You can't. Please ... No!'

Knowing what was coming, Phil bucked and screamed and begged. The hideous baying of the men swallowed up his pleas. Why were they doing this to him? What had he done to deserve this? They had to know this was wrong. Someone had to listen.

'This is your own doing,' the Beast said. 'When a man goes against the natural order, he has to expect consequences. So stop your whining and accept your punishment. You know you deserve it.'

Phil heard the rush of the whip through the air before it connected with his bare skin. The lash cut into his flesh and made him howl. Tears streaked down his face. His cries for mercy were lost to the bellows of the men around him, urging the Beast on. The lashes rained down, harder and faster, biting into him. A warm feeling ran down the back of his thighs. He lost count of the number of lashes. The pain was like nothing he'd ever known. Just when he thought he was going to black out, the whipping stopped.

Thankful the ordeal was over, Phil raised his head. As cruel and hateful as it was, he'd survived. Now he'd taken his punishment, surely these maniacs would let him go? The Beast threw down the whip and picked up a beer bottle. He downed the beer in one go, burping loudly.

'You must be thirsty,' the Beast said to Phil.

With Phil's throat dry and cracked from screaming, he could only nod. The Beast rammed the bottle into Phil's mouth, smashing his teeth. He hammered the bottle in and out. The bottle went down Phil's throat, making him gag. He couldn't breathe. Couldn't get air into his lungs. An eternity ticked by. His head became light and he drifted away. The shouting, the blows, the pain ... melted into the distance. As if it was happening to some other poor sod. Then all went black.

SIXTEEN

Desperate to escape Phil's accusing eyes, Alexei ran through deserted streets until his lungs were bursting. He collapsed against a wall, wheezing and sucking in air. When he'd recovered, he looked around. The area seemed familiar. He'd reached Back Lane, near the gay bar. His mind screamed for a drink. Anything to blot out what he'd seen.

The same barmen as before were working the bar. The little Russian held back, leaving the other blond barman to approach him. Smiling and polite, Alexei couldn't look him in the eye when giving his order. He sensed the barman looking at him. Out of breath, sweating, messed up, distant, he was coming across as strange. No matter. He felt strange. Everything felt unreal. If only it was unreal. Grabbing his drinks, Alexei sought out a dark corner. He downed the vodka. It burned, sliding down his throat. Painful. He deserved it. Another vodka went the same way. He wanted to be drunk. Out of it. Then to wake up and find it was only a nightmare.

It wasn't his fault.

'That fucking psychopath, Maxim!'

Alexei had shouted out loud. Startled, he looked around. No one had heard, the music too loud and everyone busy, dancing or finding someone to sleep with for the night. He put out the fire in his throat by downing half the beer. How had his life come to this? Easy. He was trapped by race and by blood. Nothing he could do about it. Except forget. And for that he needed more alcohol.

The same barman.

Looking.

Judging?

For all Alexei knew, the gruesome images playing and replaying in his mind were also showing on his face for all to see. The barman should just do his job and stop looking at him. A concerned look. He couldn't stand it. After what he'd done, he didn't deserve kindness. But it had all happened so fast. There was nothing he could have done.

Liar!

Phil's eyes had pleaded with him for help. He'd looked away. Done nothing. Left him to his fate. Too scared of giving himself away.

Coward!

Mumbling thanks and leaving his change, Alexei picked up his drinks and sneaked back to his hideaway. He polished off the first vodka.

Where could he go from here?

He had nowhere else to go, nothing else to do and no one else to turn to. For better or worse the gang were his family, his life. But even with them, he lived a double life. What a mess! Wherever he went, he was a stranger. He had nothing and nobody. Perhaps he never would. That would be his punishment for all the bad deeds he'd done. Condemned to live life alone.

The two barmen had their heads huddled together. Talking about him? The little Russian was probably warning his blond friend not to go near him. Alexei had seen the interest in the guy's eyes. Hell, he could sense it. That's what he did, attract men. He was the honeytrap. The blond should heed his friend and stay away from trouble. Alexei had watched from the shadows on the last occasion the blond had encountered trouble. Luckily, he'd been more than a match for the abusive fat guy who had attacked him.

Alexei guzzled down more beer. Everyone around him was having fun. None of them would guess what he'd done for fun tonight. Got someone killed. It seemed funny until the laugh turned into a sob. Alexei sought out his mouth with the beer glass and drank deeply to drown the memory. The more he drank, the more numb he felt and the better he liked it. As if nothing mattered. His life was a sham. So what? He was stuck with it.

He headed to the bar for more drink. Much more.

*

Alexei fixed his eyes on a distant lamp post. After taking a deep breath, he headed towards it ... trying not to blink ... because every time he did, the lamp post moved. He lost his balance and swerved towards the edge of the pavement. His foot slipped off the kerb and he fell. His hands and knees skated over loose gravel, burning them.

'Fancy seeing you again,' Alexei heard someone say.

He angled his head towards the voice coming from above and squinted into the face of one of the barmen from Bananas. He thanked his lucky stars it was the nice one, the blond one with the smiling face.

'Are you okay?' the barman said.

'You look like a nice guy,' Alexei drawled. 'Walk away. I'm bad news, believe me.'

'What's so bad about you?'

Alexei couldn't speak. Rocking back onto his heels, he held his face in his hands. Tears squeezed between his fingers; he couldn't hold them back. All the years of holding his emotions in check ended as the dam burst. An arm went around his shoulder and held him until there were no more tears left and then gently guided him to his feet and steered him along the road to a darkened house and up the stairs to a bedroom, where his jacket and shoes were removed and he was put to bed. Alexei closed his eyes as the barman sat beside him, stroking his hair.

*

Alexei opened his eyes. Nothing looked as it should, and his head was splitting in two. He reached for the tall glass on the nightstand and gulped down the water in one go. A plastic bucket was on one side of the bed. On the other side, a blond head poked out of a sleeping bag—the barman from the gay bar. Broken images flashed through Alexei's mind of the night before. Him. Drunk. Crying in the street, like a frightened boy. He hadn't cried since the day his parents had become victims of the treacherous winter roads around Moscow and died.

Someone else had died.

Phil.

Choked to death by Maxim.

Alexei had bolted before finding out if Phil really was dead. Stood at the back, unable to see properly, it could have been a trick of the light. Maybe it wasn't true. Maybe he hadn't died.

Alexei pushed back the cover and climbed out of the bed, picked up his jacket and shoes, and sneaked away from the sleeping barman. He had to get out of here before the guy awoke. He couldn't face seeing him. Having to talk with him. Explain. The landing was clear. Alexei crept down the stairs, cringing when a couple of them creaked. He didn't hang around to find out whether anyone had been disturbed, letting himself out of the house and only resting in the porch for a minute to put on his shoes. The sign on the wall opposite said Boy Lane. He turned left towards Vauxhall and headed home. He had to find out what had really happened to Phil. This nightmare was too bad to be true.

SEVENTEEN

Having opened the door to his house, Alexei remained on the threshold. Uncertain now about his reception from the gang, what they would say and the questions they would ask. Questions he couldn't answer without raising more doubts in their minds. About him and the kind of man he was. The stupid queer's death had ruined everything.

Alexei listened for any signs of change. Normally, at this early hour on a weekend, everyone would be in bed fast asleep. No one would be up, whispering about him. Wondering why he'd run and what he had to hide. But there was nothing. Only silence. He must have got it wrong. No one had died. He'd been tormenting himself over nothing.

He stepped inside and closed the door. In the kitchen he ran the cold tap. Seriously dehydrated, he guzzled down two large glasses of water. While wiping his mouth on his sleeve, he listened out for anyone moving about. All he could hear was a lot of snoring. He sneaked a look into the living room, the floor littered with the sleeping bags of those men unlucky enough not to have beds. Those not important enough in the hierarchy of the gang. He went into the bedroom he shared with half a dozen others. No one stirred. He let out a deep sigh, relieved that everything seemed okay. He must have got it wrong. Overreacted. Phil had lived. Life could go on as normal.

He got into bed and rested his head on the pillow. He would tell the others he'd had to bolt. That he'd been feeling unwell. A dodgy curry or something. There was no reason for them not to believe him. No proof that he was anything other than what he said he was. He closed his eyes.

Someone was shaking him. He opened his eyes and found Svetlana standing over him and looking anything but pleased. 'Get up and come into the kitchen,' she ordered him.

When Alexei entered, Svetlana was sat at the table, a mug of steaming coffee in front of her. She told him to close the door. As soon as he sat down, she laid into him. 'Why the hell did you run off like that?'

Judging by her tone, the situation was bad. A sinking feeling hit Alexei. 'What happened to Phil?'

'Phil, now, is it?' Svetlana said, giving him a searching look. 'What do you care about what happened to some sad little homo?'

'What happened with him?'

'His body was dumped in a hole on the site. It will—'

'He's really dead, then,' Alexei, said to himself, burying his head in his hands. It had been no trick of the light. It was real. Phil was dead. Killed!

'Why are you getting so upset about a dead homo?' Svetlana said, a puzzled tone to her voice.

Alexei looked up. 'Because murder was never a part of what we did.'

'Don't be so dramatic, Alexei. It was an accident.'

'The bottle didn't accidentally slip down his throat. Maxim choked him to death with it, the psychotic bastard!' Alexei slumped back in the chair, shaking his head and not caring how it looked. How could Svetlana be so matter of fact when someone had been murdered?

'Calm down, Alexei, everything has been taken care of. The body was dumped where they are laying foundations for the new buildings and covered with stones and gravel. Soon it will lie hidden forever beneath tons of concrete. Don't be so uptight. No one cares about the loss of one little homo. Good riddance!'

Alexei looked at his sister as if for the first time. She was a strong woman and had always looked after him, but she had completely lost sight of her humanity. He could see that now. It was no longer a game, roughing up a few sissy guys and taking their money. They had gone too far. He wanted no part in luring men to their deaths. 'Maxim is out of control. You need to do something about him.'

'What do you suggest?' Svetlana said, sounding as if she didn't understand what Alexei was getting at.

'That's your problem, but I will not be involved in killing people.'

'I will tell you when you can stop,' she said, ice in her voice.

Alexei sensed there was no getting through to her. She had no remorse for what had happened to Phil. He'd been disposed of like yesterday's trash. It saddened him that his sister could be so completely hard and uncaring. She couldn't see that what they were doing had crossed a line. That it was wrong.

Svetlana's voice softened. 'Look, Alexei, a weak little homo has messed up and died on us, and you're frightened of what the police might do. I get it. Don't worry, the guys will be back at the site to clean up. By the end of today, no one will ever know we've even been there. Take some time to get your head together.' She got up, gathered him into her arms and gave him a big kiss on the cheek. Then she pushed him out of the room. 'Go and get some rest, get drunk, get laid ... Whatever it takes. You need money?'

Alexei shook his head, closed the door behind him and went back to bed. He could only toss and turn, his mind too messed up to sleep, now that he knew the truth. Why had it taken a guy's death to wake him up? Make him see that what they did was fucked up. The pieces of his life—Svetlana, Maxim, the gang, the gay racket, his own queerness—were pieces of a jigsaw not meant to fit together. He was tired of playing this game. It was over.

Alexei packed a small rucksack with a change of clothing and sneaked out of the house. Out on the street, it struck him that he didn't know where he was headed. He didn't care. All that mattered was getting away from the gang. He had to if he was to have any sort of a future.

EIGHTEEN

Alexei caught sight of his Good Samaritan, walking towards him on the opposite side of the street and hid in the nearest doorway. A betting shop. He'd been so out of it that night and couldn't remember his name. He should thank the guy for taking care of him but was too embarrassed after crying like a child in his arms and then leaving the next morning with not so much as a word. He should have at least left a message of thanks or his phone number. If he had, he might not be alone now.

Alexei's insides were tied in knots, having never been completely on his own before. He would have given anything to have the guy hold him again and stroke his hair. Tell him that everything would be all right. But that wasn't going to happen. Alexei stayed out of sight until the guy and his friends entered a bar across the street. When they were safely inside the Sanctum, Alexei continued on his way.

*

Arran spotted Serge in a downstairs booth. He'd bought a couple of pitchers of beer. 'Good man,' Arran said, grabbing one and pouring out three beers. Gregor shook Serge's hand, but Jez started on him as soon as he sat down. 'Well, if it isn't Harry Potter. Didn't recognise you in long trousers.'

'Has the strip club given Red Devil a night off?' Serge shot back.

'The worm turns,' Jez said, laughing.

Arran gave the normally timid Serge a surprised look. He didn't notice. Too busy staring at Jez with a puzzled look on his face for why he'd been compared to a worm. English had to be confusing for foreigners at times. A waft of powerful scent announced the arrival of Sydnee.

'What are you talking about?' she asked them. 'If it isn't me, lie and say it is. I need lots of love and attention. You have no idea what kind of a day I've had. Plus I'm on a diet.' She glanced at the beer. 'From tomorrow. Tonight I need a drink. I've had the day from hell in Big Girls today. Sassy Symons, my most demanding customer, came in. Built like a Thames cruiser, she insisted on trying a dress that we had only one in her size and which just happened to be in the window display. As I went to get the dress off Alice—'

'Who's Alice?' Jez said.

Sydnee looked at him like he was insane. 'All my dress models have their own names and personalities.'

'Naturally.'

'Anyway,' Sydnee continued, 'I got wedged in by the Dainty Big Foot Shoe Collection. I mean, I was really stuck. People passing by the window were so rude that I had to stay perfectly still and pretend to be a dummy.'

'Must have been hard,' Jez said.

Sydnee swivelled her chin away from him. 'By the time that cute Bob the butcher from three doors down had come and disengaged me from my own display, Sassy had sashayed off to Fanny Fender's, my biggest competitor, saying that the service was too slow.'

'Is that why you're on a diet?'

Sydnee swivelled her whole body around to face Jez. 'Aren't you full of questions tonight, but answer this: Why else would it be?'

'You might have found love ... with Bob the butcher, for instance.'

'If only,' Sydnee purred. 'Anyway, enough of my trials and tribulations. How's life for love's young dreamers?'

Some surprised looks showed around the table when Serge piped up. 'I think Arran might have an admirer. Or a stalker. I'm not sure which he is.'

Arran's face burned as all eyes turned on him. He shot Serge a quizzical look.

'Remember the blond guy at Bananas?'

Arran thought it over for a moment and decided he had nothing to hide. 'He was just a guy who came in the bar and got smashed on beer and vodka chasers. He seemed so sad about something, and I felt sorry for him. I saw him later, when I was walking home along Boy Lane—'

'You never told me that,' Serge said.

Arran shrugged. 'I caught sight of him weaving all over the street. When he slipped off the kerb and ended up in the gutter, I went to help and asked if he was okay. He said something about him being no good and that I should walk away.'

'Sound advice,' Serge said. 'Hope you took it.'

'Then he started crying. Sobbing his heart out. I couldn't abandon him in that state. You never know what sickos are lurking about at that time of night. Anything could have happened to him.'

'What had happened to him?' Sydnee said.

'I never found out. He was out of it, so I let him sleep, intending to have a good talk with him in the morning. But when I awoke, he'd gone.'

'Hang on a minute,' Jez said. 'Back up. What do you mean, the next morning he'd gone? Gone from where?'

'I brought him home.'

'To our house?'

'What else could I have done? He was wrecked.'

'He could have been a thief or a murderer.' Jez lowered his voice. 'What were you thinking? Miss Givens would kill you if she knew. And it's no thanks to you that you're still alive for her to be able to do that.'

Arran was tempted to argue the point but wanted to get the conversation over and done with and so admitted he should have known better.

But Jez was like a missionary on a mission. 'What happened?'

'Nothing. I put him in my bed and slept on the floor. When I woke up in the morning, he'd gone. Didn't wake me or even leave a note.'

'Did he take anything?'

Arran shook his head.

'What was his name?'

Arran shook his head again.

Jez gave Arran a long look. 'You could have put yourself and us in real danger. Promise me you won't do that again.'

'I'll promise if you will.'

'What's that supposed to mean?'

'Well, when we were Up West that time, your friend Andrew told me that you're the one into dangerous guys. What did he mean?'

'I don't know. You should have asked him.'

'He said you were with Darius because he was dangerous.'

Jez laughed. 'He probably just meant he was an exciting guy, because he was and that was part of his attraction. I admit it. But that's all there was to it.' He fixed Arran with a steady gaze and asked, 'Are we done? Or is there anything else you want to get off your chest?'

What about all those times you go off to God knows where, with God knows who, doing God knows what? Arran wanted to say but didn't; instead, shaking his head.

Sydnee had the last say on the subject. 'You all should be very careful, because there's both good guys and bad guys out there and they all look the same.'

NINETEEN

Alexei lay in bed listening to the sounds of the new day stirring. His Pakistani landlord was setting up the newsagent shop below for the 6 a.m. opening. He rubbed his eyes, itchy and heavy. Sleep had been hard to come by lately. As soon as he drifted to sleep, Phil lay in wait. His eyes. Pleading. Then accusing. Alexei screamed that he hadn't done it. That it had been Maxim. But the eyes kept on staring until he escaped. Awoke. Tangled up in sheets soured with sweat.

A thud sounded from below. Same time every morning. The newspaper parcel being dumped in the shop doorway. Phil wouldn't be one of the news items. The gang had seen to that. The world was carrying on with one less person in it and no one cared, except him. It wasn't him being a hypocrite, even though he'd lured Phil to the honeytrap, because he couldn't have known he would die. Nothing like that had ever happened before. It was all Phil's fault for being so weak. Alexei smashed his fists down on the bed, then buried his face in his hands. It wasn't Phil he should hate; it was himself.

The gang was really to blame. The men had gone wild and overstepped the mark. But why now? The only difference between now and then was that they were in a different country. The Russian president had called Britain *a small island no one listened to*. All the men believed such thinking. They thought Russia was superior and that Russians conquered all. They were nothing if not patriotic. But if Britain and Britons mattered less, then British queers mattered not at all. The different venues for the honeytraps helped. Isolated building works that offered ready made burial sites. The scene was all set for Maxim, the king punisher of queers, to really go to town. Not long ago, Alexei had predicted that one day Maxim would go too far. Now he had. It might have been a one-off. But, then again, it might not.

The streets were cranking into life, cars and vans rumbling by, and the door bell constantly ringing as people made their way in and out of the shop. Alexei pushed back the duvet and swung his legs out of bed. He sat on the side and stared at the faded red and purple swirls in the threadbare carpet.

He never wanted to see any of the gang again, including Svetlana. Hopefully, they would soon tire of London and move on. Then he could stay. Here was no better or worse than anywhere else, whatever the president said.

After taking a swig of water, Alexei looked beyond the yellowed net curtains at the sun straining to come through the high cloud. It wasn't a bad day, dry at least. He should get out of here today and do something. The overflowing bin bag of pizza and sandwich cartons stinking up the corner had to go. Other than lazing around and driving himself mad with roundabout thinking that went nowhere, he'd done little since he'd taken the room. Not even unpacked his few belongings. This couldn't go on. He had to face up to living a future alone, taking his own decisions and making a new life. Money wasn't a problem. All the scams over the years had seen to that. But the gang mustn't find him. He had to lay low and stay out of their reach. Creaking sounds came through the barely emulsioned walls. One of the Pakistani guys next door getting out of bed. Alexei grabbed his washbag and towel and rushed to the shared bathroom for a shower. Cleaned up and dressed, he felt ready for the day. The door to his room was splintered and the lock none too secure, rattling alarmingly when he shook it to check it had locked. Not that it mattered. Nothing of value had been left inside. He clattered down the stairs and headed out for the tube station.

In the West End, Alexei found a barber's shop and lost his blond locks, emerging with a spiky crew cut. If his intention was to stay in London, he had to change his appearance; he didn't want to make it easy for the gang to find him. They would be on the lookout for him, panicking he might do something stupid. Like talking to the police. He found a greasy spoon cafe, Porky's Pantry, and had a full English breakfast, washed down with plenty of strong coffee. The cramped cafe was filled with workmen studying the horse racing pages in the red top papers, young guys in shiny suits mumbling into their phones, and young office girls in tight suits and high heels touching up their makeup. Ordinary people, living ordinary lives. The lucky ones. Life would be so much better if he was just like them. He extracted himself from the narrow seat and left the cafe.

After browsing the clothes shops up and down Oxford Street, Alexei picked out some casual clothing in blues and greys that wouldn't stand out and also bought a couple of large woollen hats. His designer shirt, trousers and leather jacket went into a bag. In the changing room mirror he checked out his new look. Grungy. The edgier hairstyle, designer stubble and loose clothing made him unrecognisable from the guy he was before. It was tempting to come up with a new English name ... Harry, Charlie, Freddie ... Except, they just weren't him. He chose to stick with Alex. He also pledged to himself that this new Alex would be a cut above the old Alexei.

From Oxford Street, Alex cut into the mesh of streets that made up Soho. In Old Compton Street, feeling in need of a beer, he looked for an out of the way gay bar before checking himself. That was what Alexei would do; he was Alex now. He headed inside Compton's, ordered a beer and sat at a window seat. The gang never ventured into Soho, anyway; they couldn't stomach the place. The gang weren't the only ones he'd deceived for so many years. He'd deceived himself, too. It had been easy to pass off two boys having a quick wank in front of each other as curiosity, a normal part of growing up. The progression to taking turns tugging on each other was natural too and nothing to get upset about. When a boy wanted to suck him off? That was just what you did when you got a bit older and girls weren't readily available. Each progression to full sex with a guy was passed off with a plausible lie he'd been all too ready to swallow. The alternative was to accept he was one of the hated and hunted perverts. Impossible. How could he be gay? He was Alexei, a handsome Russian man, the brother of the leader of a gang of gay hunters. A normal masculine man. Not one of the hated sissy boys.

Plenty of guys in Compton's were giving him the eye, seemingly interested and pleased with what they saw. Would they be as keen if they knew what he was really like? They'd take off like they were on fire if they knew what he'd done to people like them.

He took a long swig of beer, savouring the malty taste going down. That part of his life was over now. He'd woken up and didn't want to be that person anymore. He caught the reflection of the new Alex in the mirror beside him on the wall. Transformed. It would be much harder to change on the inside, forget the past, put it behind him and move on. Some of the men in the bar were in pairs. He'd never had a boyfriend. Never thought he ever would. Sex had been in the shadows, quick and furtive. He swirled the last of the beer in the bottom of the glass, fizzing it up. His Good Samaritan, the barman, had the kind of looks he liked—blond, sporty, sexy. And he was kind. What would life be like if they got together?

TWENTY

Alex pushed through the crowd at Bananas and found a spot where he wouldn't be jostled and where he had a good view of the bar. And Arran. When buying a drink, he'd heard someone call out the barman's name. A hard worker, he was run off his feet serving drinks and yet always managed to smile. He also looked people in the eye, as if he had nothing to hide. Alex felt exposed under the bright lights and had to resist the urge to shy away. Lurking in shadowy corners, furtive and shifty, was no doubt why the little Russian bartender was wary of him. He had to remind himself that now he was alone he could be open and act like he was supposed to be here. He sipped at his beer. It would take time to rid himself of his old habits.

Arran was the kind of man who could help him make new ones. Alex was desperate to make contact but saw that there was no chance of it happening here. Arran was constantly busy, and there would be too many eager ears listening in on their conversation. Somehow he had to get him on his own. They needed time to get to know eachother. Even then it wouldn't be easy. Chatting up Arran for quick sex wouldn't be difficult. That is what he'd always done. The problem was that he wanted more from Arran. He wanted to be with him and know all about him. That was something he'd never done. Even the idea of getting close to someone brought him out in a sweat, as did the thought of Arran asking questions of him. Arran seemed so open and honest that he deserved the truth, but Alex had too many skeletons in his closet for him to be completely open. The poor guy would run a mile.

Alex left the bar and sought out the river. It had been here forever, drifting along. Much like life had been for Alexei. He'd gone with the flow and done what Svetlana and the gang asked of him. There had been no point in challenging what couldn't be changed. His role in the gang had been that of the honeytrap and, rightly or wrongly, he'd known what was expected of him. His life had been simple. Without the gang, did he even exist? Did he have a future?

Alex pulled his jacket around him, reacting to the chill of the breeze off the river. But the night wasn't cold; the chill came from within. He was afraid. Afraid of being alone. Afraid of having to make a life for himself and having to take all the decisions. Afraid that Alex wouldn't be up to the task. After all, he knew nothing about the man.

*

The morning light crept into Alex's room and awakened him. His limbs felt heavy as he climbed out of bed. First into the bathroom the shower was hot and the water, soothing. Concealed inside a large hoodie and jeans, he left the flat. By night the industrial area was still. Eerily so. By day it became a rumbling, noisy place. Alex grabbed a pack of butter croissants from the shop and ate them on the walk into Vauxhall. There was no sign of life at 19 Boy Lane, the house where Arran lived. Alex pictured him sleeping peacefully in the bed he'd slept in after that fateful night and wished the future he'd daydreamed had happened already and they were snuggled up together.

Jack's Greasy Spoon cafe, hidden in a back street of Vauxhall, was open. Alex ordered a coffee. Sipping the dark brew at the window counter, he gazed at passers-by on their way to somewhere—a work meeting, a friend's birthday breakfast, the airport ready to jet off on holiday. They all had somewhere to be, somewhere they belonged. He finished his coffee and stood on the threshold of the cafe, unsure whether to go left or right.

Keeping his hood up and his eyes keen, Alex trudged around the streets of Vauxhall. The last thing he needed was to run into Svetlana, or worse, Maxim, but he couldn't stay cooped up in the dingy flat day after day. It would send him insane. He came across a park and sat down on a bench. Something felt uncomfortable in his back, a brass plaque. He shuffled along the bench and away from Artie Leonard. A couple of figures up in the distance were striking silly poses. Alex paid them no mind. It wasn't until later, as they were walking towards him, that he saw one of them was Arran, alongside a little old Chinaman. Alex kept his head down until they'd passed by, then got up to follow. At the High Street, they split up and Arran headed towards Boy Lane. Alex trailed him. Several times he went to close the distance between them, intent on talking to him. Each time something held him back. Unsure of what he would say. Afraid of a knock-back. If his plan to get with Arran fell through, Alex didn't know what he would do. He would be completely lost. He hung back, not wanting to appear as if he was stalking Arran, which was exactly what he did over the following days, finding out about his routines, biding his time until he could get him on his own and thinking over how he would play it.

Early one morning, Alex was again stationed at the end of Boy Lane when Arran emerged from his house in running gear. Heading away from Alex, he made for the river path. Alex had no need to try to shield himself from Arran's view, because he couldn't keep pace with him. After less than ten minutes Arran had been lost to the morning mist swirling in off the Thames. Alex gave up and sat heaving on the river wall, trying to catch his breath. Annoyed that he'd missed his chance. A voice caught him unawares.

'I've been wondering what happened to you.'

Startled, Alex's breathing took a turn for the worse.

'Have you had another mishap? You sound terrible.'

'It's the jogging,' Alex explained in-between deep breaths. 'I'm not used to it.'

'You don't say. But apart from lung failure, how are you? I was worried about you when you just disappeared.'

'You were?'

'Too right. You were in an even more terrible state that night.'

Alex lowered his eyes and mumbled, 'Thank you.'

'For what?'

'For looking out for me. It was kind of you.'

'You owe me big time.'

The hard tone to Arran's voice made Alex contrite. 'I know.'

'You really don't. I got into so much bother for taking a stranger in off the street. The way my housemates went on, anyone would have thought you'd murdered someone.'

Alex felt the blood drain from his face.

'Listen, you really don't look well. Let me help you back to where you live.'

On the walk through Vauxhall, Arran asked why Alex had been so upset that night. He lied, said he'd split from a boyfriend and was feeling really low. All the drink hadn't helped. Thankfully, Arran hadn't pushed for any details. When Alex led them down Boy Lane, Arran was surprised. 'This is where I live. Don't tell me we're neighbours?'

Alex indicated with his head into the industrial area. 'I live over that way. There's no need for you to go with me, I feel much better now. But I would like to take you out for a drink sometime to say thanks for helping me. If you'd like?'

Alex was crushed when Arran turned away and walked up the path to his house. Then he stopped. 'By the way, who's taking me out?'

Alex could have kissed him right there in the open. 'I am.'

'And who are you?'

'I'm Alex.'

For the first time, he really believed Alex might have a future.

TWENTY ONE

The din caused by everyone talking at once got inside Svetlana's head and made it impossible to think. She screamed at them, 'All of you, shut the fuck up!'

The grumbling and moaning fell to an uneasy silence. Svetlana could breathe again and took a moment to compose herself. The men expected too much of her. She wasn't a mind-reader. How the hell did she know why Alexei had run away or where he was or what he was doing now? She had no answers for them. She herself was struggling to work out what was wrong with him, talking about queers as if they were human and then taking off. He didn't make sense.

Svetlana was the queen of this tribe of gay hunters. A born leader, she loved having power over men, ordering them around and having them do her bidding. She had more affinity with men than women and had always preferred their company. This was her gang that she had built from nothing, bringing the men together and giving them purpose, and no one would be allowed to bring them down. Maxim irked her, sat by her side with a smirk on his face, enjoying her leadership skills being tested. Alexei had accused Maxim of being out of control. It was true he was a hothead, brutal and raw. But that was part of his appeal, along with the best sex she'd ever known. Maxim had his faults but he was loyal to the gang. No, all of this ruckus was down to Alexei. She could cheerfully have strangled him for taking off. All because of that night ...

The men fought amongst themselves to join in the punishment. Maxim was in the thick of it, choking the queer with a beer bottle. The queer's eyes became big and staring. The lips went dark. Maxim stepped back, letting the bottle crash to the floor. Everyone stopped. A flash of movement caught Svetlana's eye—Alexei bolting from the building. The queer's body was on the ground. Still. It was dead. They'd killed a queer for the first time. The men started clapping, big smiles appearing on their faces. Then the place erupted. Stamping feet beat out a rhythm, like a drum. The men hoisted Maxim on to their shoulders and paraded him around like a conquering hero. The queer's body lay trampled underfoot.

Forgotten.

Which was exactly how Svetlana intended it to stay. She looked around the room. Men were like boys. All they needed was reassurance, to be told that everything was going to be fine. It was up to her to make sure they were safe, and it killed her to think her own brother might be the only weak link in their defences. Not that she could admit it to anyone. Especially, not Maxim. Svetlana shouted above the noise, 'The most important thing is for us to stick together. Alexei hasn't been himself lately. We must find him.'

'What if he goes to the authorities?'

'Alexei would never betray us. We're his family.' Svetlana hoped for his sake he didn't do anything stupid, or she would kill him herself with her bare hands. The anxious faces and murmurings told her that the men were not convinced. She had to distract them.

Pyotr caught Svetlana's eye. Sixteen, eager and malleable—he was exactly like Alexei used to be. He would take Alexei's place.

'We're going to set up another honeytrap,' she announced.

'How can we with Alexei gone?'

'Pyotr will take his place.'

With all eyes turned on him, Pyotr paled.

'Don't worry,' Svetlana reassured him, 'Nikolay and Pavel will get you ready. They know everything you need to learn.'

Already the tone of the murmurings had changed. Men were so fickle, so easy to manipulate. 'As for the rest of you,' Svetlana said, 'get out and find Alexei. Bring him home.'

TWENTY TWO

Alex struggled to keep pace with Arran as they ran along the path by the Thames. The crispness in the air allowed him to dress in baggy jogging gear and a big woollen hat, pulled down low over his forehead. Life with Arran made Alex a lot more visible around Vauxhall, meeting up for coffee, going running, and practising Tai Chi with him and Mr Cheung in the park. But with no excuse not to do those things without making Arran suspicious, he had to be careful. The gang would be on the lookout for him. Despite the risks, he was having the best time of his life.

'Keep up, slow coach,' Arran called out over his shoulder.

Between gasps for breath, Alex called for Arran to ease up. He had a good physique he'd always taken for granted and was in shape but not fit. Not like Arran, who lived and breathed to be outdoors. Alex had caught his bug. The two of them spent most of every day out in the brisk autumn air. Alex revelled in the change to his lifestyle and the results to his body. He was leaner, harder, fitter than he had ever been in his life. Even his mind felt freer, although he had to work at that too. The nights were the worst and those times when he was alone. When Arran was working, Alex kept himself occupied by heading out of Vauxhall, usually up to the West End. The bustling streets of Soho were a pull for him. Another gay village, like Voho. People-watching from a coffee shop or bar fascinated him, seeing all types of guys pass by, those with big quiffy hairstyles or with patterns shaved into their heads, others with lush moustaches and beards, and many showing off colourful body art. The tattoos almost matched those of his countrymen, except in Russia they were usually on criminals and prisoners. In Russia gay people didn't want to stand out. Looking or acting differently would only bring trouble. In London gay people could look or be anything they chose. They had choices and didn't have to hide. Alex smiled to himself, imagining Arran's reaction if he turned up one day with a furry face and a big anchor tattooed on his bicep. Two guys went by, hand in hand. Alex had seen guys doing this before in Soho, even in daylight. He looked around, fearful for them. This would never happen in Russia. People would start yelling and attacking them. The police would be summoned.

'I remember now where I first noticed you,' Arran said. 'It wasn't in Bananas.'

Alex shot him a look, fearful of what he might say.

'It was on the first day I arrived in London. You rode the same tube as me. Damn nearly killed me.'

'I did what?' Alex said, not understanding.

'The men you were with pushed their way onto the tube and sent me flying. I think they have a thing against gay people.'

Alex held his breath. Had Arran discovered something about the gang?

'They were mocking an ad for a gay dating agency.'

'Oh, I see,' Alex said, daring to breathe again. 'Those guys. I hardly know them. Tagged onto them on the flight from Moscow and stayed with them until I found a place of my own. They're workmen types, construction. Came over here to find work on the building projects going on in London. I've lost touch with them. They've probably moved on by now.'

'You don't look like you work in construction,' Arran said. 'You never did say what you did.'

Even though the past couldn't be changed and Alex had to forget it and move on, he didn't want to lie to Arran or get tangled up in half-truths and had deflected questions about himself. A skill honed as the honeytrap. Even so, he still wanted honesty between them, as best he could manage. Arran was his new start and his future and was just showing interest. Alex had to give him something, or he would become suspicious. 'I don't have a job right now. Still looking.'

'All right for some. How do you live with no money coming in?'

'The icy winter roads around Moscow are notoriously dangerous. My parents died in a car accident. The insurance payouts are what I'm living on.'

Arran squeezed Alex's shoulder. 'I know how you feel. My dad died, too. Not in an accident, natural causes. His heart. Even though it was a few years ago now, I still miss him.'

'My parents died a long time ago, when I was a child. I barely remember them.'

'You didn't end up in one of those awful orphanages, like in Romania, did you? We saw tv documentaries showing them. They were terrible. The poor kids.'

Alex smiled at Arran's lumping all the former communist countries together. Typical Westerner. 'A relative took me in and brought me up.'

'Are they still around?'

'No,' Alex said, lowering his eyes and hoping what he said was true.

'Never mind, my friends will adopt you, and you can be part of our family. We should set up a date for you to meet them.'

It wasn't the first time Arran had mentioned meeting his friends. Alex wanted to but feared more questions. At some point he would have to face the music.

Leaving the river path they headed inland to Kennington Park to meet up with Mr Cheung, who was already in full swing. They joined in with the Tai Chi, and Alex was grateful for the distraction. Arran was so straightforward that Alex hated having to be economical with the truth. At those times, he felt just like the old Alexei.

TWENTY THREE

Arran had the living room to himself and was enjoying a morning cup of coffee. Miss Givens had headed out to the shops, and Gregor had left for work. A low sun was streaming in through the window and life had been hectic recently, so he kicked back and closed his eyes. Since arriving in Vauxhall his life kept on getting better. He'd fantasised about finding someone he could go out with every day, running, talking, fooling around and dreaming about the future. It should have been a nightmare, finding that someone ... late at night ... in the middle of the road ... on his knees and sloshed out of his mind ... and yet Alex was his perfect boyfriend. Others might disagree. The hard time Arran had been given for taking Alex in off the street was one of the reasons he hadn't yet mentioned him. He also wanted to be sure of him before announcing them to the world. Serge hadn't said anything but must suspect something was going on between them, the number of times Alex popped into Bananas and made a beeline for him at the bar. Arran tried to act as if Alex was like any other bar regular, which wasn't easy. He and Alex drew closer every day. The only niggle with Alex was his shyness. The hints Arran had dropped about meeting his friends had been ignored. He didn't seem overly keen. Alex would have to see that friends were important to Arran.

'Hi, stranger.'

Arran opened his eyes to see a smiling Jez joining him at the table.

'What have you been up to?' Jez said, pouring out orange juice into a tumbler. 'Haven't seen much of you lately.'

'Oh, just the usual, work, exercise, work, exercise ...'

'You know what they say about too much exercise ...'

Arran smiled at Jez's attempt to get a rise out of him.

'We should all get together for a night out,' Jez said. 'Let's make it soon.' His phone rang and he headed out.

The sight of Jez made the secret of Alex weigh more heavily on Arran's mind. The last thing he would ever want to do was hurt Jez. He should hear about Alex from him before someone else broke the news.

Arran had showered and was pulling on his jeans when Jez burst into his bedroom. 'Damn, I timed that wrong. Again.' Jez's mischief was like a shot in the arm to Arran. It was just like old times. Since their spat, the distance between them had grown. Nothing unpleasant; they were polite. Gone was the in and out of each other's bedroom, the constant texting, the banter. It hit Arran how much he'd missed Jez. Gregor rushed by the open door, only now arriving from work. He called out for them not to wait for him. That he would catch up with them at the bar.

'Hurry up, slow coach,' Jez shouted after him.

'Sit down before you hit the road,' Gregor called back.

Jez shrugged his shoulders. 'I don't get it.'

'One of Gregor's Russian sayings,' Arran said. 'Apparently you should sit down for a minute before heading out on a journey, to think about what is important. So take a seat.'

'We're only going around the corner to the Sanctum,' Jez protested. 'I could find my way blindfolded.'

Looking Jez in the eye, Arran said, 'I've invited a friend along tonight.' He wiped the sweat from his hands on his jeans. 'In fact he's more than just a friend. We've been seeing each other for a little while now. I wanted you to hear it from me.'

'Thank God for that,' Jez said. 'With all that nervous intensity, I thought you were about to go down on one knee and propose, what with all the talk on the radio and in the media about gay marriage. I was thinking up a way to let you down gently. That's great, who's the lucky guy?'

Arran was relieved at Jez's reaction to Alex. But with the secret out, a new feeling stirred. He felt a tad hurt Jez hadn't reacted more to his moving on. 'His name's Alex.'

'Where did you guys meet?'

Arran closed his eyes and inwardly groaned.

*

Soon after he'd left the gang, Alex had seen Arran heading into the Sanctum. This was the bar where he and his friends hung out. Apart from Bananas, Alex hadn't set foot into any gay bar in Vauxhall. Too risky. He dreaded to think what his former gang mates would do to him if they saw him going into one. But now he and Arran were a couple, they had to do normal things together, like going out and meeting his friends. Despite the danger.

Now it was happening and Alex was waiting in the entrance of the Sanctum, he felt like bolting. Arran had better get here soon. Alex closed his eyes and breathed slowly and deeply, the way Mr Cheung had taught him. On opening them, he saw Maxim.

If Maxim looked across now, he would see Alex. He lurched back into the shadows. The door to safety within the bar was out of reach and lit up by a light from above. If Alex tried, he would be seen. If Maxim saw him, he would be in big trouble. Then the situation turned even worse. Alex spotted Arran with another guy on a collision course with Maxim. Alex fell back against the wall, his heart racing. This night out had been a bad idea from the start. Life with Arran was perfect. Just the two of them. No one else. Now it would be ruined, with Alex's secrets about to be uncovered. Maxim would discover he was queer. And Arran would know his part in a gang that hunted, abused and murdered gay men. Maxim would want to kill him, and Alex would want to let him if he lost Arran. This nightmare couldn't be happening.

Maxim was yelling at Arran and his friend in his mangled English. 'Move, queer boys.' He barged through them, knocking them out of his way. The friend lunged at Maxim. Arran was caught in the middle, trying to keep them apart and appealing to his friend, 'Jez, leave it, he's not worth the aggravation.'

'He's out for trouble and he's going to get it this time,' Jez said.

They jostled their way towards Alex. Trapped in the doorway, sweat was trickling down his back. He wanted to run but couldn't move. One wrong step and his life would be over. Maxim glared at Jez, pushing him and spitting out threats. Jez fended him off. While the argument raged, Alex found his nerve and edged along the wall, inching towards the door and safety. He left the security of the shadows just as Maxim looked around. Alex froze. Maxim was looking right at him. Any second now and he'd call over and out him.

Beads of sweat scratched his face. His hand itched to wipe them away. But he dared not move. Maxim looked away. Alex darted back into the safety of the dark.

Arran was pulling at Jez's arm. 'Come on, don't spoil our night out because of this moron.' Jez held his ground, going eye to eye with Maxim. Alex begged Jez to listen to Arran, whispering over and over, 'Please Jez ... Please Jez ...' Finally, Jez listened and allowed Arran to lead him away.

Maxim smirked at them and called out, 'Run along, girly boys.'

Alex breathed a huge sigh of relief.

He was found in the doorway by Arran and Jez, who ushered him inside the bar, unknowingly shielding him from Maxim's view. If they noticed his heavy sweating, they didn't say anything. Alex heard his name spoken only moments before being suffocated by a heavy fragrance and then crushed by a bear hug from a brightly coloured person, introduced as Sydnee. The others were cringing at the sight of the crushing welcome. Alex shook hands with Jez and Serge, the barman from Bananas, who was either shy or still wary of him, judging by the way he kept his eyes lowered.

Sydnee and Serge had claimed a table and provided a couple of pitchers of beer. They asked about the commotion outside. Jez was still visibly steaming about the incident and filled them in, describing Maxim as a psychopath who had it in for gays. He had no idea how right he was. Alex heard his name being spoken. He looked up, dismayed that all eyes were back on him.

'Arran hasn't told us a thing about you,' Sydnee said. 'He's kept you under wraps and I can see why. I just want to snatch you away from him myself.' She patted the seat next to her. Alex had no choice but to oblige and sat down. He felt himself burning from all the attention. Why didn't this creature just shut up!

'We need to know all about you,' Sydnee said. 'So let's start with where you're from.'

Alex squirmed in his seat, hating that Sydnee wouldn't leave him alone. Nervous he might give something away to the Russian. He managed to get out that he was from Moscow.

'I'm curious,' Sydnee said. 'What is it with Russians and London? We're surrounded by them. And, right on cue, here comes another.'

'Another what?' Gregor said, grabbing a seat and a beer.

'Another Russian,' Jez said. 'I think the guy who keeps abusing us was also Russian.'

'He's done it before?' Alex blurted out, the words gone from his mouth before he could stop them. Fortunately, Gregor started speaking at the same time, to ask about what had happened and Alex's outburst was missed.

'I wouldn't be surprised,' Gregor said. 'It was always bad for gays in Russia, and now laws have been passed forbidding the promotion of homosexuality, the green light has been given for homophobes to go out and abuse gay people with impunity. Just because some of these people move here, don't expect them to have had a change of heart.'

Sydnee poured another round of beers and asked if organisations existed to help fight for gay rights. Gregor shook his head, a wry smile on his face. 'The big organisations, like the State, the police and the Orthodox Church, are all against homosexuality. Public polls not long ago had nine out of ten people saying that homosexuality should not be accepted by society. The same people support the anti-homosexuality legislation and are against same sex marriage. A couple of organisations do organise events for gay people. They have to keep the venues secret. Even then homophobic protestors find out and use all sorts of tactics to scare and intimidate, waiting outside to abuse and attack those guys who even dare attend or by throwing stink bombs inside to gas everybody or by calling in a bomb alert and having the premises evacuated or by intimidating landlords until venues are withdrawn. The police are everywhere, but with any skirmishes they arrest the gays and allow their attackers to leave. If gays try to report homophobic crime, the police throw them out, telling them that they don't deal with homos. Even looking or dressing differently on the street is often enough to be accused of being gay and attacked. Nowadays groups go around the streets and parks looking for gays to attack, with fists, knives, even stones.'

'Sounds like Biblical times,' Sydnee said.

'That's exactly what it's like,' Gregor said, with Serge nodding away by his side.

'Isn't there anything that can be done?'

Gregor looked at Serge and Alex. 'Move away, like we've done. In Russia gay people can have no life worth living. If you become known as a homosexual, you risk everything—your home, your job, even your life.'

'The story you told us at Halloween was true, wasn't it?' Sydnee said in a soft voice.

Gregor nodded. 'Denis is my middle name and Stephan was my friend and lover.'

Alex found it hard to witness Gregor's distress at remembering his dead lover. Arran had told him their story. Stephan had been a victim of people like him. He felt such a fraud sitting among these people and excused himself to go to the bathroom. This night was a total mess. He bent over a washbasin and splashed cold water onto his face. On standing up, Alex looked in the mirror and jumped, startled to see someone behind him.

Arran hugged him from behind. 'Are you okay?'

Alex felt sick. 'Just a little nervous at meeting everyone.'

Back at the table, Sydnee apologised to Alex for bringing up such an upsetting subject and said, 'Perhaps I should go over to Russia and campaign on behalf of gay—' Glass smashing behind the bar made everyone jump.

'I think that might be a sign from St Nicholas,' Gregor said, laughing.

'Who's that?' Sydnee said.

'The patron saint of Russia and the Disadvantaged. He was thought to be a miracle worker. But maybe the thought you would go over to Russia and petition his help was all too much, even for him.'

*

Way after midnight, Jez was alone in his room. He couldn't get the picture of Arran and Alex out of his mind. They looked good together. He couldn't blame Arran for finding someone, after he'd tried his best to get them together and Jez had blown him off. It was Jez's own fault the chance had been missed. He should have known that with Arran's good looks he wouldn't be single for long.

He opened up his laptop and went online to find some comfort.

TWENTY FOUR

'Are you okay?'

Not for the first time the gay had asked that question. Pyotr felt nervous, and when he was nervous he came across as surly. He had to fight the nerves. Trevor was his first honeytrap, and Pyotr wanted it to be successful, to prove himself and gain standing within the gang. The gay was a little sensitive and needy, always looking for reassurance. Pyotr had to find some common ground with him. It wouldn't be easy; he had nothing in common with dirty queers. He decided to tell the truth. 'Sorry, I'm just nervous. This is all new to me, living in London and chatting to guys online.'

'Don't worry,' Trevor said, 'we're both strangers in a strange city. Where are you from?'

Pyotr narrowed his eyes, wary. 'Is my accent that bad?'

'I love your accent. It makes you sound strong and mysterious.'

'My strength comes from working on the building sites,' Pyotr said, flexing his biceps. Pleased when Trevor looked impressed. 'What brought you to London?'

'I'm from a small town in Scotland you won't have heard of.'

That explained his own strange accent.

'It's the kind of place where you don't talk about being gay. It wasn't easy, trying to find people like me to be with. Even when I did, they were only interested in the sex. Probably in relationships or married, most of them. I met them on the Internet, like we did. I couldn't wait to get out, but London isn't what I thought it'd be.'

'Don't you go out to bars?' Pyotr said.

'You've probably seen me there,' Trevor sighed ...

Not bloody likely!

'... I'm the one standing on his own, waiting for some guy to hit on him, who turns out not to be the right one and then gets accused of wasting the guy's time.'

Now Pyotr had the gay talking, he wanted to keep it going. 'It can't be all bad?'

Trevor shook his head. 'I love my independence, making my own way, earning a living and having my own place.'

'What is it you do?'

'Sell books in a quaint old bookshop near St Paul's Cathedral. I love being around books ... that woody smell ... the promise of hidden treasures held within the pages ... people's heart's desires written down ...'

Pyotr had never read a book for pleasure in his life and struggled with the right look on his face to match Trevor's words. He sounded like he was having an orgasm. Ugh! He gave up trying and changed the subject. 'What about the people you work with?'

'They're lovely, but they have families, so I don't see them outside of work. We have nice chats in work about all sorts, books and plays and films. But they're not nosy and don't poke into my private life. Not that there's much to tell. I go to work, come home and that's pretty much it. The people I live with are friendly enough when I run into them in the kitchen or on the stairs, but there's no one I'm really pally with.'

Pyotr shook his head. 'What's pally?'

'Friendly with, close to,' Trevor said, smiling.

Pyotr smiled too. Grooming a queer wasn't so bad, once you got started. All you had to do was look good, show a little interest now and then, and let them do most of the talking. Already he was learning everything he needed to know about Trevor, and it looked like he would be the one. The only obstacle might be Christmas. 'I suppose you'll be heading home to see your family over the holidays?'

Trevor seemed to brighten up at the mention of Christmas. 'I thought I'd stay in London and see how it compares.'

Trevor was looking at him with a definite twinkle in his eye. It was Pyotr's job to trap the queers, but the thought of the two of them ... He felt sick. 'Compares?'

'All the festive attractions, the Christmas lights, the wonderful window displays in the big stores, the fireworks ... In my mind, I still picture London over the festivities as a Dickensian Christmas ...'

Pyotr didn't even want to ask what kind of queer Christmas that was. Not that it mattered. He had what he needed to know. Trevor wouldn't be going away for the holidays. Away from his family, isolated and lonely, he would be in need of a friend. Pyotr smiled while Trevor continued to babble on about trees and fairy lights and shit, confident he would deliver him in a honeytrap. That would be his Christmas gift to the gang and the world.

Pyotr made his excuses and cut the connection with Trevor in the personal chatroom. He looked over at Nikolay and Pavel and was given the thumbs up. They went off to report to Svetlana, leaving him alone.

Pyotr sat back and let out a huge sigh of relief. This was his chance to be someone within the gang, and he was determined to seize it. As he went to log off the main site, another message flashed, inviting him to chat. He was feeling pretty cocky after Trevor and decided to go ahead.

The guy was several years older than Pyotr, with wavy brown hair and bold eyes. Said he was called Jerry. This one was a hell of a lot more confident than Trevor and started chatting right away, getting straight into the sexual stuff, telling Pyotr what he was into and what he liked being done to him. Pyotr had never even heard of some of the stuff he was talking about and was taken aback by the speed of the guy but careful to disguise his disgust at what he was hearing. Out of his depth with this kind of talk, Pyotr stuck with him until he stopped telling and started asking and then made an excuse to leave. The pervy guy's eyes never left Pyotr, making him promise to hook up with him again soon.

Pyotr wasn't sure Pervy was their type but mentioned to Nikolay about the chance encounter. Nikolay told him to concentrate on Trevor for now. He could keep the other guy dangling for the future.

TWENTY FIVE

Alex didn't recognise himself in the van's rear-view mirror. He looked happy. When had be been truly happy before? Nothing had ever satisfied him for long. Not the easy money from the honeytraps. Not the underaged drinking in nightclubs. Not even the illicit sex in the shadows with other men. Always there had been something lurking inside him that had tainted his happiness. He'd never delved too deeply, didn't want to know, no point. He didn't feel that way anymore. He felt light and free and ... happy.

After hearing Gregor's story and learning what the victims go through, Alex had struggled to put the past behind him. Without Arran, he wouldn't have made it out of bed of a morning. Alex had been so right about him—easy going, genuine, loving—and loved being around him, trips to the cinema, out for drinks and meals, and then burning off the calories with hard exercise and even harder sex. He didn't even mind when told he was Arran's guinea pig for practising to be a fitness instructor. Arran inspired Alex to want to be a better person. He felt wonderful and couldn't keep his eyes out of the mirror, loving his short spiky hair and rugged facial stubble. Everything about him was different. Better. His breath quickened as he ran a hand over his ripped abs where Arran's hands had been. They couldn't get enough of each other.

Now Alex was living as an openly gay man, he felt a part of the world and not just a bystander. He had a boyfriend and gay friends, went out to gay bars and eating places, listened to singers like Sam Smith, read books by Paul Burston and Rupert Smith, and watched films like God's Own Country shown on a normal tv channel. Amazing. He saw gay people everywhere—on the streets, in the parks, in magazines, on television. They were unafraid to be visible. Newspapers and news channels carried issues that mattered to gay people—job rights, health, marriage, having kids. And many people and organisations championed the rights of gay people to have everything everybody else took for granted. He'd known none of this in Russia and wouldn't have believed life could be like this for gay people if he hadn't seen it with his own eyes. The life options made Alex dizzy. Jez had narrowed them down for him: 'Hot guys, hot sex, every day, and twice on Saturdays and Sundays.' Arran had laughed, shaking his head at Jez. These guys took all their liberties for granted.

Alex envied the guys their jobs and wanted to work. It wasn't that easy for him. He didn't have the paperwork in the UK to get a legitimate job and couldn't tap the Russian community for work and risk word of his whereabouts getting back to the gang. It came as a shock when Sydnee offered him seasonal work, driving her van to the supplier for stock and keeping the back room ordered. He had readily agreed to take the job, even though Sydnee was still a mystery to him. Nothing in his life had prepared Alex for Sydnee—or her van. He had almost resigned on the spot when he first saw the signage on the side, advertising Big Girls and its particular lines of merchandise, having expected a grubby work van with nothing written on it. Trust her not to care that everyone saw what she did for a living. Arran and Jez had teased him, advising Sydnee to dress him in a special driver's uniform to display clothing from the boutique. They gave Alex the idea to disguise himself in overalls and a hat. The supplier was a Bangladeshi outfit in East London. The workers who helped him load the van didn't seem to speak much English and never commented on the specialist stock. It seemed to be all just business to them.

When Alex wasn't driving, he did the lifting and carrying behind the scenes in the boutique. Unable to make head nor tail of Sydnee's own chaotic stock control set up, he rearranged it into an orderly system. Sydnee complained she couldn't find anything, and Alex became indispensable in locating the stock she would come running breathlessly into the stockroom to find. He came to enjoy her witty comments about the customers who came in. Sydnee always seemed to be in a good mood and was infectious to be around. She was also a strong businesswoman and lived life on her own terms. Alex got pretty choked up when he asked her why she'd offered him the job and she said because he was family now.

Alex parked the van behind Big Girls. The boutique was closed. He let himself in with the key Sydnee had entrusted to him. She had asked him to help with a new window display for Christmas that would rival the big stores of the West End. He loved her ambition. Nothing was too big, too bright or too garish. She had designed a new party season range she wanted highlighted in the window to generate more sales at Christmas.

They got to work stripping out the old display, removing the fittings and taking the clothes off the dummies.

'Don't call them dummies, you'll hurt their feelings,' Sydnee told Alex. She pointed out each of her models—Alice, Betty, Mavis, Eunice, Karen and the one with the bowed legs was Hilda.

Nothing surprised Alex about Sydnee, not even naming and talking to her shop models. She talked to herself all the time—thinking out loud, giving herself little reminders and pep talks—and didn't seem to care who heard her. Alex picked up Hilda.

'Where are you taking her?' Sydnee said, suspicion in her eyes.

'Into the back to fix her wonky legs.'

When Alex re-emerged, Sydnee asked him how he'd got on. He said he'd done the best he could, but she would never regain full straightness of her legs. He laughed when Sydnee sighed, conveying great sadness. He looked at what she'd achieved in his absence. White card had been stapled to the ceiling and walls of the window area. Together they hung giant snow crystals. 'What are we aiming to create?'

'The White Christmas Tranny Masked Ball,' Sydnee announced, grandly.

She'd overlooked that the models were girls, and Alex didn't have the heart to disillusion her. While she dressed the models in her finest fashions, including fake jewel Venetian masks, Alex made a snow scene with the white polystyrene shapes he'd been asked to save from the stock boxes. He then hung a white Christmas tree upside down from the ceiling, and they decorated it together. 'What's the meaning of the upside down Christmas tree?' he asked her.

Sydnee shrugged. 'Nothing, it just looks different. Arty people will come up with their own pretentious meanings and connect it with God, the devil or some secret society. The more mysterious, the better. Word will spread and people will rush down to see it for themselves. All publicity is good, right?'

Alex nodded. 'People love a mystery.'

He passed slender pieces of white furniture to Sydnee, who took forever in placing them just right—a side table and two spindly-legged chairs. Finally, the dressed models took centre stage. Sydnee said she wanted them to look as though they were dancing and having a fantastic time. Ages they spent, bending limbs and torsos in an effort to create the right effect.

'Look what you've done to Alice,' Sydnee said, chastising Alex. 'She looks contorted.'

'You can talk. Isn't that Mavis dancing backwards?'

'So she is. No wonder Betty and Eunice look confused.'

When all the models were arranged—looking fabulous and dancing the right way—Alex did the honours and flicked the on-switch of a lava lamp to rave them up. He joined Sydnee outside. The earth shook as she jumped up and down, clapping her hands and hugging Alex. The orange and blue lava light flowed over the models, making it look like they were moving—dancing in some bizarre Christmas themed nightclub in Venice.

'Is it how you imagined?' Alex said, grinning inside.

Sydnee sighed. 'It's perfect.'

She insisted on taking Alex to the Sanctum for a thank-you drink. The other guys were already in there. Sydnee couldn't hold back her glee in describing the miracle display she and Alex had created. They all had to sit through repeat showings of the thirty-two second video she'd taken on her phone. She predicted the new party season range and the revamp of the fancy dress line would make it the best Christmas ever for Big Girls. She wasn't in the least bit amused when Jez suggested that all her merchandise was in fact fancy dress. She didn't speak to him for close on two minutes.

Alex resurrected Sydnee's good mood by making a toast to wish the boutique success at Christmas: 'To Big Girls and all who wear her.'

TWENTY SIX

The honeytrap was so close that Pyotr could almost taste it. Every day he met up with Trevor online to keep him keen and to make sure nothing happened to ruin their plans. Although Pyotr hated the other pervy gay he'd met online, with his dirty sex talk and greedy eyes that made him feel naked, he'd learned a lot from him about how to sex chat. Trevor was now right where Pyotr wanted him. Only the details were left to set. Trevor thought they were meeting for a night out, followed by home to his place for the Christmas holidays. Pyotr's smile came naturally. 'I'll pick you up in my car.'

'What's it look like?' Trevor said.

'A Mercedes-Benz CLA250 Coupe.' Trevor's smile flattened and Pyotr thought he mustn't be impressed.

'I don't know anything about cars.'

Typical. Queers were not real men. They knew nothing about cars and sport and fighting. Pyotr hid his derision and said, 'It's a big black car, very stylish. You'll like riding in it.'

'I'm sure I will.'

Pyotr ignored the odd smile playing on Trevor's face and gave him the pick up details. Pyotr knew the location to take him—the site where a new factory was being built over towards the west of the borough and less than ten minutes by car. He'd driven the route a couple of times and knew all the quiet side roads to take to get there safely. The last thing he wanted was to be stopped by the police for any reason. That's why the gang kept the car in pristine condition. Several of the guys were working on the building site, including one on the security detail. They would have total control of the site and would not be disturbed. The honeytrap was set for the evening of the final working day before Christmas. The holiday period would leave the site deserted for over a week. None of them could believe how easy it was in this stinking country to do whatever they wanted with no questions asked.

'I can't wait,' Trevor said. 'I'm so happy you're coming to my place for Christmas. I've been out shopping ...'

Typical. All queers knew about was shopping, buying frilly things and face creams, like girls.

Trevor was still prattling on. '... I want everything perfect for our first Christmas together. You'll love what I've done with my place—massive floor cushions so we can lounge around and watch telly or listen to music or something, a couple of arty prints that jazz up the walls, a sweet little Christmas tree already dressed with tiny baubles, a gorgeous new duvet cover ...'

A duvet cover! Pyotr shuddered at the picture of the two of them in the same bed. Naked. Trevor pawing at his body with his queer hands. It was enough to make him create his own arty print all over the wall. The disgust must have shown on his face because Trevor asked what was wrong. Again.

'Nothing,' Pyotr said, covering his slip. 'I was hoping you weren't getting into debt on my account.'

'Don't worry, my gran left me some money in her will. She passed away not long before I came down to London. Normally I don't touch it, it's my nest egg. But this is a special occasion ...'

Pyotr gave Trevor a big smile. Although he hadn't understood half of what Trevor had said, he did pick up that he had savings money. This was the gang's first Christmas here, and it would be the best—the final honeytrap of the year, followed by lots of turkey and shit, fags and booze, and all bought at Trevor's expense, courtesy of yours truly, Pyotr. The gang would love him for delivering Trevor—and his money. He would be a hero, like Maxim.

'... You should have seen me struggling to carry everything back from the shops,' Trevor went on, 'squashing onto the packed tube, struggling up the hill to the house and squeezing up the narrow stairs to my room. I collapsed with exhaustion when I got through the door. When I got my second wind, I started cleaning—dusting everything, then running around with the hoover—before putting out all the new stuff. I tackled the shared bathroom last. Torture. I was in there for an hour, scrubbing at the tidemark and rust around the plughole. Could see my face in it when I'd finished.'

Shouldn't have bothered. Pyotr was bored out of his mind.

'I changed the bulb in the lamp to one of those soft mood bulbs to create the right atmosphere. I also put a little something under the tree for you.'

'You did what?' Pyotr said.

'I bought you a present. I hope you'll like it, but just in case ... I've kept the receipt.'

Christmas presents hadn't even crossed Pyotr's mind. Until now. How could he get his hands on it without giving the game away?

'There's no use looking like that because I'm not going to tell you what it is. It's a surprise. And before you say another word, I wanted to do it. You've been so good to me, wanting to know everything about me and I feel so selfish that there's never any time for you to speak about yourself. So that's why. I don't expect anything back, either. So don't worry about that. Anyway, listen, I'm going to have to cut it short today. I've got a date—'

Pyotr shot bolt upright, worried something was about to go badly wrong. There wouldn't be time to set up another honeytrap at this late stage. The gang would blame him. This had never happened to Alexei. 'A date?'

'With a barber,' Trevor said, laughing. 'See you soon. Can't wait.'

*

Pyotr leaned back in the chair and relaxed, feeling pleased with himself. The honeytrap was set. He had stepped into Alexei's shoes with ease, delivering a honeytrap at his very first attempt. Now the gang would give him the respect he deserved, and Trevor would get what was coming to him. Roll on Christmas.

TWENTY SEVEN

Arran was in the cellar at Boy Lane, digging out the Christmas decorations to trim up the house. 'Look at this place,' he said to Jez. The cellar was typical Miss Givens—whitewashed walls and everything stored in boxes or bags complete with handwritten labels. It made their task super easy. 'There's no dust, cobwebs, spiders or rats in sight, present company excepted.'

'Ha, bloody, ha,' Jez said. 'Miss Givens loves the traditions around Christmas, and trimming-up day is officially the start of our Christmas celebrations. It's a house ritual.'

Arran was looking forward to Christmas Day, when Alex, Sydnee and Serge would join them. He was also horny for Christmas night, due to the amnesty on overnight guests. He and Alex would get to spend the whole night together, officially. Unlike the first time they'd met. They'd also get to have sex in a bed, which would be another first. Sex in the great outdoors was a turn on but a bit chilly at this time of year.

As they climbed the narrow stairs, each balancing several boxes, they heard music playing. In the living room, they found Gregor and Miss Givens. Gregor was opening up a bottle of cranberry vodka. 'Hey, don't start the party without us,' Jez said. 'And what is that music playing?'

'Classical,' Gregor said, sounding and looking defensive, as if expecting an argument from the two of them.

Jez nodded. 'I like it. A nice change from the Christmas pop songs played on loop in all the bars and shops. They're enough to drive anyone insane after the first two hundred hearings.'

They knocked off the ice cold vodka in Russian style—straight back in one go. While Gregor was topping them up, Arran asked him how come freezing cold vodka burns. When pouring out the drinks and shaking his head at the same time proved too difficult, Gregor resorted to, 'I don't know.'

'Is this a Russian Christmas custom?' Miss Givens said.

'Drinking vodka is an all year round Russian tradition, but religious occasions were out in the time of the old Soviet Union because they didn't fit with communist theory. After the fall of communism, people went back to the Russian Orthodox Church that follows the Gregorian calendar, which is why Christmas Day is celebrated in Russia on January 7.'

'Are you a churchgoer, then?'

'No, he's just a goer,' Jez said, pumping his arms and leering at Gregor.

Gregor laughed and shook his head. 'I do believe in God, but the church is one of the main drivers of anti-homosexuality feeling in Russia. They preach that homosexuality is morally unacceptable and a sin and talk about gay marriage leading the world towards doomsday.'

Miss Givens tugged at the string on the storage boxes. 'It never fails to surprise me how intolerant religious organisations and their followers can be sometimes. Some straight people think they have the monopoly on God and religion.'

Arran had never seen Miss Givens rattled. He joined her in freeing the decorations and then spread them out over the floor, so that they could see what was what. Lamps and candles were lit to compensate for the waning winter sunlight. Arran and Jez started to assemble the Christmas tree. Miss Givens went to hand them the baubles but then seemed to change her mind and kept hold of them.

'Don't you trust us with your baubles?' Jez said.

'They're antique,' she said, eyeing the fragile gold and silver baubles painted with little nativity scenes.

'Not half—'

Arran nudged Jez in the ribs. 'We promise to take care of them as if they were our own.'

Miss Givens handed over the baubles to Arran and gave Gregor a wreath to hang on the front door. As she was trailing fairy lights around the window, Arran clocked the sideways looks she gave him and Jez as they decorated the tree. They managed to hang the prized baubles without mishap and were then handed a sheet of webbing. 'What is it?' they said.

'Angel web,' Miss Givens said, going on to explain that it was used in Christmas decorations because it had appeared during apparitions of the Virgin Mary.

'We mean,' Jez said, 'what do we do with it?'

Miss Givens gave them a demonstration of how to tease it out like spider's web and then watched with visible distress as they tortured it into place. The final glory task was left to Miss Givens in placing the antique fairy on top of the tree. Arran's dig to his ribs caused Jez to swallow the comment on the tip of his tongue.

*

Arran suggested to Miss Givens that she should have joined the military such was her level of planning for the big day. Each of the housemates had their orders. Miss Givens had planned the menus and picked up the meat ordered from Bob the butcher, at Sydnee's insistence. Arran and Gregor were charged with fetching all the beverages. Jez pointed out that he was in charge of finding all the fresh produce—vegetables, salad, fruit. And nuts.

'Man nuts don't count,' Arran said.

Jez pulled a face. 'Spoil sport.'

'If we fail in our tasks, do we get jankers?' Arran asked Miss Givens, digging up the term from his Scout camping days.

She gave him a look. 'Don't be lewd, Arran, it's almost time for Jesus to come.'

He laughed.

Arran welcomed the opportunity to spend time with Gregor. He was a real friend, dependable and warm. He could also be funny, with a dry sense of humour. They catered for every need—wine, beer, shorts and mixers, medicinal brandy and the morning-after recovery fruit juice. Gregor easily strolled along, pulling one of Miss Givens' shopping trolleys behind him. Arran had point blank refused a trolley and was now struggling to carry his share of the drinks in flimsy cardboard boxes.

After their Christmas duties had been completed, the guys set off for the Sanctum. The bar was heaving. Over countless heads, Arran spotted Alex, waving from one of the booths at the far end and pointing at the bar. Sydnee and Serge were with him. Arran got the message and went to the bar, noticing the overflowing tips jar while he waited to be served. Donny was doing well, as were he and Serge. They'd been run off their feet for weeks in the build up to Christmas, with Bananas busier than ever. The punters were in festive mood, and the tipsier they got the more tips they gave. Arran intended to use his share to buy his Secret Santa gift and was made up to have drawn Alex. Bearing gifts of three pitchers of beer and assorted crisps and nuts, he joined the others. He shouted above Wizard's *I Wish It Could Be Christmas Every Day*, 'We're back to the same old Christmas songs. I wish they'd let Gregor be DJ.'

'Yeah,' Jez said, 'we could bop till we drop to Beethoven and his mate, Bach.'

'What are they talking about?' Sydnee said.

Gregor shook his head. 'Ignore them.'

Alex pointed at a Christmas tree, flashing away above the bar. 'I don't get the connection between Christmas and trees.'

Sydnee set down her packet of marmite crisps on the table, a big smile broadening her painted face. 'I had a friend who was a White Witch—'

Jez pulled a face. 'Where do you meet all these weird people?'

'They're not weird, they're just like you and me. Anyway, she always complained that the Christians had pinched a lot of the old Pagan customs. She said that in olden days trees were dressed up with edibles, like fruit and nuts, for the Winter Solstice celebration to remind everyone of the bountiful Spring to come. They were also dressed gaudily to ward off evil spirits.' Sydnee jangled her brightly coloured earrings and bangles till they sang, drowning out Wham. 'You could say that I'm a human Christmas tree. Stick close to me and I'll keep you safe from evil.'

Jez suggested she might benefit from Secret Santa bringing her a course of professional styling sessions, only to be given a clip around the ear for his cheek.

'Talking of gaudy dress—'

'Steady on, Gregor,' Sydnee said.

'I only meant that a fancy dress Christmas Day would have been nice, if only to give Arran much needed practice for next year's Halloween party.'

Arran nearly choked in trying to swallow down his drink and defend himself at the same time. 'I thought my Teen Wolf character was a classic.'

Alex patted him on the back.

'You're in a minority of one,' Jez said. 'But don't worry, mate. Next year I'll help you with your outfit.'

Arran groaned. 'I can just imagine. You'll have me running around half naked, like you do.'

'What's wrong with showing skin? Gregor earns his living from it.'

Sydnee leaned into Gregor. 'How about a blow by blow account of your rubbing technique?' She described Gregor's resulting skin colour as radioactive red, the same as her hair.

'We should nickname him Chernobyl,' Jez suggested.

On the walk home, Sydnee insisted they go by Big Girls to admire her and Alex's creation one more time. She stood for ages, gazing at the White Christmas Tranny Masked Ball. Then, on her top note, she wished the whole of Vauxhall a very merry Christmas. 'I hope you all get exactly what you wish for,' she said, finishing off with a hearty hiccup.

TWENTY EIGHT

When Pete turned off the main road and drove through an opening between closed down work units, Trevor was surprised. When his door opened and two men joined them, it was a shock. When they took hold of him and dragged him out of the car, he was panicked. There was something badly wrong with this situation.

Within minutes of Pete picking him up in his big black car, his dream come true had turned into a nightmare. Whatever Pete's motives were for this ambush, every fibre of Trevor's being told him he had to get away. When one of the men slipped on frosty gravel, Trevor lashed out at the second guy, catching him on the eye. Freed, he took off in the direction of the street. He left behind a frantic scene, Pete yelling, car doors slamming and tyres skidding over the loose surface.

Trevor sprinted to the main road, searching up and down for help. No one was about. He spotted a car in the distance and marched down the middle of the road, shouting and waving his arms to catch the driver's attention. The car's brake lights glowed red as it approached. Relief flooded over Trevor in waves. He would be safe. The car crept towards him. The driver was a middle-aged man. His startled eyes told Trevor how nervous he was. Suddenly, the car revved up. Trevor pelted towards it, banging on the roof and shouting for it to stop. It veered away from him, sending him sprawling to the ground. The car accelerated away, quickly receding into the distance and taking his chance of safety with it.

Pete's car was now in sight. He was in the driver's seat, his eyes like slits and so very different from the guy Trevor had known on the Internet. These guys meant to do him harm. But why? What could he have possibly done to them? He picked himself up and ran on. Heard the whine of Pete's motor as it came after him. When it neared, Trevor changed direction, causing it to swerve. The side fender caught him on the hip, knocking him over. He climbed to his feet and limped away, his side throbbing. The sound of car doors being flung open and heavy footsteps giving chase made him whimper. His eyes locked on a fallen tree branch. He picked it up and turned to face the men, coming at him from either side. He swung the heavy branch and caught one of them on the arm. The second guy darted in and wrenched the branch out of Trevor's grasp. Defenceless, the men jumped him and wrestled him to the ground. He screamed for help as he was dragged to the car and thrown in the back. No one was around to hear. The wheels screeched as the car spun around and sped away. Trevor lay on the floor, catching his breath and feeling sick with fear. If only the man in the other car had stopped ...

Trevor couldn't keep track of all the twisting and turning of the car and stopped trying to memorise the journey. Eventually the car slowed, gates creaked open and they rattled over rough ground before coming to a stop. Despite his hip complaining with every bump, Trevor gathered his strength for another attempt to escape. The men must have sensed this and shackled him between them, giving him no chance to run. Screaming and squirming to free himself from their clutches, he was dragged into a nearby building and sent sprawling onto hard concrete, grazing his hands. His last hope of escaping died with the slamming of the heavy metal door.

Trevor looked around. They'd brought him to some sort of warehouse. Flames were leaping out of oil drums and the air reeked of smoke and booze. It was a hellish place from which there was no way out. The windows had been boarded up, and he was surrounded by a shedload of men. Their eyes were on him. Hard, hateful eyes. He shrank from their gaze. A couple of them grabbed Trevor by the arms and hauled him towards a stinking metal pail. They dunked his head into the steaming yellow liquid and held him down. Warm piss stung his eyes and soured his mouth. He thrashed his legs about to get free. Held in a vice like grip, he couldn't escape. His panic rose.

They were drowning him!

He was pulled out of the pail and snatched a lungful of air. Then his head was plunged back into the piss. He squeezed his lips together, holding on to the precious breath. Seconds ticked by like hours. His lungs were screaming, and his heart was hammering out of his chest. He couldn't hold on much longer. Even though his brain was ordering him to keep his mouth closed, his body was begging him to open up and breathe. His body won. He opened his mouth. Piss flooded in. They wrenched him up and let him collapse to the floor, coughing and gasping for air. In-between precious breaths he begged for no more. A woman's voice came to him.

'It's okay, relax. We just wanna have a bit of fun with you.'

'This ... isn't fun ... it's sick,' Trevor managed to say, his chest heaving.

'C'mon, get up. Let's have some fun and then you can go.'

A sliver of hope opened up inside Trevor. He ignored the pain in his hip and struggled onto his feet, wanting this ordeal over with as quickly as possible.

'Strip,' the woman said, a bemused expression on her face.

His ears were full of piss. He couldn't have heard right. 'What did you say?'

'Strip! Strip! You fucking moron.'

When the men started to hum the Stripper music, Trevor felt like an act in a grotesque burlesque show. His head was reeling and he couldn't make sense of what was happening to him. This situation was too surreal for someone living at the centre of the civilised world and not some heathen outpost. He had to be the victim of a sick joke. He searched out Pete. His face showed no trace of humour. This wasn't the same guy who had shown such an interest in him. Trevor felt such a fool for all the trouble he'd gone to in making his room look festive for the two of them for Christmas. What kind of Christmas would he have now after this sick charade? Pete had seemed so nice, so interested. Now he looked as pitiless as the rest of the men in this cesspit. Trevor searched again for a way out. Surrounded by viciousness, there was no escape. He would just have to ride it out.

A punch to the head sent Trevor reeling. He rubbed his head and cowered from the vicious thug screaming at him. 'Dance! Strip! You fucking little nancy boy.'

Hands gripped Trevor from behind, moving him in time to the ridiculous humming. He twisted around to see Pete mocking him and asked why he'd done this to him.

'Because you're a dirty queer.'

'But you're gay, you told me so yourself,' Trevor said, not believing what he was saying even as he said it. This man had tricked him.

Pete went berserk, punching Trevor in the face and busting his lip. Spit flew out of Pete's mouth as he screamed, 'Don't call me a fucking pervert, you little cocksucker! Now do as you're told and strip.'

This was real. Tears rolled down Trevor's face. It was futile to appeal to the better nature of these people, including the woman. He would have to put up with their antics until they grew bored and let him go. He began to dance in a stiff, disjointed way to the insane accompaniment, slowly removing his clothes. The men clapped his efforts, catcalling and jeering. He stripped down to his underwear and stopped, too embarrassed to continue. Pete yanked down his boxers, leaving Trevor naked before them. His attempt to shield his genitals was cut short. Forced to raise his hands to fend off the cans and bottles being lobbed at him. These people were deranged. But not mad enough that they hadn't planned this whole elaborate set up. The police had to do something about them. As soon as he was freed, he would go straight to the police and report them. They couldn't be allowed to do this to anyone else.

The vicious thug got in Trevor's face. 'Down on your knees, cocksucker.'

Wary of him, Trevor did as he ordered. The thug grabbed Trevor's hair and yanked his head back. To the hum of the Stripper music, he ground Trevor's face into his groin. The men went crazy from laughter. Trevor registered surprise at feeling something stirring. The guy was turning himself on.

'Look, he likes it,' the thug shouted. 'Let's see if he likes this.' He drove his fist into Trevor's stomach, winding him. As Trevor tried to roll away, the thug grabbed him. 'You're only getting what you deserve.'

'I haven't done anything wrong.'

'You're a queer, a kiddie fiddler, a pervert,' the thug screamed. 'Say it.'

'I'm not!' Trevor screamed back.

'Say it! Say it!'

'Let me out of here you sadistic maniac. Let me out! Let me out! Let me ...'

Trevor's mantra sent the thug into a frenzy, punching and kicking him.

Trevor tried to fight back, his puny punches not even touching the big alpha male. The pack of men closed in around them, snuffing out the light and laying into Trevor with their fists and boots. One big mass of pain, he was terrified he wouldn't be able to hold on. Too many of them stood against him. Their hate too strong. The sad part was that he had no understanding of why. What had he done to them? To anyone? To deserve this cruelty, this punishment.

Helpless on the floor, boots laid into Trevor from all sides ... stamping on him ... mashing his head and body ... crushing his insides ... His screams reduced to whimpers and his ability to fight weakened. His resolve to hold on dwindled with every blow. The hope he would return to his life was fading ... draining away ... Until no hope remained.

TWENTY NINE

Frost crackled under Alex's feet, the white coating making the world look innocent. And there was no one about to ruin the illusion. Except him.

Already he'd been up for hours, flattening the clothes he was wearing with a borrowed iron, wrapping and unwrapping and rewrapping a Secret Santa gift, and waiting impatiently for the clock hands to say it was a decent hour to set out. He was keen to get started his first English Christmas—swapping presents, eating turkey and Christmas pudding, wearing silly hats and telling cracker jokes. However, Arran had warned him to be serious through the Queen's speech or risk Miss Givens's wrath.

On arriving at Boy Lane, Alex knocked on the door and went in. Arran rushed out of the living room and gave him a hug. Alex wrinkled his nose and pushed him away. 'You're all sweaty. Have you been out running?'

'Why should Christmas Day be different from any other day?'

'I thought it was.'

'You and Miss Givens, both. When I told her I was committed to exercising, she told me I should be committed—to a lunatic asylum for going jogging on Christmas morning.'

Alex smiled. 'What's all that noise?'

'Miss Givens going at it in the kitchen—Operation Christmas Dinner. She's been up since the crack of dawn, banging and chopping and whisking up a storm.' Arran made for the stairs. 'Come up and talk to me while I get ready.'

'Where do I put this?' Alex said, waving his Secret Santa gift in the air.

'Drop it in the sack behind the door.'

Three quarters of an hour later, as they were coming back down the stairs, they heard a big commotion and found Sydnee in the hall on her knees. 'What are you doing down there?' Arran said.

'Some idiot left this sack trailing and I caught my foot in it.'

Alex hid behind Arran, who told her, 'That was probably Alex—'

Alex nudged him in the back. 'Traitor.'

Miss Givens came running out of the kitchen.

'Do you have a turkey?' Sydnee growled at her. 'If not, I'm going to wring Alex's neck when I get up off this floor. He damn nearly killed me.'

Alex tore down the remaining stairs and offered his arm to Sydnee. The two of them wrestled to get Sydnee back on her feet. Jez and Gregor came bouncing down the stairs and abruptly stopped.

'It's a bit early for dancing, isn't it?' Jez said.

Sydnee growled.

A knock came at the door. Serge appeared, looking overwhelmed at the sight of everyone gathered in the hall to greet him. 'Happy Christmas,' he called out.

Sydnee growled.

Miss Givens waved everyone into the living room. Sydnee requested a drink, for the shock. Miss Givens urged Gregor into the kitchen, to bring out the Bucks Fizz. After slaking half the contents of her glass, Sydnee surveyed the room. 'Love the decorations. They're beautiful.'

'We did them,' Arran and Jez said, their voices in chorus. 'We're thinking about a career in window display. What do you think?'

'Don't give up your day jobs,' she said, winking at Alex.

Gregor finished setting the table and called everyone over to take a seat. The vibrant oilcloth showed the lady of the house fussing over rosy cheeked children while the man of the house stood at the head of the table with two big carving knives in his hands, ready to carve an enormous steaming turkey.

'That family looks just like us,' Sydnee said, laughing.

'That's what I thought you were going to do to me,' Alex said, eyeing the turkey.

'I had something much more inventive in mind for you. I was going to make mincemeat of you first, then stuff you—'

'Dig in while they're hot,' Miss Givens said, handing around plates of salmon and scrambled eggs with chives on hot buttered muffins.

The clinking of cutlery on china was the only sound heard until Jez started to wonder out loud what Secret Santa might have brought him.

'Don't talk to me about Secret Santa,' Sydnee said. 'I'm still having a funny turn from when he grabbed me.'

'He'll make up for it,' Jez said. 'What is your must have for this year?'

'I don't care what I get—as long as he's gorgeous,' she roared.

'In that case, you'll need your strength,' Miss Givens said, bringing homemade fruit loaf and cups of hot chocolate out of the kitchen.

'I'm stuffed,' Alex said.

Arran glanced at Sydnee. 'You very nearly were.'

Miss Givens suggested that the Christmas morning carols service might be uplifting. Dressed in winter gear against the frosty chill, they wandered along to the park. The haunting brass band sound of the Salvation Army came floating through the air. As they approached the entrance, the band struck up *Silent Night*.

'My absolute favourite,' Sydnee declared, clapping her hands and rushing towards the band.

Jez raised his eyes. 'I didn't think you could even spell *silent*.'

Sydnee ignored him, swaying around to the music and getting tangled up in the lead of a Labradoodle puppy that had pulled away from a young boy while trying to bite at a shiny blue bow around its neck. As Sydnee started to tumble she called out, 'What the—'

'Language, Sydnee, there's young ears about,' Jez said, making a grab for her arm and steadying her.

Sydnee recovered only in time to duck down under a remote controlled helicopter on a trajectory towards her head. 'What the—'

'Sydnee!'

They came to a consensus that it might be safer to take a stroll away from where people were congregated. When they came alongside a spread of bushes, Arran nudged Jez. 'I'll cover for you, if you want to make a quick recce and see if there are any hotties lurking inside.'

'Ha bloody ha!' Jez said. 'These days, you have as much al fresco sex as I do.'

Arran grinned. 'Yeah, but not tonight.'

After taking several turns around the park and singing along to the carols, they headed back to Boy Lane. The streets were largely deserted of people and traffic, and all the shops were closed. Sydnee abruptly came to a halt and shushed them.

'What is it?' Alex said.

'I'm sure that's my security alarm I can hear sounding off.'

Sydnee started to hurry towards Big Girls, with the others following on behind. The closer they got the more convinced was Sydnee that it was her alarm. When they got to the end of the street, they could see a gang of men loitering outside the boutique. Sydnee yelled at them to bugger off. The men looked in her direction before moving off in the opposite one, laughing and jeering. Sydnee gave chase. The others ran after her, calling out for her to be careful. She didn't even break stride. The men up ahead hotfooted it away. Alex and Arran overtook Sydnee and went after the men. The gap between them closed to where Alex could make out the culprits. He stalled. Stumbling, he slipped off the kerb and turned his ankle. Arran raced after the men alone. Sydnee called out for him to stop; he couldn't take them on by himself. They gathered around Alex and helped him to his feet. He hopped about for a while before regaining a normal walk. By this time the men had disappeared.

The group trudged the rest of the way to Big Girls. Sydnee sank to her knees in the middle of the road. Alex patted her shoulder. Where the window used to be was a gaping hole. The White Christmas Tranny Masked Ball was a crime scene, the girls sprawled in a mangled heap, one with her head caved in, and all of their fineries torn and crushed. The Christmas tree had been felled, scattering broken baubles out into the street. The back of the window display had been demolished. Broken glass glistened everywhere like deadly frost.

Miss Givens took charge. She directed Sydnee to open up the boutique and turn off the alarm, still wailing away. The inside of the shop was devastated, the culprits in plain sight. House bricks lodged in smashed counters, embedded in ruined displays and nested in ripped merchandise.

Sydnee sounded forlorn. 'Look at what they've done to Big Girls. She's like a hag with no makeup. On Christmas morning, too. The makeover will take forever.'

Alex put an arm around her. 'That's why you've got us.'

'Don't worry,' Jez said, 'if anyone can perform a miracle on Big Girls, you can.'

Sydnee's eyes narrowed in their scrutiny of Jez. Miss Givens shoved him and the others into the back room, where they took off their coats and readied for action.

Sydnee rang the police to inform them of the attack on the boutique. 'I know it's Christmas Day ... So you haven't anyone you can send out? ... No, the men that did it aren't still around, we chased them off ... No, of course we're not vigilantes ... Look, never mind. Just give me an incident number for the insurance.' Sydnee wrote it down on the wall by the phone. 'Fuckers! The way they treat you makes you feel like the wrongdoer and not the wronged.'

Alex squeezed her arm. 'What did they say?'

'That the men will be long gone ... Unlikely ever to be caught ... Probably just pranksters ... Basically, just to get on with it.'

'Then that's what we'll do. Let's get stuck in and restore Big Girls to her former glory.'

Sydnee nodded, setting her mouth in a determined looking line.

Miss Givens sounded upset. 'I hate to have to leave, but the food—'

'You go see to the food,' Sydnee said. 'We'll all be starving by the time we get this place tarted up.' Then she got back on the phone to a window glazier. 'You cannot be serious ... No, don't come out, I'll see to it myself.' She banged the phone down and made a face. 'You wouldn't believe the charge the glazier wanted to make just for coming out. I'd need a second mortgage. The window can be boarded up for now and reglazed after the holidays.'

'We have some boarding at Flesh,' Jez said. 'Give me a hand, Arran.'

On returning, they boarded up the window and made it secure. The big clear up then got underway. Sydnee and Alex made a start of stripping their cherished display, removing the damaged furniture and Christmas tree, and untangling the girls. Hilda was a gonner.

'I can't believe,' Sydnee said to Alex, 'that she's struggled all these years on bandy legs only to be murdered by crazed loons. There's no justice in this world.'

Alex patted her arm, words failing him.

Jez found a transistor radio inside a size 16 red patent leather shoe. It still worked when he switched it on. He twizzled the dials and came across a radio play. As they toiled, they listened to the tinny voice of a narrator telling the story of Scrooge. Arran and Serge removed all the offending bricks, rescued what contents they could, then carried the damaged counters and displays out into the backyard. Jez swept up the shards of glass from inside the boutique and then did the same from the pavement out front. There was no mention of Christmas as the hours slipped by and the light began to fade.

A squeal of wheels announced the arrival of Miss Givens, pulling her shopping trolley behind her. Out of it came everything needed for an improvised Christmas dinner. Stands and racks were pushed back to make a clearing, and boxes were set out in a circle. In camp style, they passed around the plates and cutlery and food containers from one to the other until piece by piece they each assembled a Christmas dinner. Before they tucked in, Miss Givens gave a toast. They all raised their plastic cups of cranberry juice 'to family'.

The harrowing flight of Scrooge through time to the scenes of his meannesses was interrupted for a news and weather bulletin: Before the tube had closed down, a reveller had hung mistletoe on one of the trains and almost caused a riot with people trying to kiss underneath it; a Muslim man had been pictured handing out Christmas presents to the homeless; and the Met Office had issued a yellow warning for a severe storm approaching the south east of England.

'This is the best Christmas dinner I've ever had,' Alex declared, restarting the conversation and taking the opportunity to turn down the radio. The haunting of Scrooge was enough to give him indigestion.

'This is the only Christmas dinner you've ever had,' Arran reminded him.

'That too,' Alex agreed.

Sydnee smiled. 'Those vandals did me a good turn. What I mean is that at times like this you find out who your real friends are. You've done me proud today. Thank you.'

'But what about all the mess they caused?' Alex said.

'With the insurance money, I'll make this place even better and brighter. You wait and see.'

'I hope Secret Santa got me shades for Christmas,' Jez said, covering his eyes.

'Don't talk to me about Secret Santa,' Sydnee said, fanning herself with a black leather bra. 'I still haven't got over the attempt on my life this morning. What a day this has been.' She winked at Alex.

*

Alex stood naked in the dark, mesmerised by the storm raging outside. The house felt small under its power. Rain was lashing down and a violent gust of wind rattled the window. Alarmed, he stepped back and felt his ankle complain. Still sore from when he'd gone over on it that morning. The shock of seeing Maxim and some of the other men. It wasn't fair what they'd done to Sydnee's boutique. Queers were weak; that's what they'd always said. Not true. Sydnee was strong and laughed in the face of hardship. She didn't deserve their derision.

Seeing the gang again brought back the past. Reminded Alex of the hurt he'd caused to undeserving people. He felt sick to his core.

Arran came up behind, put his arms around him and kissed his neck. Alex turned and led him to the bed. He wanted his mind and body consumed by Arran, so that there would be no room for anything else.

THIRTY

Svetlana felt like wiping the smirk right off Maxim's face. He could be so annoying and stupid at times, like a big kid. 'What did you think you were playing at?'

Maxim's smirk turned into a sneer. 'Can you believe in this country full of lousy Muslims and Jews that I couldn't find a shop open. They don't even believe in Christmas. They have no right to shut up shop.'

'So you attacked another shop that wasn't even open?'

Maxim shrugged his shoulders, as if it was no big deal. 'It wasn't a real shop. Just this pervert's place, full of tent dresses and barge shoes for poofs pretending to be women.'

'You could have been caught by the police.'

'It was driving me mad,' he said, twirling his finger in the air, 'walking round and round, looking for somewhere open. When we came across that pervy shop, I just flipped.'

'What if you'd been seen? Have you thought of that?'

'We were,' he said, grinning. 'Some big freak came running down the street, screaming like a witch. It was hilarious.'

Svetlana launched herself at him, pummelling him with her fists and screaming. 'You could have put us all in danger. Brought the police to our door, asking questions—'

'You should have been there,' Maxim said, fending her off. 'We found this pile of bricks and started chucking them at the window. It began to crack, like ice. Then the whole lot came crashing down, like an avalanche. You should have heard it. We smashed that sick display to pieces. I nearly came in my pants.' He pulled her hand to his crotch and said, 'feel,' then fell to the floor and rolled around, laughing hysterically.

Svetlana stood over him. 'While you're pissing yourself, the police are out looking for you from the description given by the freak.'

'Relax,' Maxim said, trying to pull her down to join him on the floor. 'No one got close enough to recognise us. By the time they got to the shop, we were gone. No harm done.'

Svetlana pulled away from him and went off to their bedroom, banging doors behind her. The incident with Maxim wasn't the only thing bothering her. Alexei's no-show at Christmas had her wound up. This was the time she'd felt sure he would come home. She kicked one of Maxim's trainers. It smacked into the wall and slid down. He was forever leaving them lying around for her to trip over. There was concern among the men that Alexei might betray them by talking to the police. Svetlana couldn't believe her own brother would do that to her. Nevertheless, she regularly checked the local radio, TV news bulletins and newspapers for any mention of missing homos. There weren't any. And no knocks came at their door in the early hours of the morning, the police come to arrest them. Some of the men believed they were protected by God for doing his work and punishing homosexuals. Svetlana wasn't into religion and didn't go along with their thinking, but if it made them happy and kept them in line, she could put up with it. It was her job to keep the gang safe, and she would do anything to make that happen.

She lay down on the bed. Why had the homo's death unnerved Alexei so much? And what the hell was keeping him away? None of them wanted to end up behind bars, but the shock must have worn off by now. No one was that sensitive, not even Alexei. He had to know she would protect him. That's what she'd always done. He was such an ingrate. It made her angry to think on how much she'd done for him only to be repaid in this way. With silence. She took a deep breath, letting the air out slowly and trying to manage her anger. Maybe Alexei had been in an accident. But even if he had, someone from the hospital would have contacted her by now. The next time she saw him she would give him an injury for causing her all this upset and torment.

At least Pyotr taking over the honeytrap had placated the men. He was doing well and was searching for a new victim. After letting them know of a guy he'd kept dangling that he was unsure about, Maxim had sneaked a look at him on the webcam. Recognising the guy from somewhere, Maxim had gone into a wild tirade, ordering Pyotr to wind him in. He didn't care what he had to promise to make it happen.

*

Pyotr had a bad feeling about Jerry, suspecting that he wasn't telling the truth about himself. He daren't voice his concerns to Maxim and carried on meeting up with him. Pyotr hated the sick things Jerry asked him to do but couldn't say no and risk losing him. Maxim would have battered him black and blue. Pyotr waited until no one else was in the room before doing what was asked of him. He stood up and turned slowly around to let Jerry check out his body. He heard the perv whistle.

'Pull up your shirt,' Jerry whispered.

Pyotr lifted his white cotton t-shirt to reveal a ripple of tight abs, honed by all the heavy lifting and running about he did every day on the building sites.

'Now run your hand up and down your chest.'

Pyotr could hear Jerry's breathing getting more laboured and could imagine what he was doing. Disgusting pig!

'Run your hand down your stomach and undo your jeans. Open the flaps. Let me see what you're wearing.'

As Jerry gave his instructions, his voice was coming out raspy. Pyotr felt sick and humiliated. It should be him that was in charge and not this perv. He wished he'd never mentioned him to Nikolay. He would never again make the same mistake.

'Ease down your jeans,' Jerry whispered. 'Slide your hand down inside your boxers ...'

Pyotr gritted his teeth and did as asked. Soon the boot would be on the other foot. The perv would be trapped and at his mercy. Then he would pay for putting him through this sick display. The guy was whispering again, asking to see more. Pyotr moved his hand around and teased him without exposing himself. The pig let out a moan and the webcam picture shuddered. It was over.

Pyotr vowed never mention to anyone what had happened. He didn't want the men talking about him like they did Alexei, when Svetlana wasn't around. They speculated that the reason for his disappearance was that he was too sensitive and weak. If he hadn't been Svetlana's brother they would have beaten him up, just like the homos. Maybe Alexei was a homo, they joked.

THIRTY ONE

Jez was setting up Flesh for the start of business when a knock came at the door. 'You're too keen,' he called out. 'Come back when we're open.'

'It's PC Dent,' came the reply.

They sat at a table where the police community liaison officer laid out a couple of flyers.

'These are missing people?' Jez said.

'They've been reported by their families as missing. They live away from them.'

'Here in Vauxhall?'

'Both are from neighbouring boroughs but may have frequented the bars here.'

'They're gay?'

'That's why I'm here,' PC Dent said. 'I thought you might recognise them.'

Jez picked up each Photostat flyer and studied their faces. He shook his head. 'Sorry, neither one is familiar.'

'That's okay but let me tell you what we know about them. Maybe then you could ask around. Your regulars might have run into them. This,' he fingered one flyer, 'is Phil Backman, nineteen years old, from just outside Reading. Mother and father split up and remarried and were in irregular contact with Phil. They have no idea what has happened to him. He was working at a men's outfitters in the West End. His colleagues say he was hardworking and friendly, but none of them saw him out of work and didn't know any of his friends. He was expected back after having a Friday afternoon and Saturday off but failed to turn in.'

'Did he call in sick?' Jez said.

PC Dent shook his head.

'Didn't the manager think it odd?'

'He said young guys do a disappearing trick all the time. They find another job, move on and don't even bother serving their notice. He seemed more annoyed than concerned.'

'What about where he lives?'

'A houseshare in Wandsworth. A stopgap kind of place where people say hello in passing but don't get involved with each other.'

Fingering a second flyer, PC Dent said, 'Similar story with this other guy, Trevor Beech. Came down from Scotland around nine months ago. The family only reported him missing when they couldn't get hold of him over the holidays, so he could have gone missing at any time over that period. He worked for an independent bookseller near St. Paul's Cathedral. Struggling a bit, so they weren't displeased, let's say, when he didn't turn in after the holidays.'

Jez shook his head in dismay.

'I know what you're thinking, but that's the reality of the times we live in. People come and go, and no one gives much thought as to where they've gone to. I can't preach since the police don't spend much time investigating the missing, unless there is evidence of foul play. The exception being kids and vulnerable adults. What I'm doing now is more than we usually do and only because Phil's father used to be a local government councillor and Trevor's is a Methodist minister.'

'It's not what you know but who you know,' Jez said.

PC Dent smiled. 'The way of the world.'

'Have you no clue what has happened to them?'

'Well, both cleared out their current and savings accounts, so—'

'Themselves?'

'The cashpoint camera at Trevor's bank shows someone dressed in a big padded jacket with the hood up. Could have been anyone. The one at Phil's bank was on the blink. Both PIN numbers were known.'

'Typical,' Jez said, raising his eyes. 'CCTV everywhere, but when you need it most, it doesn't work. What do you think has happened to them?'

Jez was spellbound by the insight into the world of missing people that PC Dent gave him before taking his leave. He then bluetacked the flyers to the wall outside the toilets.

*

Jez finished his shift and joined Alex, Arran, Gregor and Serge at their table, shuddering as a sheet of rain smacked into the massive plate glass window opposite them. 'What awful weather,' he said. 'No Sydnee?'

'On her way,' Alex said. 'She just texted me.'

Jez poured himself a beer from the pitcher and was in mid-drink before he stopped, his eyes widening. Sydnee flew by, in a blur, water dripping everywhere. A whole pitcher of beer later she emerged from the bathroom, poured herself a beer and demolished it in one go.

'What, no burp?' Jez said.

'Thirsty work creating a work of art,' she told him, running her hands down her generous body.

'Talking of work,' Arran said. 'How are things at the boutique?'

'Those thugs did me a favour. I remodelled Big Girls with new streamlined fittings that display her assets to their best advantage and allow me to swish up and down the aisles like a supermodel.'

'You are a good swisher,' Jez acknowledged.

'Did the police come out to see you?' Gregor said.

'Not a chance. Unless you can supply them with a cast iron name and address of who did it and take them round there by the hand, they don't want to know.'

'You haven't seen any of those thugs hanging around, have you?' Alex said.

Sydnee took a swig of beer, shaking her head. 'I wouldn't recognise any of them even if they were.'

'I thought one of them looked familiar,' Arran said.

Jez agreed. 'One of them looked like the guy we had the set-to with outside the Sanctum. Wouldn't be surprised. He was a real homophobic headcase.'

'But what a strange thing to do on Christmas morning,' Gregor said.

Sydnee laughed. 'Probably had his eye on a rubber cat suit and was pissed because the boutique was closed.' She eyed Gregor. 'You can never tell.'

'Stop,' he said, his face turning bright red.

'Chernobyl!' They yelled, took a swig of beer, then banged their glasses down on the table.

'Those thugs,' Sydnee said, 'will be lying low or with any luck will have slunk off to pastures new.'

Alex suspected she was wrong but wished she was right.

'That reminds me,' Jez said. 'The community bobby came into Flesh today to ask about a couple of gay guys gone missing. I didn't know them, but he told me some interesting facts about the world of the disappeared. For instance, did you know that a few hundred thousand people go missing in Britain every year? Can you believe it? That's like the population of a town like Northampton ...'

Alex glanced at Arran, remembering that he came from that town. Arran was shaking his head at Jez, and Alex cottoned on that Jez had been stirring. The guy was such a tease.

'... Many thousands of the missing are never seen again. Amazing, since Britain is the CCTV capital of the world.'

'What happens to them?' Gregor said.

'They go off grid. Survive by taking a new identity, cash in hand jobs and bunking down in squats and hostels ...'

Alex squirmed in his seat, this conversation too close to home for his liking. But Jez was in full flow. '... Some of them have mental health problems or amnesia.'

'I saw this film,' Sydnee said, 'about Agatha Christie, the author, going missing for eleven days. A nationwide hunt ensued. The husband came under suspicion before she was found in a hotel in Yorkshire. I don't think she ever really explained what had happened to her. The film invented a love story, but I remember reading that she may have had post-traumatic amnesia since her mother had recently died and her husband had confessed to having a mistress. The cad.'

'Spot on, Miss Marple,' Jez said. 'A big shock, like an accident or an attack, can cause people to lose their memory.'

The dazed faces of the guys the gang had trapped over the years paraded in front of Alex's eyes. No wonder they were traumatised after being beaten and humiliated and then tossed out, bloody and broken. Had they got their lives back on track and learned to trust again? Or had they only papered over the cracks and were living half a life? And they were the lucky ones to have survived. His eyes skipped past Phil. Arran was asking about some of the other reasons people would walk out on their lives.

'Some people end up living rotten lives,' Sydnee said. 'They may not see any other way but to walk out and leave it all behind.'

The lights in the bar flickered, then went out. Jez's voice came out of the darkness. 'Some of them are trafficked as prostitutes or slaves. Some are murdered.'

A streak of lightening lit up the bar, turning faces a ghostly white.

'I hope those boys are safe wherever they are,' Sydnee said, before crashing thunder drowned her out.

Alex looked out on the storm. He pictured Phil, dumped in a lonely hole in the ground. Abandoned. His family would be unaware of where he was and desperate for news.

The lights blinked back on.

Alex excused himself and went to the toilet. The missing persons' flyers on the wall caught his eye as he went by. He backtracked for a closer look. Then rushed into the toilet and locked himself inside a cubicle, sliding down the wall with his head in his hands. It was Phil, staring down from the wall, his eyes accusing Alex just as he'd done on the night he'd died. It was stupid of Alex to think he could just forget Phil and all the others and just start again. Now he was right back at the beginning.

Only, this time, it was worse.

The police knew of Phil. What else did they know? Were they on to the gang? If so, it would only be a matter of time before they came for him. Alex felt sick with fright and shame. The new life he'd built would come crashing down around him. His friends ... Arran ... would find out all about him. Who he was. What he'd done. Alex left the cubicle and bent over the basin to splash water on his face. He stood up and looked in the mirror. Saw a face staring back at him. Not his own. 'Don't do that,' he said.

'Sorry,' Arran said. 'I just wanted to check you were all right. You seem not yourself.'

Alex was shaken to find Arran there. Watching him. Suspicious? What did he mean by *not yourself*? 'I'm a bit off colour. Probably just a cold coming on. This weather ...' Alex ran the hot tap and scrubbed at his hands.

Back at the table the talk speculated on what could have happened to the missing guys. Alex wished they would move on and talk about something else. Anything. He couldn't stand much more of this.

'Wasn't there a serial killer targeting gays in London some years ago?' Arran asked Sydnee.

'The question is directed to me because I'm wiser or older? On second thoughts, don't answer. I can recall a couple of notorious ones, but I can't believe there's another making the rounds now. There must be some other more likely explanation for why those boys have disappeared. I really feel for their families. They must be going through hell, not knowing what has happened to them. Made worse by it happening over Christmastime. Someone out there must know something. They should speak up.'

Alex jerked his head up. For one frightened second he'd imagined that Sydnee was talking to him. As if she knew he was the one. What a fraud he was. He did know what had happened to Phil. The boy's blood was on his hands.

The talk got inside Alex's head. These people had changed him, with their friendship, honesty and openness. Made him so as he couldn't hide secrets deep inside like he used to. Their truth shone a light through the walls he'd constructed in his mind to be able to stand another day. It poked its way into all the dark compartments where he'd hidden what he wanted to forget. It was the only way he'd known. But if the walls came tumbling down and his truth emerged ... things between them might never be the same again. His new life would be over. He'd have to face a bleak future by himself.

They took advantage of a lull in the storm to head home. When it was time for Alex to continue on to his place, he reassured the guys he would be fine and not to worry. His call of goodnight faded as he headed alone into the darkness.

THIRTY TWO

Arran jogged on the spot, clapping his hands to keep warm while waiting for Alex. In case he'd overslept, he gave him an extra ten minutes on their usual time before setting off without him. Even though the storm had subsided, a chill wind was still blowing and he wished he'd worn an extra layer. Without Alex running by his side felt strange. They were a team now. His non-appearance wasn't a surprise, as he'd seemed a bit subdued in the bar. Just a cold coming on, he'd said. A day or two's rest and Alex would be back on the team.

Arran ran along the river path, dodging the after effects of Storm Dolores—blown down tree branches, blown away advertisement signs and blown over rubbish bins. The sight of congealed fat on leftover burgers and kebabs was enough for him to consider turning veggie. He shooed the crows dining on them out of his way. On the homeward journey he picked out Vauxhall in the distance, looking miserable under a black sky. The rotten weather was a permanent fixture these days. Once on Boy Lane he sprinted along, ready for a hot shower.

That night the talk in Bananas among the punters was of the missing gay guys. Arran joined a group of regulars at the end of the bar, chatting about some serial killer from back in the Nineties.

'He was known as Jack the Gripper,' Jonny said.

'Sounds kinky,' Des said.

'Of course he was bloody kinky. That's the point of being a serial killer.'

Jonny seemed to know what he was talking about. The lads around him were all ears, including Arran.

'His real name was Colin Ireland. He used to pick up guys in the Coleherne pub in Earl's Court. Closed down now.'

'That's a shame,' Des said. 'Why was that?'

'Why was what?'

'Why did it close down?'

'Well, funnily enough, business dropped off. Anyway, as I was saying ... he picked these men up and went back to their place, promising them a spot of hanky spanky. The rough stuff was a handy excuse to tie them up. Then he throttled them.'

'That's a bit rich, murdering them in their own gaff.'

'That was the point,' Jonny said, giving Des a look. 'Left him free to rob the place. He'd been done before for burglary. Been in and out of borstal and prison. He even strangled the cat of one victim.'

'Now that's going too far. He should have been stopped. Where were the boys in blue when all this was going on?'

'Do you even need to ask? There was an outcry in the newspapers, accusing the police of not bothering to investigate properly because the victims were gay. They denied it, as they do.'

'Not bothered about us.' Des took a glum sip of lager through a straw.

'Didn't have a clue what was going on, did they? All these murders of gay men in the papers and they didn't think to look for a serial killer.'

'Psychopaths the lot of them.'

'Who are?'

'Coppers.'

'You're not wrong. Another serial killer, up in Muswell Hill, used to be a copper. Dennis Nilsen, his name. He liked to kill guys, dress them up, put them around the dining table and sit chatting to them.'

'Wonder what he said to them?' Des said.

Jonny grinned. 'Talk to me. Not just going to sit there looking glum, are you? Oh, well then, chop chop ...'

'Chop chop?'

'Chopped them up like a dog's dinner and flushed them down the loo.' Jonny grinned at the faces around him, screwing up with revulsion. 'That's how they got onto him. A sewers inspector investigated complaints of a foul smell and found all these body parts floating in the—'

'Don't! I've heard enough,' Des said, fanning his face with a chewed up beer mat.

Arran had also heard enough and moved off to clear up the empty glasses. He hoped nothing like what he'd heard had happened to the missing guys here. They were only around his age and far too young to die. The mention of the Coleherne pub put him on edge. He checked out the punters in Bananas ... Any one of them might be the serial killer, hiding in plain sight. At times like this he was glad he was fixed up with Alex.

THIRTY THREE

'Alex has been out of touch for four days,' Arran said to Jez. He wasn't sure whether he was rattled by all the bar talk of missing guys and serial killers or by the suspicion that something might be seriously wrong with Alex. It wasn't like him to not answer calls and texts. They were walking around the industrial area of Vauxhall where Arran thought Alex lived.

'How come you don't know?' Jez said.

'He never asked me to go there. I got the impression that it's a little run down. Anyway, we spend nearly all our time outdoors, and we've only recently bought bikes. We like to take off and explore places along the river. He loves Greenwich. And we often stop off for a drink in Wapping at the Hangman's pub.'

Jez shivered. 'This place gives me the creeps, little twisting turns, big old warehouses and dark corners everywhere. Doesn't it get to you when you're walking home from Bananas in the dead of night?'

'It didn't used to. Now with everybody and his husband talking about a gay serial killer, a guy can't help but keep looking over his shoulder when here in the pitch dark, on his lonesome, and his footsteps echoing off the cobbles like in some black and white horror film. It's the perfect place for a killer to be lurking in the shadows, waiting for some unsuspecting drop dead gorgeous guy to walk by.'

'I get the picture,' Jez said. 'You don't really think anything bad could have happened to Alex, do you?'

Arran took a moment to answer. 'I honestly don't know what has happened to him.'

'What if this is his way of telling you it's over between you?'

Arran shook his head. 'I would have known ... seen the signs. But it wasn't like that. We were good. Life was good.'

They continued searching until it started raining again and then headed back to Boy Lane. Miss Givens was waiting in the hall. 'Any news?'

Arran shook his head. 'It was a hopeless task to begin with, thinking we might accidentally bump into Alex in the street.'

'Don't worry, we'll get the others round here later and put our heads together.'

*

That evening, Sydnee and Serge joined the Boy Lane crew in the living room. Miss Givens put out a homemade carrot cake. Sydnee, wearing a dejected look on her face, pushed it away, saying it would ruin her diet, as her willpower was reducing faster than her weight.

Arran felt all eyes on him as everyone pitched in with their answers to the Alex question. He welcomed their positivity. They latched on to the idea from Miss Givens that some emergency might have arisen. Sydnee supported the suggestion. 'At times like that, everything goes out of your head. You just have to do what you have to do, there's no time for anything else. Which would explain why Alex hasn't contacted you yet.'

Arran saw the logic in their thinking, except that Alex had been gone for four whole days without a single call or text.

Gregor thought he might suddenly have had to return to Russia. 'As well as the emergency, he would have had to arrange a flight and travel over there. What do you know of his family?'

'His parents died in a car accident years ago, and I'm not sure he has any other family left. He never talked about anyone.'

'If he has gone back to Russia, it would be tiring for him to make the journey and then deal with the issue. Communications between there and here are not that straightforward, even today.'

'He might be in shock and not thinking straight,' Sydnee added. 'If that is the case, then I'm sure he'll be in touch with you in the next few days after the shock has worn off.'

Everything they said made sense to Arran. He started to feel a little easier, knowing Alex's disappearance could be explained rationally.

'What if something has happened to him?' Jez slipped into the lull in the discussion.

Arran's thoughts stumbled back into the dark.

When the silence in the room dragged on, Jez said, 'I don't want to upset you, but we should consider every possibility, however far-fetched it might seem to us.'

'You mean he might have become a victim of the gay serial killer, don't you?'

'We should contact the police.'

'First we should find out if he's had an accident,' Miss Givens said. 'He could have been knocked off his bike by a car and be lying unconscious in one of the hospitals. We should check.'

*

Arran avoided brooding about Alex's disappearance by concentrating on Jez as they walked to Vauxhall police station on Kennington Road. 'What are you getting up to these days? Seeing anyone?'

'Don't worry about me. I'm much too busy with work at the minute to give guys any attention.'

Arran considered Jez's guileless face, knowing there were times when he had no clue whether he was telling the truth or not. In so many ways he was incredibly open, but with respect to that one aspect of himself—what he got up to, with whom, where and when—he played it very close to his chest. Arran wasn't convinced a gay killer was stalking the streets of Vauxhall, but they had first hand experience of at least one angry homophobe living here. And where there was one, there might be others. Like vermin. Whether they might be tempted to go one step beyond verbal abuse and start attacking people if the right situation presented itself, he wasn't sure. However, he did believe you could end up getting hurt by being in the wrong place at the wrong time. What worried him about Jez was that he seemed to relish that location.

At the station they approached the front desk, where Arran said he would like to report a missing person. The desk sergeant reached for his pad to take down the details. 'Person's name?'

'Alex.'

'Alex what?'

Arran looked at Jez, who shook his head. 'We don't know.'

131

'How long has this Alex been missing?'

'Four days.'

'Address?'

Arran shook his head. The sergeant shot them a look before moving on. 'Employer's name and address?'

Arran looked at Jez. It passed unspoken between them that they couldn't give Sydnee's name as she'd paid Alex cash-in-hand.

'Then do you have a recent picture of Alex?'

Arran had pictures on his phone. He hadn't remembered to print off a hard copy and promised to drop one in.

'Do you know of any reason he would have taken off?'

'He may have been called back to Russia for an emergency. We're just so worried because we don't know for sure.'

'Alex was Russian?' the sergeant said. 'If he wasn't working, what was he doing here?'

Arran and Jez shook their heads.

'So, for all you know,' the sergeant said, 'he could well have ended what was a holiday and returned to Russia. Which means that the only crime committed was that he didn't let you know he was leaving.'

'Except,' Arran said, 'what about the other guys who have gone missing around Vauxhall recently? Alex's disappearance could be linked with them.'

'It could,' the sergeant conceded, 'except we don't have enough information on those guys or your guy to make any concrete links, do we?'

Arran's head dropped. 'So what happens now?'

The sergeant didn't look hopeful. 'Not much I can do without even the most basic information to register your friend as missing.'

'So that's it?' Arran said.

'Listen, most missing people turn up of their own accord within a couple of weeks. You'll see ...'

Arran hoped he was right. He felt such a dick for not knowing the most basic things about his own boyfriend. Not even his bloody surname. Now he was left wondering who Alex really was.

THIRTY FOUR

Donny gave Arran a tray to carry the drinks. The way upstairs was completely clear. Only a couple of handfuls of men were hanging around the bar, looking lost. The diehards. 'This place is dead,' Arran said to the others as he placed the tray on the table and handed around the drinks.

'Just like all the other gay bars around here,' Jez said.

'The Sanctum isn't living up to its name as a refuge these days,' Sydnee said. 'The gay serial killer chatter is keeping everyone away.'

They were sitting close to the open fire in the upstairs bar. Gregor pointed to what was going on outside the windows. 'This stormy weather doesn't help. I got soaked again going to work this morning.'

'When I was out running, I almost got blown away,' Arran said.

Sydnee snorted and slapped her rump. 'The chance would be a fine thing.'

'Diet not going too well?' Jez said.

Sydnee shook her head, a sorrowful look on her face. 'But there's always a bright side. I might be on a forced diet soon, the way this serial killer talk is killing my sales. Today I counted the number of customers that came into Big Girls. Thirteen. Before closing up I rang my good friend Dora Matt and told her to pop into the boutique, pretending to be a customer. Just to make sure I didn't attract bad luck.'

'Does that count?'

'Better to be safe than sorry.'

Arran felt all eyes on him. He'd let his mind drift, thinking about his missing boyfriend and all that he didn't know about him. 'I'm fine, honestly.'

'Until you know otherwise,' Gregor said, 'you should give Alex the benefit of the doubt.'

'I don't know what to think. Every day I go through the motions, sticking to the usual routines and hoping Alex will reappear with some flimsy excuse, so that I can forgive him and we can get back to normal. Whatever that means. Because the more I think about it, the more I realise I have no idea who Alex is. Did he confide in any of you?'

'It would seem our Alex is a man of secrets,' Sydnee said, after the others had shaken their heads.

'How does Alex make his money to live?' Gregor said.

Sydnee uttered a guilty sounding little cough. 'Well, it wasn't on what he made working for me. Anyway, it was only part time-ish.'

'He told me he's living on the insurance payouts from the deaths of his parents,' Arran said.

'You once mentioned to me that his parents died when he was a kid. The insurance money wouldn't stretch out forever. Even if it has, the exchange rate of the Russian Ruble to western currency is low and the West is an expensive place to live. He would have to supplement his income in some way. He may have become involved in making some easy money. The situation could have turned nasty, and he had to make a run for it or go into hiding. What brought Alex to London in the first place?'

Arran recalled seeing Alex with the roughnecks on the tube. 'He came with a group of other Russians that worked in construction. He gave me the impression they'd moved on.'

'What if it is something bad, like smuggling drugs or people trafficking?' Jez said.

Arran pulled a face. 'I can't believe that of Alex. He isn't the kind to be a heavy duty criminal. If it is criminal, it would be something small.'

'Sorry, I got carried away for a minute. Alex is a friend to all of us and, you're right, he isn't like that.'

'Look,' Sydnee said, 'we're talking in circles here. Let's go along with what Gregor suggested and give Alex the benefit of the doubt. We should keep our eyes peeled for a sighting of him, just in case he is lying low in Vauxhall for any reason.'

Arran nodded. 'I've already been out with Jez, Gregor and Serge at different times to see if we could spot him.'

'Did you print off a photograph of Alex for the police?' Jez said.

'I gave them a copy of this one here.' He pulled a photo out of his pocket to show them.

'This one has him half turned away from the camera. Don't you have a better one?'

'When I opened up the picture file on my phone, I couldn't believe I had only two photos of Alex and this is the best one. I could have sworn I'd taken more.'

'Could he have deleted the rest?'

'This is getting too weird.'

Sydnee raised her eyes. 'Let's not get started on the conspiracy theories again.'

*

Jez felt for Arran over Alex. The poor guy didn't know what to think or do about his boyfriend. It was like Alex had never existed. Putting aside the gay serial killer theory, there had to some reason for why he would split without a word to anyone.

Jez opened up his laptop, went online and searched for UK missing persons' websites. He found a couple and clicked on the first. Even though Alex had kept his personal life hidden from them, there may have been someone he'd been close to. A close friend or relative. When not with Arran, he often wasn't around. He could have met with them then. They might be worried and have posted him missing. They could fill in the gaps about Alex and would have more of an idea of where to start looking for him.

PC Dent hadn't been kidding. Page on page showed pictures of adults and children who had disappeared. He quickly scrolled down the recent posts without coming across one for Alex. It was the same story on the second site. He closed down the window. Finding Alex without his full name was like searching for a needle in a haystack.

He switched to a forum covering the Vauxhall area and read the posts. They gave the low-down on what was going on in the area—social gatherings, music events, crimes, gang issues ... Nothing caught his eye that might relate to Alex. Some posts did make mention of a killer targeting gay men. Others ridiculed the idea. He scrolled down but could find nothing else of interest. An online search for Alex had been a long shot at best.

In need of company, he logged on to a sex chatroom. Within a minute of him posting a message, he received one to connect. Recognising the guy's handle, he went ahead. The guy really turned him on. When they opened up their webcams, Jez could hardly believe his eyes. The guy wasn't his usual distant, surly self; he was smiling. 'You seem pleased to see me tonight.'

'I've been waiting for you?'

Jez felt a tug in his groin. 'I had some business to finish up. What did you want with me?'

'I think it's time we meet up in person. I'm free on Friday night. What do you think? You up for it?'

Jez looked down at himself. 'Oh, I'm definitely up for it.'

THIRTY FIVE

Alex was cold, the coffee hot, and Jack's Greasy Spoon cafe a shelter from the persistent wind and rain. The out of the way cafe wasn't used by anyone he knew. He held the coffee mug in both hands, savouring the warmth. At least the foul weather gave him an excuse to hide inside baggy clothing. He looked like nobody and everybody. Perfect for the task he'd set himself.

It hadn't been easy walking out on his new family. Arran and his friends represented everything Alex wanted to be and gave him security. He disliked being completely on his own but lacked the courage to come clean with them. He'd seen them around Vauxhall, searching for a sign of him, in the bars, in the park, along the river path; all the places he and Arran had frequented. Their concern for his welfare touched him. At those times he'd wanted to run up to Arran or Jez with some made up excuse—he'd been sick, delirious or had an accident, been out of it—and have them welcome him back into the fold. It had been a struggle for him not to do just that. He was forced to remind himself of the mission he'd set himself. The gang would never end their vendetta against gays. It was up to him to stop them. Only by demonstrating he wasn't the same man that had done the same terrible things to gay men could he return to his friends. Even then it would take a lot of understanding on their part to forgive him. But that was a chance he'd have to take. Living a lie was no longer an option; the lie always present, like a cancer, eating away at him.

Seeing Phil's face on the wall at Flesh, hearing Sydnee's concern over what the families of the missing would be going through, and knowing what Gregor had lost at the hands of abusers like himself had demolished the walls he'd built in his mind to house his darkest secrets. Exposed to the light, he could no longer ignore them. If he wanted to live openly as a gay man, he had to be honest about the man he used to be. He had to confront his past, which meant confronting the gang.

The incident at Christmas, the wanton vandalism of Sydnee's boutique, had reminded Alex of the gang's presence. Half his problem would be solved if they moved on. But it was merely wishful thinking. It didn't seem they had any intention of leaving. The gay hunting here was too good to pass up. While nursing his sore ankle outside Big Girls, he'd sensed it was only a matter of time before he was in the wrong place at the wrong time and the gang would find him. If Arran or one of the others was with him when that happened, their lives might be put in danger. Phil was dead. How many others had the gang killed? From what Jez had said, dozens of people went missing every single day in this city alone. Was Trevor Beech missing or dead? Had the gang acquired a taste for killing? If so, the killing spree couldn't be allowed to continue. The gay hunting had gone too far. Only Alex knew about their activities. It was up to him to stop them. The mere thought brought him out in a sweat. If he tried and failed, he was doomed. The gang would never forgive him the ultimate sins of perversion and betrayal. He doubted Svetlana would be able to save him, even should she want to. They would beat him to within an inch of his life. They might even kill him.

He was running a big risk by taking on the gang. But by seizing control he had the chance of a better life. An honest life. He hoped he was up to the task. After all, he'd never shown that level of courage before.

Alex finished his coffee, then headed out of the cafe. Within ten minutes he reached his former home and was ready for another day of trailing his old family members. He kept watch from the grounds of the church at the end of the street, stamping his feet to keep warm. The gang owned two vans. Those men he couldn't follow. Only those who travelled to work by public transport. If he wanted to find out what they were up to, he had to get close enough to hear them talking. It was fraught with danger, but there was no alternative.

At twenty past seven the front door opened and out came six men, including Nikolay and Pavel. They walked by him, heading for the bus stop. Alex hung back until the bus arrived, jumping on at the last minute and burying himself within the mass of early morning travellers, close to his quarries but out of their eyeline. With his hood up and a scarf hiding his face, he felt confident they wouldn't recognise him. The men spoke to each other in Russian, confident it was unlikely they would be understood. Mostly they were grumbling ... the awful weather, the bland food, the weak beer, the British, the blacks, the Muslims, the Jews ... The list of complaints ran on and on. Alex shook his head, feeling ashamed. How could he have been a part of them for so long, sharing their lives, agreeing with their views, laughing at their jokes and being their bait for trapping vulnerable men to punish?

The other people around had no idea of the characters they were travelling alongside. The Asians had no idea the men were saying how they would like to stone the greasy-headed wogs to death. The women had no idea the men were describing how they would like to spear them with their big Russian tools. Where once Alex would have dismissed such talk as harmless men-talk, now he was disgusted by it.

He followed when they left the bus. They led him to a building site where a former church was being converted into flats and disappeared from view.

Frustrated because he could follow no further and because he hadn't learned anything of interest, it was some time before Alex recognised his surroundings. He'd been here before. He walked on for a couple of streets until he came to the Russian Baths. He'd been inside just the once, with a couple of the other men. It was a magnificent building. On the opposite side of the road a bus pulled in and Gregor got off. Alex darted behind a van. Through the glass he followed Gregor until he disappeared down the alleyway at the side of the baths. Hunched over against the wind, his friend seemed weighed down. Was he the reason for Gregor's downbeat look? Were his friends missing him as much as he was missing them?

It grieved Alex he was causing his friends so much torment. The sooner he brought the gang to justice, the sooner he could return to them. How they would receive him, when the truth was out, he couldn't think about.

Not yet.

THIRTY SIX

Gregor pulled from his pocket the picture of Alex he'd picked up from the hall table when leaving for work. Arran had printed them off to jog people's memory when searching for him in and around Vauxhall. No one had seen Alex, not recognising the shot of him looking off into the distance and seemingly unaware the photo was being taken. Gregor hoped Alex hadn't come to any harm, wherever he was. It seemed strange they'd all spent so much time together and yet knew next to nothing about him. If Alex had deliberately withheld information about himself, he may have known he might have to disappear. But from what or who? Apart from them he didn't seem to have had any ties in London. Certainly no one he'd spoken about.

Despite Arran putting on a brave face, he was hurting and conflicted, not knowing if Alex was in hiding or had fallen foul of someone. Gregor didn't buy the serial killer talk. More likely, Alex had upset someone he'd been doing business with. If Alex was in trouble, someone in the Russian community would know something and Gregor was best placed to find out what that something was. Even so, he couldn't picture Alex as a criminal. He acted like an ordinary guy, into spending time with his boyfriend, times out running or biking and nights out with his friends. And he definitely couldn't be into anything heavy, like drugs or people trafficking or being in truck with the Russian mafia. Gregor hoped it was true. He didn't want to put himself and the others in harm's way; the Russian mafia were pitiless.

Alex might have kept his identity a secret and gone into hiding without a word to protect them. The story of him still living off insurance payments after all this time didn't wash. Yet he wasn't short of money. He'd purchased a new bike, went on nights out and always bought his round. So he had to get his money from somewhere. Maybe he'd stolen it from someone. Someone he shouldn't have. Someone who would do anything, and hurt anyone, to get it back. Gregor felt the urge to retreat into his own world of books and classical music; a world divorced from thinking about missing people, hardened criminals, stolen money or whatever was actually going on with Alex.

After glancing at the time, Gregor went to collect his first customer of the day. New to him, he was a middle-aged businessman type with a little potbelly. Gregor was an exponent of the Russian massage technique he'd learnt at his local gymnasium in Moscow and honed in Budapest en-route to London. From bitter experience he knew to give new customers a brief explanation of massage techniques to offset their preconceptions, which ranged from the downright sleazy to expecting a miracle cure for everything from back pain to depression to love problems. Each thirty-minute massage was like a workout for Gregor and kept him trim. At the end of the massage, Gregor showed the guy the picture of Alex. 'My cousin,' he explained. 'He may have got into a spot of trouble and has done a disappearing trick. I promised my aunt I would ask around. She's worried sick. Have you seen him?' The guy couldn't help and left.

Gregor wiped down the massage plinth before taking another look at his work diary. The gaps towards the end of the day would most likely be filled as the day went on. Failing that, the receptionist would put out announcements to entice more customers. The rest of the day passed quickly with one customer after another as the free slots were filled. Gregor drew a blank with each of his customers. None of them recognised Alex.

His second to last client was also a new face. In his early twenties, the brawny man seemed edgy. He climbed onto the plinth, keeping tight hold of his towel. Gregor asked if he had any particular areas he would like him to concentrate on. The guy used a hand to indicate his neck, shoulders and lower back. Gregor started lightly at first, to get the guy used to massage and to gauge his reaction. When he responded well, sinking into the massage rather than flinching away, he gradually increased the depth and intensity of the strokes. Under his sensitised fingers he felt the muscle tightness and knots easing away. Some tension showed when Gregor moved up his legs. Taking the hint, he kept well away from anywhere private. At the finish, he had the guy sit on the edge of the plinth until he came to terms with having to move again.

'How do you feel?' Gregor said.

'Great,' the guy grunted.

The guy didn't give much away. Gregor was unsure of him but decided to show him the photo of Alex anyway. It couldn't hurt. He took a long time examining the picture, and a flicker of something seemed to cross his face. Surprise? Worry? But when he gave it back, the response was the same as all the others—a shake of the head.

Gregor's final customer of the day didn't recognise Alex, either. It had been a long shot to think any of them would since to Gregor's knowledge he'd never visited the baths. Still, it was worth the effort to try to find out what had happened to Alex, if only to put Arran's mind at rest. After scrubbing down the plinth, Gregor took his work diary back to reception and changed out of his uniform. He left Alex's photo in his locker.

Gregor opened the door of the back entrance that led into the alley beside the baths. With no lighting, he viewed only a long streak of dark. He closed the door behind him and set off walking. The wind drove the rain into his eyes, making it difficult to see. He treaded carefully in an effort to avoid the deep puddles that collected when it rained. A blow to his back came out of nowhere. A kick to his leg sent him down onto the wet tarmac. His head was yanked back and a face appeared close to his, the features hidden behind a hat and scarf. Gregor put out a hand to ward off further harm. 'What do you want?'

'We'll ask the questions,' the man said, his voice deep, like the rumbling of an underground train. He shook Gregor. 'Why are you asking around about Alexei?'

'Who's Alexei?' The words were out of Gregor's mouth before his brain kicked in.

A sharp punch stung his face.

'Don't play games with us. You were showing his picture to everyone in the baths.'

'Tell us, now!' another voice hissed in his ear.

Gregor had predicted that asking after Alex might bring trouble. Now it was here and these men meant business. It was frightening when he had nothing to offer them; he didn't know anything. They pushed him around, slapping him and prodding fingers in his face and continually asking questions. How were he and Alexei connected? What had Alexei been up to? Who would hide him? 'I don't know,' Gregor said. 'That's the truth.'

142

'He's just messing us around,' a third voice said.

'He'll talk after this!'

Gregor dived to the ground and curled up. Dull heavy thuds sounded on his sodden clothing right before the pain exploded in his back and head. He cried out, hoping someone would hear before they did him serious damage.

THIRTY SEVEN

Alex returned for dinner to Jack's cafe and ordered the special of the day, chicken casserole. Something warm inside him was what he needed. Satisfied, he left the cafe and headed for the library, finding a comfy armchair in the book section. Now he needed quiet, to think. He had to find out what the gang was up to. Turning up at the house and confronting Svetlana head on meant tackling Maxim as well. Only one way that confrontation would end. Badly. For him. It also would be risky getting closer to the men, but they hadn't picked him out so far. No doubt picturing him as he used to look and dress, longish hair, smart trousers and fitted jackets. Now he was unrecognisable from that person, concealed in an oversized Parka coat, cargo trousers and a large woollen hat. He would just have to bide his time and wait for the gang to get careless and reveal their plans. Only then could he act against them. He picked a book off the nearest shelf and started reading. With most of the library users in the computer section, the book area was peaceful and no one disturbed him. He found his countryman, Dostoevsky, heavy going and drifted off to sleep a couple of times.

At seven o'clock, Alex made his way back to the house to wait for any of the gang leaving for the shops or the pub. Usually a few of them went out in the evening if only to get out of the cramped house for an hour or so. The huge church at the end of the street, with a roofed gate by the entrance and a bench nearby, provided a good vantage point. Just before eight, the front door opened and four men came out, Dmitri and Vadim among them. They made their way to a pub a couple of streets away. Alex had been inside the pub before and was familiar with the layout. A quaint old place, all frosted glass and ornate mirrors. He kept an eye on the men through the window and waited until they had moved from the bar before heading in. While waiting for his drink to be served, he kept a sharp lookout in case one of the men came back. The old fashioned pub was laid out with lots of little recesses and snugs. Several men propped up the bar, and a few couples were tented together over small round tables. No one paid him any attention. With a drink in hand, Alex treaded warily around the bar, searching for the men. The unmistakable sounds of his own language came to him from a snug up ahead, and the shapes of four men showed through the frosted glass. He took the one before and sat down close to the wood and glass divider. He pulled out his new mobile phone and laid it on the table.

To catch their conversation, Alex leaned as close to the divider as he dared. The talk was only about work. Two of them were working on a building site a few miles away, putting up a new factory to make the charging units for electric cars. They were saying that real men didn't drive electric cars. Alex sat back when they continued to talk about other work sites and took a sip of ginger beer, wishing it was just beer. But he had to keep a clear head. He put down the glass when he heard chair legs scraping the ground and leaned over the table, pretending to be engrossed in a game on his phone. Two of the men passed by, not even glancing Alex's way. Tempted to follow them, he couldn't, the risk too great.

Less than ten minutes later they came back, carrying more drinks and complaining about having to go outside in the wind and rain to smoke. That got them talking about all the crazy health and safety rules they had to follow on the building sites. They named one site in south-east London that had sent a worker home because his metal-capped boots were cracked. Madness, having to lose a day's pay over something so trivial. The Brits were nuts. Another site, further afield, had been closed down for a few days because bones had been found. They laughed so hard that the table and chairs rocked. The bones had turned out to be dog bones. They then said something about being careful before two girls went clomping by in heeled boots and Alex missed the rest. He heard them whistling after the girls, who didn't even bother to comment.

Alex's ears pricked up on hearing Pyotr's name. It appeared he had taken Alexei's place in the gang.

'Pyotr's a good guy,' Dmitri said. 'He'll do well setting the traps.'

'I'm glad Alexei's gone, the arrogant prick,' Vadim said.

Alex could feel his heat rising at the slight to his name. Although he'd never been popular among the men, with having to maintain a distance to preserve his secret, he had thought they at least respected him. Now he knew different.

'He only survived with us because of his sister, hiding under her skirts.'

'Not that he'd know what to do under there.'

Alex burned with fury at hearing them mocking him, laughing and banging their fists on the table.

'There's something not quite right about him.'

'Wonder what he's doing now?'

'It had better not be anything to betray us, or he'll get the same treatment as the queers get.'

As they continued talking, Alex's ears pricked up. 'Pyotr ... hooked another ...' He looked up with frustration as two guys went by, chatting and drowning out the rest of the men's words.

Seconds later a chair leg scraped against the floor. One of the men passed him, heading for the toilets. He sensed they were about to leave the pub and headed out first, loitering outside. He trailed them back to the house, too distant to hear anything more.

On the way home he paused outside 19 Boy Lane, drawn like a moth to the warm lights burning within. Would he ever be welcome inside their home again? He shut down such feelings and allowed his feet to drag him away.

His room was freezing. Alex curled up and tucked the duvet in around his body. *Never listen at keyholes* was a saying he'd heard since coming to London. Even though he wanted to stop the gang and bring them down, he couldn't help the hurt feeling inside. It was as if he'd never really been one of them. Always the outsider, never belonging anywhere. This shouldn't have bothered him, considering the men were narrow-minded bigots, who put down innocent gay men only for their own amusement. Still no one liked to be the one on the outside, looking in.

The men had sensed Alex was different and would do to him what they'd done to other gay men if they ever found out the truth. Already he'd been replaced; Pyotr was the new honeytrap. His mean young body would be hard for gay guys to resist. Someone had already fallen for him. The next honeytrap was on.

THIRTY EIGHT

The rain was lashing down and Gregor was soaked to the skin. He couldn't move, pinned to the ground by heavy men kneeling on his chest and legs. They showed no signs of giving up, even though he couldn't answer their questions. He was scared out of his wits that they would leave him half dead before they were through. He should tell them something. Anything. Just to make them stop. It didn't have to be the truth. It couldn't be, when they both wanted the same thing: To find Alex. The man kneeling on his chest grabbed a handful of hair and slapped his face. He clung on to the hand, pleading, 'No more ... Please ... I don't know anything, I swear.'

'You're lying. What are you to Alexei? Tell us or we'll—'

A sliver of yellow opened up in the darkness. Two figures step out of the light. Gregor took his chance and called out to them, 'Help! Help me!'

The figures started shouting and waving their arms. The man holding Gregor slung him down and left him with a warning: 'We know where to find you.'

The three thugs walked off towards the street. It chilled Gregor that they didn't even bother to hurry. They didn't fear being caught.

Gregor was helped to his feet by Yuri and Valeriy and taken inside the baths. He was a mess, his clothes wet and torn, his face covered in red marks and blood leaking from a head wound. He winced, cleaning himself up. His work colleagues looked on, concerned.

'You're going to hurt bad when the adrenaline wears off,' Yuri said.

'What happened to you?' Valeriy asked. 'Who were those men?'

Gregor didn't want to get into a lengthy explanation and dismissed them as thugs out to get his wallet. He patted his breast pocket proudly, indicating they hadn't succeeded.

'How many times have we complained about the lack of lighting in the alley?' Valeriy said, with Yuri nodding alongside.

'I'm grateful you came along when you did. Otherwise ...'

Gregor wanted to go for a bus. The two wouldn't hear of it, insisting he wasn't in any fit state to travel alone on public transport. They rang for a taxi to take him home. He sat in the back, clenching his teeth at the jolts over the potholed streets of London.

At Boy Lane he fumbled with his key at the door long enough for Miss Givens to open up for him. 'Oh my God!' she cried. 'What on earth has happened to you?' As she helped him in, she called up the stairs to Arran and Jez. Their heavy treads sounded on the landing and stairs. When the boys appeared, she was settling Gregor into an armchair. The three of them crowded around him, taking in the damage to his body and clothes. Then came the questions ... In a rush ... All at the same time ... Gregor couldn't answer, overwhelmed.

'Let him breathe for a minute,' Miss Givens instructed the boys. She went to the drinks cupboard and poured out four large brandies. 'Medicinal.'

Gregor took a sip and started spluttering. They waited for him to settle down before starting again with the questions.

'Were you mugged?' Jez said.

'Three men jumped me in the alley outside the baths, asking questions about Alexei.'

'Asking about Alex?' Arran said. 'Who were they?'

'I was showing around one of the photos you left on the hall table. They got wind of it and wanted to know my connection to him.'

'What did you say?'

'Nothing. I didn't really know what they meant. I mean, we're just friends.'

'They must have thought you were involved in whatever he's mixed up in. Did they say why they wanted him?'

Gregor shifted position, grimacing with pain.

'They must want him awful bad for them to beat you up like this. Did you know any of them?'

'The alley's dark, no lighting. Hats and scarves hid their faces.'

'What about CCTV? Did you report the incident to the police?'

Gregor started to shake his head and stopped. It hurt too much. 'No CCTV and no police.'

'You should go to the police,' Jez said. 'What if they come back to finish the job?'

'Stop scaring him,' Miss Givens said.

Gregor was scared. He didn't want those men coming back. Nor did he want to get involved with the police. Russian police had the habit of changing victims into criminals, and he didn't think it was too much different in London. 'The police wouldn't do anything. Those men are long gone by now, and I couldn't even give them a decent description. Best to let it go.'

'What has Alex got himself into?' Arran said.

Gregor shrugged. 'But at least it seems he's alive and not the victim of a serial killer.'

'For now. What about when those men get hold of him?'

Gregor rested his head on his hand.

'That's enough for tonight,' Miss Givens said. 'He's been through the mill. We can talk tomorrow. Jez, help Gregor up to his room, then bring down his torn clothes for me to wash and mend.'

*

The following morning, Yuri's words came back to haunt Gregor. Every part of his body complained when he moved.

Miss Givens wouldn't hear of him going in to work and sent him back to bed. She rang the baths and told them he was in too much pain to come in. Breakfast in bed was bacon sandwiches and a pack of painkillers. 'You should have those ribs checked out,' she told him.

'No point. They only tell you to take painkillers and rest up. Exactly what I am doing.'

Arran and Jez came into his room and sat on Gregor's bed. 'You look awful,' Jez said.

'Thanks for that. I feel so much better now.'

'I just meant that the swelling and bruising has broken out on your face, today.'

'I'm sorry,' Arran said. 'I feel terrible for what has happened to you. If it wasn't for me and—'

149

'For what? Those men did this to me, not you and not Alex.'

Arran still looked dejected. 'I hate leaving at a time like this. It's just that I promised mum a visit, and I can't let her down after staying in Vauxhall for Christmas.'

'Go and see your mum and dad,' Miss Givens said. 'Don't worry about Gregor, we'll take good care of him.'

Jez shoved him on his way.

'See you all when I get back,' Arran called out over his shoulder.

THIRTY NINE

Alex paced around in the shadow of the church, his eyes fixed on the door of his old house. He was certain the gang had another honeytrap planned. Some poor mug didn't have a clue about what was happening to him. Most people thought grooming was only about children. Adults rarely fully considered the dangers to themselves of meeting strangers on the Internet.

Rain was falling. It never seemed to stop. His hat and coat were soddened, scarcely having the time to fully dry. Too pumped up to sleep much, he'd been out on the streets virtually night and day, hoping to hear more details of the honeytrap. If only he'd heard the rest of what Dmitri and Vadim had said in the pub. They may have given away the location. That's what he desperately needed to know. Following the gang on the night would be hazardous. He might easily lose them. Since that time, days of trailing various gang members to their workplaces, shops and pubs had gone by without him finding out another scrap of information.

Today was Friday. If anything were going to happen this week, it would be tonight. He leaned back against the church door and made a conscious effort to control his breathing. His body was high on adrenaline, anticipating the struggle ahead. He needed to keep a cool head to deal with whatever trials the night might bring. He'd brought along his bike. Tracking the gang would be easier on two wheels. If only Arran were by his side to share the burden. Except then he would want to know everything about the gang, and the whole sickening story would come out before Alex was ready. Arran wouldn't understand how one gay man could do the things Alex had done to other gay men. Alex still hadn't fully processed it himself. He supposed it took a certain kind of strength to have lived the way he'd lived, done the things he'd done, kept the secrets he had, and not cracked up. Now he wanted to use his strength for good and to make things right. The past was the past and couldn't be changed. All he could do was to stop any further abuse of gay men by the gang. For that to happen he had to stay strong.

Alex detected movement. Out of the door came Pyotr, looking good in a black leather jacket, dress shirt and jeans, and his blond hair shining. The image of how Alexei used to look. He headed for the car.

The honeytrap was on.

Alex took a deep breath. This was it, the chance he'd been waiting for. Now it was him against the gang. He was the only one who knew about the honeytraps. The only one who could put a stop to them. He went under the roofed gate at the entrance and mounted his bike. Two other guys joined Pyotr in the car and they set off. Alex waited for them to pass before following. From the direction taken, he was sure they were still using the same pick up point and headed in that direction. He hoped so because the car was soon no more than a speck in the distance.

If he managed to arrive before the victim got into the car, Alex thought over what he should do. If he went flying in, shouting and waving his arms, the guy would dismiss him as a lunatic. Even if he somehow stopped him from getting in the car, the gang would have been alerted to Alex's presence and threat. He would become the hunted, not the hunter. He concentrated on pedalling hard to make sure he reached the pick up point before the car disappeared again. He had to see the direction of travel if he were to have any chance of finding the site chosen for the honeytrap. He sped along Boy Lane, past nineteen, towards the industrial area. Quieter at this time of the evening, there was only light traffic and few pedestrians. The factories and units had all closed for the day. Down the street he spotted the familiar black Mercedes pulled in at the kerb, illuminated orange by a nearby streetlamp. Only a dark silhouette could be seen climbing into the passenger seat. Alex couldn't make out his features. It was too late to warn him now. The gang had their victim. The poor guy didn't know his only chance lay with the guy pursuing them.

The honeytrap had been sprung.

Alex stopped and took a breather. He noted which way the car headed—down the road and right at the end. After taking a deep breath, he set off in pursuit. The roads were in poor shape due to the heavy vans and lorries toing and froing from all the factories and warehouses in the area. The infrequent street lighting made potholes difficult to spot. He slowed down, not wanting to risk a puncture or coming off and damaging the bike. At the right turn the car had taken, it suddenly reappeared. Alex swerved to avoid it. The bike went from under him. He landed on his hip, his momentum taking him towards the front fender hurtling towards him. The car wheels were spinning over the loose surface. He raised his hands and turned his head from the shower of gravel pelting him. The car was almost on top of him, the screech of the brakes blasting his ears. He curled up and made himself small. Thought about death. And the wasted opportunity to take down the gang. How more innocent men would die because of his failure. The noise reached a crescendo. Alex closed his eyes. A massive thud hit his back. Then the noise stopped. The engine had died. The next second it roared into life and revved up. Alex opened his eyes. The car was speeding away. He'd survived. They hadn't even bothered to check on him.

Breathing a massive sigh of relief, Alex got to his feet. He felt okay. The adrenaline coursing his veins had to be numbing the pain in his back and hip. Tomorrow he would pay for his injuries; tonight he had to forget them. His hands and knees were grazed and bloody but wouldn't stop him from biking.

The bike!

He rushed over and checked it. The handlebars and wheels seemed fine. He'd been lucky. With no time to lose he straddled the bike, pointed it in the direction of the car and set off.

He had an idea where the honeytrap would take place.

In the pub, Alex had overheard the men mention two building sites. The first was towards Sydenham and would take him three quarters of an hour to reach. The shock of the accident had slowed him. He picked up the pace. He had to make it in time. Someone was depending on him. When he was sure of the honeytrap, he would put in an anonymous call to the police. Pedalling flat out was hard work. He thanked Arran for all the fitness training he'd put him through. Neither of them had known then that it might be crucial in saving someone's life. Breathing hard and with sweat running down his back, Alex spotted the outline of the site. He slowed down to avoid signalling his arrival. The site perimeter was boarded up and lit by hazard lights attached at intervals. A strip of work units on the opposite side of the road was in darkness. Other than one or two cars that went by, the area was quiet. Leaving his bike propped against a telephone pole, Alex trotted over to the main gates. A gap to one side allowed him to see through. The site had a deserted look and feel. No obvious signs of activity came from within—no lights, no noises, no vehicles. He remained still and listened. Nothing.

The honeytrap was taking place somewhere else.

Alex shot back to his bike and took off for the second site in the Beckenham area. Time was against him. By now the gang would be laying into their victim, softening him up with kicks and punches. The guy wouldn't know what was happening to him. Then they'd strip and humiliate him. Make him feel like nothing. Because in their eyes that was what he was. Nothing. Alex had to get there before the gang seriously hurt him. Or worse, killed him. The gang had become killers. Phil had just been the start. He wished he were wrong. Whatever the truth, he had to find the gang soon. His leg muscles were screaming from fatigue, pushed to their limits. The police had to catch the gang in the act, putting the evidence beyond doubt. They would be caught, convicted and put away with no clue Alex had betrayed them. That simple. It had to be. With heavy legs, he forced down on the pedals. He was slowing and the site was still nowhere to be seen.

If he'd made a mistake with the route ...

It didn't bear thinking about. Fuelled by his desire to make amends, Alex pushed through the pain barrier to keep going. Buildings were becoming less frequent, more scattered. A grassy wasteland. In the distance the jagged outline of a building stood out against the night sky. This had to be the second site. The gang had to be here. If they weren't, the victim was on his own. Alex would have failed him.

He couldn't fail.

On the approach, Alex listened for telltale signs of activity coming from the site. None. But that meant little. The gang were experts at insulating the buildings used for the honeytraps. The perimeter boarding displayed *DANGER KEEP OUT* signage at intervals. As badly as Alex wanted to obey, he forced himself to press on. Time was short. The metal gates formed a solid barrier with no way to see inside. Underfoot he felt the ground sloping and noticed a hollow below one of the gates. After dropping onto his back, he levered himself underneath and into the site. Creeping forward in the dark interior, he was sure anyone around would be able to hear his heart drumming out of his chest. A large, partially constructed building lay on the opposite side of the site. He moved towards it, past three other smaller buildings that shielded several vans and the Mercedes car. The gang were here. He'd found them. A new feeling stirred within Alex.

Fear.

These people had been his family. Now he was afraid of them, what they were doing, and what they would do to him if they found him poking around. Already they didn't trust him. This would be proof. Alex pictured Maxim, savage and brutal, revelling in the violence and wondered just how far he would go. How far had he gone already?

Alex hurried along under the scaffolding, looking for a breach in the securities to see what was going on inside. Muffled noises came to him. Taking hold of a corner of boarding, he peeled it back. Shouts and screams quickened his hands. He had to see inside. Make sure. Then he would make the call. After that it would be in the hands of the police.

A swishing sound came through the air. Ducking too late, something hard connected with Alex's head. He sank to his knees, clutching the back of his head. Felt something sticky on his fingers. Two figures appeared from out of the darkness, dragged him inside the building and flung him on the floor. Boots came flying in. Alex curled up into a ball to protect himself.

When the kicking finally stopped, Alex lifted his head. After a few seconds his eyes adjusted to the flickering firelight inside the building. Someone was lying alongside him. Staring at him.

FORTY

Arran awoke refreshed on Sunday morning. Back in his bed at Boy Lane, he extended his arms and legs, arched his back and stretched out the kinks. His Northampton bed had seemed smaller than he remembered. The home visit had flown by. His parents had raised their eyebrows when he'd produced a bottle of Rioja red wine at his welcome home meal. He'd raised his own eyebrows at the VW Campervan they were restoring. When it was finished it would look fantastic. They were planning to take it on a road trip around the British Isles, including a spell in the Dales, as his mum was originally from Yorkshire. He was filled up at seeing them so happy. They were concerned for him, on hearing about the disappearance of Alex and the other guys. But in Northampton, talk of missing guys and serial killers had seemed less real.

Miss Givens and Gregor were in the living room when he went downstairs for a late breakfast, yawning a belated good morning to them. On opening his eyes fully, he noticed their worried faces.

'Jez hasn't come home since he went out on Friday evening,' Miss Givens said. 'Jon Jacks from Flesh rang to see why he hadn't turned in for his shift. Staying out is one thing, but Jez is not so irresponsible as to miss work without calling in to give some sort of excuse. We're really worried for him.'

A knock at the door signalled the arrival of Sydnee and Serge. 'Any news on Jez?'

Jez. Missing. Arran couldn't get his head around it. 'What could have happened to him?'

'He's gone AWOL before,' Gregor said. 'Maybe—'

'This is different,' Sydnee cut in. 'He's out of touch and his phone's dead. Jez would never just disappear completely without a word to at least one of us. Where would he go? And why? And especially not after all the upset over Alex. Something strange is going on around these parts. Guys are going missing and not being found. Are they being kept against their will?'

'For what?' Arran said.

'Quite a few cases have come to light of people being kept as slaves for years. Not just abroad, but in this country too.'

'I don't know about that, but could there really be some substance to the serial killer talk?'

'I've never really bought into it. But now I don't know what to think.'

'Jez was one for taking risks ...' Arran stopped talking, fearful about where he was headed.

'Let's not get ahead of ourselves,' Sydnee said. 'We've been through this situation before with Alex. We know what to do.'

Sydnee, Serge and Gregor set about contacting the local hospitals—Guy's and Tommy's, Charing Cross and the Hammersmith. Meanwhile, Arran uploaded images of Jez from his phone onto his laptop and printed out several copies of a clear headshot. Miss Givens made tea and put out slices of banana cake on a plate. The practical matters didn't take long, with all their enquiries drawing a blank.

Arran could still feel his face burning from his last visit to the police station and suggested they drew up the information the police would ask for. He rifled through a drawer in the sideboard, found a pen and notepad, and volunteered to act as a scribe. Most of the information came from Sydnee and Miss Givens.

Full name: Jeremy 'Jez' Matthew Truman
Home address: 19 Boy Lane, Vauxhall, London.
Last seen: At home, Friday morning, by Miss Givens, landlady.
Description: 6 ft, 12 stone, wavy dk brown hair, dk blue eyes, smooth shaven.
Date of birth: 1st July 1999
Parents:
Rita Truman (Deceased)
Simon Truman (Whereabouts not known)
Employer: Flesh Bar, Vauxhall. Manager, Jon Jacks Telephone: 0207—
Reason for going out: Went on a date with a man unknown.
Mobile phone no: 079—

Arran pinned a photo to the information page and slid them inside a manila envelope. It was agreed that if Jez hadn't turned up by Monday morning, he and Serge would go to the police station to report him missing.

*

At Bananas that night Arran looked over the thin crowd. The place had never been so sad looking. So empty and quiet. The serial killer talk had really kicked in, and people were staying away in droves. Jason had handed over a long list of cleaning tasks.

Serge was wiping down the lower shelves and tapped him on the leg. 'With Jez gone, that makes four disappearances. What is going on around here?'

Arran shook his head. 'I wish I knew.'

'Do you think the killer finds his victims in the bars? He could be here right now.'

'It's hard to know what to think.'

'Someone must know something.'

'I do know Jez liked to take risks and was into sex with strangers. The first time I ever saw him, he was heading into the park bushes with a pick-up. I hope he hasn't got himself into a situation he couldn't handle.'

Arran slept badly that night, disturbed by the wind and rain trying to batter their way inside. By morning he felt drained. He breakfasted with Gregor and Miss Givens on tea and toast. It was all they could manage. The only sound came from the radio droning on in the background, news of potential strikes by train and postal workers, the attempted murder of an ex-KGB spy on the streets of Winchester and floods in the north of England. 'Shall I turn off the gloom box?'

Miss Givens glanced across. 'Best leave it on for the local news, just in case ...'

When Gregor left for work, Arran walked with him to the bus stop, for something to do. Gregor was apologetic. 'I feel bad for going off to work and leaving you to deal with the police again. I know it wasn't a pleasant experience for you the last time.'

Arran waved away his apology. 'I can handle it, don't worry. We'll keep you informed of any news.'

Before climbing onto the bus, Gregor took hold of Arran and hugged him. The warm gesture from the normally reticent Gregor was almost enough to open the flood barriers. The two people Arran was closest to in the world were missing. First Alex, now Jez. The world was turning upside down and inside out.

Heading out from under the shelter the driving headwind and rain bent Arran in half, his coattails slapping against his thighs. Vauxhall was a very different place from the sun-blessed gay village of his arrival, besieged by the wintry elements and emptied by talk of a killer on the loose. He dodged the spokes of a discarded brolly, thrown at him by the wind. But as bleak as it was, Arran couldn't imagine a world without his two best mates in it.

FORTY ONE

Alex came to in the dark not knowing where he was, his head and body aching and cramped. Stretching out, his foot struck something solid. Then he remembered being secured in the cupboard under the stairs of his old home. He put a hand to the soreness at the back of his head, wincing as he hit a sticky lump and recalling how it had happened. Painful images came to mind. Despite all his good intentions, he'd made a mess of the situation and everything had gone wrong. Now there was nothing he could do about it. The cupboard door opened and a face looked in on him.

Nikolay wrinkled his nose and ordered Alex into the bathroom. 'You have twenty minutes to wash off your stink.'

Alex crawled out of the cupboard on hands and knees, and climbed to his feet. Nikolay shoved him in the back to hurry him along, then threw clean clothes after him into the bathroom. Unable to look at himself in the mirror, Alex rested a hand on the basin to steady himself while he peeled off the torn and bloodied clothes stuck to his body. He ran the shower on hot, flinching as it struck the cuts and bruises from his beating. The water swirled red at his feet.

Blood.

Again he had blood on his hands. Another boy had died. Captured by the gang, Alex had been taken inside the building and thrown down. Alongside him lay someone else. He looked into his staring eyes. The last time he'd seen them, they'd been alive and full of mischief. Now his body was a mess, destroyed. Almost unrecognisable. He must have died in great agony. Alex begged the dead boy's forgiveness for not saving him.

The hot water was burning Alex's skin. He deserved it. Arran and his friends would never forgive him now. They would ask why he hadn't told them about the gang. They would say he should have gone straight to the police. They would want to know why he'd waited. They would work him out. See him for what he was—a failure and a coward. Afraid of the police finding out about his involvement in the honeytraps. Afraid of the gang finding out he'd betrayed them. Alex slammed his fist into the tiled wall.

'What's going on there?' Nikolay shouted. 'Get a move on.'

When Alex had finished cleaning himself up, he was pushed into the living room. Only Svetlana was inside, standing perfectly still by the window. Nikolay directed Alex to a chair and commanded him to stay put. Alex stared at Svetlana's back, reluctant to say anything. She wasn't his sister. She was the leader of a homophobic gang. A murdering gang, who saw him as a loose cannon. When she turned he shrank back into the chair, unable to meet her gaze.

'You look a mess,' Svetlana said. 'All your own fault. You've brought all of this down on yourself.'

Alex didn't say anything.

'Where did you go?'

Alex had to tread carefully. The quiet, controlled tone of Svetlana's voice gave away that she was angry. One wrong word and she would erupt. His only hope was to lie to her. The truth about the people he'd met and the person he'd become would kill her. And him. He went to speak and found his voice wasn't there. He coughed to clear his throat before trying again. 'I had to get away for a while, on my own, to clear my head.'

'What did you do?'

'Nothing special. Walked around a lot. Drank a lot. Tried to forget what had happened.'

Svetlana moved towards him, her eyes blazing. 'Why would a queer dying bother you?'

Alex bit his lip. The guy might have been a queer, but he was still a somebody. A person. Someone's friend. Someone's flesh and blood. Whatever he was, he hadn't deserved to die in torment and agony. 'I don't know. It all happened so fast and I freaked out.'

Svetlana's eyes burrowed inside Alex's head. He felt hot. Started to babble. 'This gay hunting has got out of hand. Before, everyone had their fun beating up on the gay guy, and, yes, there was violence but it stopped well short of murder.' Alex couldn't look at Svetlana but didn't stop. 'It's all your fault for not controlling that pig, Maxim—'

Svetlana flew at Alex and smacked him across the face. 'How can you side with these filthy queers against your own people and against me? Me! Who stuck by you. Stopped you from being dumped in one of those orphanage holes. Kept you fed and safe. Put money in your pocket. How can you say such things about us? We're the only family you have.'

Svetlana was wrong about family. Still, he'd pushed her too far. He had to tread more carefully. 'I know, I know, everything you've done for me,' he said, raising his hands and gesturing for her to calm down. 'But we're not in Russia now. It doesn't matter how we see these people, the West sees it differently. If we're caught, we'll be punished. How many gays have died?'

'A couple. What does it matter? Is that what is really bothering you, that you will be punished by the authorities?'

Svetlana was pushy with the questions, as if she had some sort of hidden agenda. Somewhere inside the dark recesses of her mind, did she know about Alex's sexuality? She called him sensitive. Did she really mean gay? Alex was tempted to say it, to tell her he was gay and have her deal with it. He daren't. Too afraid. But he had to tell her something. 'Of course I don't want to be put in prison in a strange country. I'm young and don't want to waste my life behind bars. Nor should you.'

Svetlana's face softened and her shoulders dropped. 'Don't worry, no one will find the bodies buried under tons of concrete and bricks. And without a body, there is no crime. Right? Besides, there is no one looking for these queers. I know. Everyday I check—radio, tv, newspapers. It's my job to keep you safe. Isn't that what I've always done?'

Svetlana was unaware the police knew gay guys were going missing, and Alex didn't correct her on that score. But she was right in the sense that the police were unlikely to actively investigate when they had no idea about the gang or that any crimes had been committed. 'I know you look out for us,' Alex said, placating her.

'I was a little concerned you might go to the authorities. Tempted?'

Alex looked at Svetlana, on his guard again, ready to say whatever she wanted to hear. 'How could I go to the police? Like you said, these are my people and you're my sister. I was rattled that's all.'

Svetlana stared at him for a long time, her eyes searching his face. 'Are you telling me everything?'

'What else is there?' Alex met her eyes briefly before looking down at the floor, his face heating up. What else did she know?

'Who is Gregor Gregorovich?'

The sweat poured out of Alex. 'Why do you ask?' he said, trying to buy himself time to think. He could only imagine what had happened. His friends had been concerned for him, and Gregor had volunteered to ask around within London's Russian community. His enquiries must have come to the attention of someone in the gang.

'Because he's been asking questions about you. Now why would he do that? How do you know him?'

Alex cast around for some plausible reason she might buy. 'I spent some time at the Russian Baths where he works. We got talking and became friends. I borrowed some money from him. He probably just wants his money back.'

'How much money?'

'A few hundred pounds.'

'Why would you need to borrow money when you have plenty?'

'I called about a room when I was at the baths. I didn't have enough cash on me for the bond, so he loaned me the money. I meant to pay him back straight away, but I forgot.'

'He must be a good friend to lend you that amount of money at a moment's notice.'

Alex wondered what Svetlana was driving at. Did she know Gregor was gay? He shouldn't have said they were friends. The sweat was itchy, irritating his face. He daren't go near it. If Svetlana suspected he was lying, she would push all the harder. He would admit nothing. 'I barely know him, an acquaintance. He was just around when I needed a favour.'

Svetlana seemed to accept what Alex was saying but then switched tracks again. 'You've always been a bit more sensitive than the others. A sensitive boy, Alexei. Is that all there is to it?'

Alex ran his hand across his face, wiping it dry. The game was up. She knew. She fucking knew! If he was going down, he wasn't going to make it easy for her. 'I'm not an animal, like some I could mention. If that's what you mean?'

Svetlana didn't react like she had the last time he'd attacked Maxim. Her voice remained level. 'The men mutter among themselves that you have more sympathy for the queers than is normal. Why do you think they say that?'

Even as he said it, Alex was disgusted with himself. 'I've played my part in these games. A bigger part than most of the others. So maybe it's jealousy. Or maybe they're jealous because I'm your brother. Or maybe they think I get preferential treatment.'

'Maybe, maybe, maybe,' Svetlana repeated in a mocking tone. 'Whatever the reason, you need to watch your step with them. You need to make it up with them and make things right.'

'How do I do that?'

'You're a smart, sensitive boy,' Svetlana smirked, 'so I'm sure you'll figure it out and that an opportunity will present itself. You can leave now.'

Alex's heart leapt. Once he was out of this place, he would finish what he'd started and go straight to the police and tell them all he knew. This time there would be no mistake. He would have no more blood on his hands. But Svetlana wasn't finished. He heard her say that his place and his bed had been taken by Pyotr, so he would have to bed down where he could. He didn't care, having zero intentions of staying. He was impatient for her to finish so he could be on his way.

'One more thing,' she said. 'You are not to leave this house.'

All Alex's newfound hopes crashed. 'Why not? You can't keep me a prisoner here.'

'You will do exactly as I say. Until such time you have proved your loyalty to us, beyond any doubt, you will remain inside this house.' With that bombshell dropped, Svetlana left the room.

Alex slumped down in the chair, banging his fist on the arm. Any hope of making things right was over. He was back in the same hopeless situation he had tried so hard to escape from. Only, this time, it was worse. Before, he'd been part of the gang and accepted. Free to come and go as he pleased. Now, he was their prisoner. Despised and distrusted by all of them. How he would be made to prove his loyalty to the gang, he had no idea. But the look Svetlana had given him as she'd said it filled Alex with dread.

*

Svetlana found Nikolay at the kitchen table, drinking coffee. 'What did Alexei have to say for himself?' he asked her.

'He said he only knows this Gregorovich from the baths. That he was trying to find Alexei to get the money back he'd lent him. Find out what you can about him.'

'If he proves to be a threat?'

'End it.'

FORTY TWO

Another dead night in the Sanctum. So quiet that Arran could hear the gentle crackling of the fire. 'Tell me about Jez,' he said to Sydnee, conscious of the empty space between them he usually occupied.

'If this wasn't such a dire situation, there would be no way we would be having this conversation,' Sydnee said. 'You know that, don't you?'

'I know you would never betray a confidence.' Arran stared into the molten orange of the fire. 'But we owe it to Jez to do everything we can to find him. I need to get inside his head and understand how he thought, so I can figure out what he might have done and where to start looking for him.'

Sydnee ran her finger around the base of her glass before beginning to tell Arran the story of Jez's life. 'He arrived in Vauxhall on the day he turned sixteen. Here because it was as good a place as any, having lived in children's homes from an early age. Ended up in one after his mum died of cancer. His father was a bit of a drifter and couldn't cope with looking after an eight-year-old boy, so he gave him up into the care of the State.

'For the next eight years Jez spent his life in a succession of homes, interspersed with a couple of short periods of fostering. The sad truth is that most people who adopt want a baby and not a half grown child. Some children were adopted, but Jez wasn't one of the lucky ones. I think because his cheeky ways were interpreted as mischievous and wilful, people shied away from taking him, which was a great shame. If only one couple could have seen beyond it, he could have brought them such joy.

'Jez said life was tough in the homes, looking after yourself in a large group of kids, each with their own problems and hang-ups. For the most part he kept to himself, with just one or two friends close to him at a time. The kids at school with parents tended to look down on them and treat them differently, being unkind as only kids can sometimes. And, of course, there were no parents for parents' evenings and no money for trips and extras. The carers at the children's homes were paid to do a job, their attitudes ranging from kindly to indifferent to cold. I suppose Jez was lucky in that respect, given some of the stories that have emerged of the widespread and organised abuse of children by paedophiles in State-run homes.

'He was less lucky with some of the other kids. When Jez was fourteen he was noticed by a group of three older boys, who picked on him and abused him sexually for a couple of years. By day the boys called him names and even gave him a few slaps, out of earshot and sight of the adults. By night they came to his bed and got him to service them. The code in the home was that you didn't tell the adults what was going on with the kids, so he took what they gave and never complained a word. These children had been rejected by their parents and no doubt felt that poor care and even abuse was their lot in life. Despite the older boys abusing him sexually, they were the ones who called him poof and queer.

'When Jez turned sixteen, he'd had his fill of state care and left the home for good. I got talking to him here in the Sanctum, which is why we've always considered it to be our special bar. He was sat on his own, drinking a coke and looking all shiny and new. It worried me, seeing the old chicken hawks checking him out. I didn't want them taking advantage of him because, despite looking street smart, he also looked young and in need. I decided to get in first before anyone else could. We started chatting and Jez told me he was new in town, looking for a place to stay and a job. That made him vulnerable. He would have been eaten alive by people wanting a piece of him, which would have made him hard and that would have been a tragedy.

'I couldn't abandon him to his fate. So I took him home and got him a job in one of the bars, collecting glasses and sweeping up. You should have seen him. You would have thought he owned the place, so proud was he of working and earning a living. A cocky little thing with the punters, too. He made me laugh, watching him flirt and tease them. But because he had somewhere to live and a wage coming in, he didn't need to go off with anyone for board and lodgings. He had sex, for sure, but with partners of his own choosing.

'Once he'd found his feet and had a little money behind him, I arranged a room for him with Miss Givens. Between us we subsidised him for a couple of years, but he was a smart kid and soon started to move up. When he reached eighteen, he could work as a barman and after that there was no stopping him. He's just a gorgeous young man, inside and out. That's saying something, given his start in life. The rest you know ...'

Arran looked at Sydnee, both happy and sad at her recollection of Jez's early life. 'I never would have guessed his background. He's one of the most positive people I've ever met.'

'He works at it and doesn't let things get him down for long. I think that's what some people don't realise. Even though life can be hard, you still get to choose how you react and what face you present to the world.'

Arran nodded. 'You both helped me out, just like you helped Jez.'

'I suppose it was Jez's way of paying back a kindness with a kindness. You probably reminded him of his younger self, arriving here with a head full of dreams and not much else.'

Arran thought over the abuse Jez had suffered. 'Did he talk to you about his sex life?'

Sydnee admitted she was aware of some of the riskier scenes Jez was into—sex with casual pick-ups in the park or at some other deserted spot. 'I'm no psychologist, but his tastes probably trace back to his first experiences of sex. From what I've read it can be difficult to shake them off, even if they aren't particularly good for you. Whatever the reasons, at the end of the day, that's what excites him. I worry for him because you never know who or what you're going to run into, and he never seems to have any limits or even any safeguards to fall back on. But he's a grown man. All I can do is to keep on at him to be careful.' She raised her eyes and looked at Arran. 'He mentioned you to me, you know?'

Arran hadn't known. 'What did he say?'

'He's a little bit in love with you. Obvious from the way he looks and talks about you. He mentioned that something could have happened between you but hadn't. No specifics. I think he's conflicted within himself. On the one hand he's drawn to you, and on the other hand he's drawn to the riskier scenes he craves. As far as I know he's never had a relationship with someone more or less his own age. Darius was a little bit older. Jez had his head turned for a while with the money and the high life, but it was never going to last. He's never been with someone like you. You're very together for a young guy, straightforward with your emotions and affection. I think that's what he admires in you and what he aspires to. I don't think he knows how to be with you on that level yet because he's not in the same place. He wants to have a regular, honest and loving relationship with a guy, but he doesn't know how and doesn't want to hurt you by trying and failing. Remember, he's still only twenty himself and still working through the issues in his life, including his sexuality. Am I starting to sound preachy?'

Arran's eyes were pricking him, and he had to fight to stop tears forming. After what Sydnee had told him, all that had passed between himself and Jez now made a lot more sense. 'I liked Jez from the moment I met him and made it known to him. When he didn't make a move, I was hurt and puzzled, because we get on so well and because I knew an attraction existed between us. When *we* didn't happen, I thought Jez loved me more as a friend than a lover and didn't push it any further because I value his friendship so much. We think that life is black and white. I can see now that for Jez it is much greyer.'

Sydnee covered his hand with hers and patted it for a few moments. 'It's very difficult for Jez to explain himself, so don't blame yourself.'

They sat in silence, the only sound coming from the fire crackling away, the flames licking at the logs, reducing them to ash.

'It's been almost a week since he went missing,' Arran said. 'Each day I check with the police ...' He shook his head. 'They never have anything to report, on Jez, Alex or any of the missing guys.'

'I've hardly slept and Miss Givens is beside herself,' Sydnee said, 'but what more can we do?'

'We can't leave it up to the police. They don't take missing people seriously, apart from kids or the rich and famous. None of the missing guys have turned up. They're no more than a statistic, and Jez is on the way to becoming the same.'

'Disappearing isn't a criminal offence. All the talk in the bars about a serial killer targeting gays is just that, talk. No murdered bodies have been found, which is a good thing, but that's why the police haven't investigated.'

'They collect information, add it to a data sheet and wait. But this is Jez we're talking about. Our friend. We know him. He wouldn't just up and leave. He wouldn't do that to us, especially knowing our reaction to Alex's disappearance. If we want to find Jez, we're going to have to do it ourselves.'

'But how? I'm just some plain old shopkeeper and don't know the first thing about investigating missing persons.'

Arran almost choked on Sydnee's description of herself. Plain Janes didn't come in six foot bright red packages. But he didn't know anything of investigations, either. 'I can't sit around on my hands when Jez could be hurt or in the clutches of a maniac somewhere and relying on us to find him.'

'Okay,' Sydnee said, 'let's start at the beginning. What do we know?'

They quickly realised they didn't know much. Not who Jez had met. Not where they'd met—at Flesh, one of the other bars, out on the street or online. Not where they'd gone on their date. Not whether Jez had remained with the guy or headed off with someone else after the date. Or even during, knowing Jez. Not whether he'd been attacked and abducted on the way home or if he'd left on a whim. Not a lot was what they knew.

'Do you think Jez and Alex's disappearances are connected?' Arran said.

'I don't see how. Apart from both going missing, the only other connection is us.'

'Do you think a cult could be recruiting gay guys?' he asked, his voice barely above a whisper.

'What did you say?' Sydnee said. 'A cult?' She shook her head. 'Surely we would have heard rumours.'

Jon Jacks appeared at their table. 'Any news of Jez?'

Arran shook his head. 'His disappearance remains a mystery.'

'PC Dent called in at Flesh to ask about him,' Jon said. 'I told him the truth. Jez's happy in his work, doing well and had no reason I knew about to leave. He asked about problems with the other staff or customers. There hasn't been any. Jez is well liked by all. Dent did say the police have no clues about any of the missing guys, leaving me with the impression they were a low priority. As the police community liaison officer, he dealt with Jez at Flesh many times, which is why he's making an effort. But he seems to be as much in the dark as we are. Anyway, I'd better get back to the bar. I thought you'd want to know how things stand.'

After Jon had took his leave, Arran said, 'There you have it, official. If we want Jez back, it's down to us to find him.'

FORTY THREE

Despite the rattle of the bus making Gregor's ribs grumble, he felt much better. After a few days back at work, he was less fearful of running into the men who had bashed him. Even so, he remained careful and left work at the same time as others to avoid being alone in the alley.

The incident suggested Alex had disappeared of his own volition, and Gregor could understand why Arran would think that but he wasn't as sure. Guys going missing from the same place and at the same time seemed more than mere coincidence. Arran was determined to find Jez, and Gregor had offered to help in any way he could. It struck him later that the best way he could help was by finding Alex. No obvious link connected the two disappearances, yet there had to be one.

Because Gregor couldn't identify his attackers, he was fearful of stirring things up, but he admired Arran for taking the initiative and wanted to do the same. With his ties to the Russian community, he was best placed to find Alex. This time he would be more discreet. The thugs who had attacked him were Russian and must have been in the baths to hear him asking around about Alex. Unless someone had tipped them off. He hated to think badly of anyone, especially his work colleagues, but until he knew better he had to consider all possibilities.

Gregor let himself into the baths and changed into his uniform. Still early, the building was at rest as he moved through to reception to pick up his work diary. He had an idea. Flicking back to the appointments on the day of his attack, he ran a finger down to his second to last appointment—Nikolay Borzov. The memory of him was clear—early twenties, sore neck and back, edgy. Gregor had taken care with him. Borzov had spent a long time looking at the photo of Alex. The flicker Gregor had seen cross his face may have been recognition. Gregor headed to the membership card filing cabinet. While infrequent users to the baths wouldn't be members, regular users would have taken out membership as it was cheaper. He flicked through the suspension files and found a card for Borzov. Ludmilla, the receptionist, was away from her desk, in the kitchen making coffee, so Gregor pocketed the card and left.

No customers were booked in for the next half hour. He laid the card on his desk. Nikolay Borzov was twenty one. When he'd joined, around five months ago, he'd given an address in Vauxhall.

Vauxhall.

Gregor tried not to race ahead with wild speculations. Thinking logically, Alex *plus* the other missing gay guys *plus* Borzov *plus* the Vauxhall address did seem to add up. To what? The answer was in there somewhere, Gregor was convinced. He pictured the edgy Borzov in his mind. The complaints of an aching spine would fit with him working in construction. Alex had mentioned to Arran that he'd travelled with men looking for work on the building sites. The timeframe would also fit with Alex's appearance on the Vauxhall scene. The two men had to be tied together in some way. Gregor wrote down the address on a scrap of paper and put it in his pocket. What he'd discovered was useful and had to lead somewhere. At the very least it was something concrete to build on. The identification of Borzov also reassured Gregor. At least now he knew from which direction an attack on him would come.

As a member, Borzov would be a regular user. Gregor took to walking around the main chamber and poolroom in-between his massage customers. He was in an ideal situation to find out who Borzov hung out with and what they talked about, even though the idea of getting close to such violent men terrified him. He needn't have worried. Despite keeping up a constant vigil, Borzov failed to appear.

On the bus home, Gregor considered sharing his discoveries before deciding to keep them to himself for the time being. Borzov and his friends were dangerous. The last thing Gregor wanted was for Arran to rush over to the house and get himself in trouble. Neither did he want to raise hopes when there was so little to go on. Borzov was suspicious, to Gregor's way of thinking but he had yet to prove anything.

Borzov had seemed tense and guarded during the massage, keeping his towel tightly wrapped around him. His behaviour had made Gregor edgy, too. Had Borzov suspected he was gay? Was he uncomfortable to be practically naked in front of Gregor? A homophobic attitude might turn out to be Borzov's only vice. While being unsavoury and unpleasant, it was hardly a novelty in today's society. Neither did it make him a criminal.

Back in Vauxhall, Gregor stopped off at a store. For what he had in mind, he needed a disguise.

FORTY FOUR

Arran spent a restless night, trying to link together the bizarre happenings in Vauxhall. Although Jez and Alex knew each other, he couldn't imagine they'd run away together. Too far-fetched. The only link connecting all the missing guys was their sexuality. Not much to go on.

The talk with Sydnee had given Arran an insight into Jez's early rotten life of orphanages, bullying and sexual abuse. He had no idea how Jez had managed to become the great guy he was. It still hadn't helped Arran to figure out where to start looking for him.

At first light Arran got out of bed, showered, dressed and wandered into Jez's room for inspiration. His laptop was on the desk. Flipping it open, he tried to log on—password protected. He rummaged around the desk, looking for the password. No luck. Resting a hand on the laptop, he considered handing it over to the police ... Except, Jez might not like that idea.

Arran closed the laptop and made a search of the room for bits of paper with names, emails, phone numbers ... anything that might help him. He included a diary in his search, although Jez hadn't mentioned keeping one. But then there was no reason why he should; diaries were private affairs. Arran ran an eye over the bookshelves without spotting one among the many books. If only he could find something to identify Jez's date or where they'd met up that night.

Arran lay down on the bed. The house wasn't the same with Jez gone. It felt like a morgue. Jez's sweatshirt hung from the bedpost. As Arran played with the frayed cuff, he noticed a few photographs tacked to the side of a bookcase. One was of Halloween. Arran cringed at his forgettable Teen Wolf costume. Jez looked hellish in his Red Devil costume—more skin than fabric. Arran missed him, his teasing, his bursting into his bedroom, his crossing swords with Sydnee ... Every noisy thing about him.

Where are you, mate?

Another photo showed Jez in a crowd of people, standing outside a bar. People that Arran didn't know. Jez had a life outside the one Arran was familiar with—friends, lovers, places to which he disappeared. A secretive life. Arran had to gain entry into that secret world.

*

The tube clattered through dark tunnels, heading for the West End. Arran surveyed the sea of faces surrounding him, sitting down, standing up, hanging from the ceiling straps. Thousands of people came and went from London every day. Not too long ago he'd been one of those new arrivals. A lot had happened since then, good and bad. How was he ever going to find Jez or Alex in the throng of people inhabiting this city? Were their disappearances connected? Did they even want to be found? How could he find them when they were as secretive as each other? Clearly, both had things to hide.

Arran left Oxford Circus tube station and headed for *Tapas* in Charlotte Street. Goyo, the manager, was tied up on the phone when he enquired after him at the bar. He ordered an orange juice and waited. The lunchtime trade was in full swing and most of the tables were taken. The rich aromas drifting Arran's way reminded him of the day he and Jez had spent together; the time they'd almost become lovers. It was tempting to think he wouldn't be sitting here now if they had. Goyo's arrival interrupted the walk down what-might-have-been lane.

'You probably don't remember me,' Arran said. 'I came in a little while back with Jez.'

'Ah, Jez, yes ... How is he?' Goyo said, taking Arran's hand and shaking it.

'He's the reason I'm here. Has he been in here lately?'

'I haven't seen him, but let me check.' Goyo fired off some rapid Spanish to the barman, who then disappeared into the restaurant interior. When he returned, Goyo translated what he said for Arran. 'Jez came in two or three weeks ago.'

'Was he with anyone?'

'He was with a guy, tall, dark hair, the staff they didn't know him. Is everything all right with Jez?'

Arran shook his head. 'I'm not sure ... He might have disappeared ... In fact he's been missing for a week now.'

Goyo laid a hand on Arran's arm and squeezed it. 'That's terrible news. Tell us what we can do to help.'

'The police have been notified, but ...'—he shrugged—'so I'm trying to find him. That's why I'm talking to people who knew him. Hopefully, someone will have run into him and know what he's up to, where he's gone.'

'Keep in touch,' Goyo said, handing Arran his business card. 'And let me know if you need any more help.'

Arran left *Tapas* and crossed over Oxford Street into Soho, heading for the bar with no name to catch a word with Jez's friend, Andrew. The bar was almost empty when he entered. Andrew wasn't one of the few.

Soho was its usual busy self as Arran strolled around, hoping for a sighting of Jez or Alex and wondering about the guy seen at *Tapas* with Jez. He popped his head into the gay bars in the area, coming away disappointed. In Rupert Street he picked up a chicken burrito at one of the outdoor food stands. He made his way through Chinatown to the little park in Leicester Square and sat down on a bench to eat it. Lots of people were about, nibbling on sandwiches and chatting. No one he recognised.

Towards early evening Arran headed back to the bar to look for Andrew, finding him the second time around and asking for a private word. They found a table away from the group Andrew was with. He was shocked to hear Jez had gone missing but hadn't seen him around lately. Arran asked about Darius. Andrew looked like he might not answer but then said, 'Darius hasn't been seen for a week or two now, ever since splitting up with his latest boyfriend. Everyone assumes he's lying low somewhere, licking his wounds. That's what he's always done before.'

The timing of Darius's break up seemed to Arran as suspiciously timely. 'Do you think he and Jez could have hooked up again?'

Andrew shrugged. 'Anything's possible.'

'You hinted to me when I was here before that Jez liked Darius because he was dangerous. What did you mean?'

On this occasion, Andrew seemed to sense Arran was genuinely concerned for Jez and was more open. 'They're both gorgeous looking guys, and there was an instant attraction when they met. Darius wanted Jez. Used to getting what he wanted, he chased him until he gave in. Jez lived the good life, with Darius picking up the bill. However, with Darius, there is always a price to be paid. He can turn the charm on and off like a tap, and he has a cold edge to him. I think it was that which Jez responded to more than the charm or the money. Darius dominated him in and out of bed, treating him like a dog at times. Even in front of us here, he would order Jez about or cut him down with an icy rebuke. Jez took it all. Maybe he enjoyed it or maybe he needed it, I'm not qualified to judge. But just when it seemed he was a lost cause, he turned, dropped Darius and stopped coming here. The day I saw Jez with you was the first time he'd been seen here since the split. I guess he has more steel to him than any of us knew. Darius was furious, cursing Jez left and right and threatening to make trouble for him. I don't know if he ever made good on his threats.'

'So, he hasn't been seen for a while?' Arran said.

'No, he hasn't, but I can't say he's exactly disappeared, either.'

'Do you have his phone number to call him?'

Andrew took out his phone and placed the call. Arran hoped the news would be good. That Darius and Jez were back together. Mystery solved. The phone rang and rang ... and, eventually, Andrew ended the call.

'Is he capable of hurting Jez?' Arran asked.

'You know what they say about love and hate being the flip sides of the same coin. But didn't I hear about a gay serial killer stalking the Voho area?'

'That's the talk. A number of gay guys from there, including Jez, have disappeared. The police are just logging them as missing persons. As far as they're concerned, these cases are no more mysterious than any of the other thousands of people who go missing each year in London. No bodies have been found, which means there are no crimes to investigate. With two of my friends missing, I can't stand by while the police do nothing.'

'Who's the other guy?'

Arran told Andrew about Alex. How he'd gone missing after a night out in just the same way Jez had.

'Could their disappearances be connected?'

'I have no idea. One last question. What does Darius look like?'

'I'll send you his photo.'

They swapped phone numbers before Andrew returned to his friends. Arran took a sip of beer. Darius was the key to finding Jez. He fit the description of the guy seen with him at *Tapas*. He would run the picture by them. With any luck, the two were back together, and it wasn't a case of Darius exacting his revenge on Jez. Only when Darius was found would they would know which was true.

Conscious of a few looks directed his way from Andrew's crowd, Arran finished his beer and made his way out of the bar. Intending to walk along Oxford Street to the underground station, he headed for Soho Square. The centre was boarded off for reconstruction work, leaving a narrow, dimly lit passageway around the perimeter. The film company buildings and churches had closed for the night. Hearing sets of footsteps running up behind him, he moved aside to let the joggers pass. A blow to his back sent Arran head first into the boarding. He landed face down on the pavement, hitting his head a second time. A knee in the middle of his back pinned him down. Hands were all over him. Then he felt nothing more.

FORTY FIVE

The burglar counted down the stairs at Boy Lane, avoiding the creaky sixth and ninth. At the bottom he stopped and listened.

Nothing.

He hadn't been caught. He crept out of the house and sighed with relief at having evaded Miss Givens's detection. If she'd found him dressed from head to toe in black and his face hidden behind a hat and scarf, she would have asked too many difficult questions and Gregor wasn't a convincing liar. But he couldn't risk Borzov catching him spying.

Gregor set off walking in the direction of the Borzov house, drawing his new scarf in tighter around his neck to protect against the sly wind. His time in Britain had made him soft, the winters here nothing like the brutal cold of a Moscow winter that could freeze breath as it left the body. Passing through Vauxhall, Gregor glanced into the half empty bars. Businesses were suffering from all the talk of a serial killer on the loose. Jez was well known on the bar scene, and his disappearance had made people even more afraid and wary.

Gregor found the street he was looking for and slowed to a leisurely pace, his eyes searching out the house numbers. Many weren't clearly visible. Wandering too far, he had to backtrack to locate the right house. He took out and lit a cigarette as he gave the house the once-over. A large detached place, with three or four bedrooms. A dark Mercedes and two grubby white vans were parked in front of a stand alone garage. Gregor took a drag and blew the smoke out without swallowing. A waist high wall bordered the front of the yard, the barrier made more substantial by a tree and a couple of bushes in need of pruning. The house looked in reasonable condition and not dissimilar to all the other houses in the street. Ordinary people living in an ordinary house? Or criminals hiding in plain sight? Moving shadows behind the curtains suggested a number of people inside. Gregor had to find out if Borzov still lived here, what he was involved in and how he was connected to Alex. The sudden slam of a door made Gregor jump. Farther down the street a man appeared. He climbed into a car and drove off. Gregor had known staking out the house would be risky, but he was jumping at his own shadow.

He took a quick puff on the cigarette to calm his nerves. Not wanting to look suspicious to the neighbours, he'd bought them as a prop but didn't want to develop the habit again. A dog would have been another option, except no one he knew had one to lend. A sliver of light opened up at the house. Gregor pitched back into the shadows, dropping the cigarette. The end glowed like a beacon, pointing in his direction. Someone was looking out of a window. He pressed himself against the garden wall and was grateful for the cover of overhanging tree branches. He couldn't make out the face, whether it was Borzov or not. Whoever it was, their gaze was on him. He hardly dared breathe. If they were suspicious and came out, he didn't know what he would do. He cursed himself for not thinking through his intentions and coming up with a plan. Now he was trapped and couldn't think straight. A flicker of movement caught his eye, the curtain dropping. Gregor's gaze darted to the front door. Scared it might open. Scared of the trouble it might bring. Another beating. Seconds ticked by and nothing happened; the door remained closed.

Gregor took the chance to hurry away. At the end of the street he found a bench by a large church and lit another cigarette, taking a long drag and holding it until he felt the nicotine hit. Slowly exhaling, he watched the white smoke swirl about in the cold night air. This wasn't him. Someone who sneaked about in the dark, spying on violent men, possibly hardened criminals. After taking one last drag, he stubbed out the cigarette and set off for home.

On the way back, Gregor called in at the Sanctum for a quick drink to settle him down. No one he knew was in. Poor Donny looked lonely, with the bar almost empty. It still felt good to be here. Safe. He drank down half his pint. What had he been thinking? Going off half cocked. Tonight had been a huge mistake. Even if he'd seen Borzov, he had no way of finding out what he was up to. It wasn't like he could beat it out of him. He just wasn't built for this kind of detective work. He finished his drink and left.

The back streets were several shades darker and quieter than the main roads. Gregor fought against his overactive imagination. He didn't necessarily believe in the serial killer theory, but there was something strange going on in Vauxhall. Guys didn't just up and disappear. Not ordinary ones, anyway. Guys like Jez and Alex.

Something sounded behind him. The scrape of a shoe? Gregor feared the worst. Borzov must have seen him hovering around near his house and had followed him.

The sound came again. Louder this time. Footsteps, definitely. Borzov was gaining on him.

Not daring to look back, Gregor picked up his pace. He couldn't go through another beating at that brute's hands. He'd end up dead.

Heavier now, the footsteps. Closer. Gregor stiffened, fearing a blow from behind. A hand grabbed him. He threw it off and bolted for home.

'Gregor! It's me.'

Gregor recognised the voice. He stopped running and turned around. 'Arran, not funny! You trying to kill me off? I was imagining all sorts ...'

Arran doubled over, reaching out an arm to him. Gregor rushed to his side and saw the mess he was in. He helped him down the street and banged on the door until Miss Givens let them in. 'I hope you haven't lost ... What on earth has happened to Arran?'

Gregor got Arran inside and settled in an armchair. He had a nasty looking head wound that wouldn't stop bleeding, and his clothes were messy and torn. Between them they tended to his cuts and bruises. Miss Givens muttered under her breath about having warned him to be careful. 'First Gregor and now you.'

'Don't worry, it's not as bad as it might look,' Arran said. 'I was mugged by two chancers up in Soho.'

'Did they get anything?' Gregor said.

'Wallet and mobile phone. Luckily I had my tube ticket in my pocket, or I would have been stranded.'

'Drink this,' Miss Givens said. 'Medicinal brandy.'

'How come you're back so late?' Gregor said.

When Arran had finished telling them what he'd been up to, Gregor was quick to make the connections. 'Do you think someone tipped off Darius that you were asking about him and sent a couple of thugs to give you a warning?'

'Just opportunistic thieves, I reckon. I was in the wrong place at the wrong time.'

'But what if it was a warning?'

'Then that would tell us Darius has something to hide. I'm convinced he knows something about Jez's disappearance, and I intend to find out what.'

'How will you do that when Darius seems to have disappeared, too?' Miss Givens said.

'Somehow,' Arran said, 'I have to get into Jez's laptop.'

FORTY SIX

The next morning found Arran and Miss Givens getting into some awkward positions in turning Jez's bedroom upside down, searching for the password to his laptop that Arran was convinced held the key to unlocking the mystery of his disappearance. Arran strong-armed the bed for Miss Givens to get down on her knees and look under. As she did so, she gave him a wary look.

'Don't worry, I won't drop it on your head.'

'Never crossed my mind,' she said, peering under from the outermost edge.

Arran did most of the lifting, while Miss Givens did most of the searching and tidying up. No stone was left unturned or out of place. Arran crawled on hands and knees, pulling up and scanning under the corners and edges of the carpet. Miss Givens poked around inside jacket pockets and in-between folded shirts and jumpers. Arran took a look under the desk, behind the chest of drawers and on top of the wardrobe while Miss Givens ran a hand over the picture frames and bookcase. The quiet methodical work was only punctuated by Arran straining to lift the heavier furniture, Miss Givens's creaking joints and the forlorn reports of *nothing here* and *nothing here, either.*

Together they began to go through each book on the bookshelves—Now & Then, Tin Man, The Friend ... flicking the pages to see if anything dropped out and checking the front and back covers for concealed slips of paper.

'Do you think Jez's read all these books?' Arran said. 'I can't picture him staying still long enough to read a whole chapter never mind a long book.' He detected a flash of yellow inside The Winker. 'I think I may have it,' he said, plucking out a post-it with writing scribbled on.

When Arran opened up the laptop, the screen came alive with the login page. He entered **J_tru_man#** and gave Miss Givens a hopeful look before pressing *Enter*.

The text box shook.

'What's happening?' Miss Givens said.

'It doesn't like the password.'

They looked at each other in frustration. Arran concentrated on the password and then retyped it as **J_tru_man1**, explaining to Miss Givens that the number one indicated the current month, which allowed Jez to update without having to change the whole password. She nodded her head in his direction. The screen changed and the home page came up. Miss Givens clapped her hands. Arran dismissed the uncomfortable feeling he had at delving into Jez's private world. It had to be done if they wanted to find him. He clicked on the Mail icon and was surprised and dismayed at how organised Jez was in managing his emails. The majority were new messages, having arrived in the last week and most of them junk. He skimmed down the names of the remaining messages without finding Darius's name among them. He opened up a few personal messages to check they were from who they said they were. And, unfortunately, they were. He told Miss Givens, waiting silently by his side, what he'd found. Her face dropped. Arran added that Jez could have deleted Darius's messages before he left but failed to convince even himself. He'd been so sure he'd find evidence that Darius was behind Jez's disappearance.

Opening up the Internet browser history, Arran scrolled down to the days before Jez had gone missing. One website stood out—ManConnector. The opening page showed a members-only gay website, requiring a username and password. The racy home page—sexy models in skimpy underwear—enticed them with the suggestion that such men were available at the click of a button. His hand hovered over the keyboard ... Without the necessary information they were barred from the site. Arran went back into the browser history. Jez had been on a number of gay porn and chatroom sites over the previous months, but he'd been on the ManConnector site more than any other, including on the three consecutive nights before his disappearance.

Jez's picture file showed photos of themselves in happier times ... Halloween ... Christmas ... In others, he was with his mates from Flesh. Arran had hoped there might be snaps of Jez as a boy. Not a single one. It hurt him to think that no one had bothered to take any. But maybe it was just that Jez didn't want any reminders of those dark days. Miss Givens began to sniffle at seeing Jez so happy and full of life. Arran put the laptop to sleep. He came away feeling frustrated at not making more headway. He'd been so sure.

They were discussing what to do next over a cup of tea when the information on Darius arrived from Andrew. Arran opened up the attached file to reveal a photo of Darius and Jez together. Darius had black hair and was slightly taller than Jez. He looked and held Jez as if he possessed him. Jez's rejection must have hit Darius hard. Had he sought out Jez for revenge? Or had they got back together and forgotten the rest of the world existed? They could have; they had that kind of intense air about them. Jez must have been missing Darius for him to revisit his old haunts recently. He would have known that word would have reached Darius of his reappearance. Maybe that's what he'd wanted to happen. There was only one way to find out. Arran punched Darius's number into his phone. The ringing went unanswered. 'Why doesn't he bloody answer?' he said, slamming his phone down.

'Jez arranged a date with someone,' Arran said, voicing out loud what he was thinking for Miss Givens's benefit. 'It may have been Darius, or he could have met someone new on the ManConnector website. He and Darius's paths may even have crossed again on the site. If I could get Jez's password to go on ManConnector as him, then I may be able to smoke out whoever it was. It doesn't mean that person was connected with him going missing, but they may have information that could point us in the right direction. Darius is still the main suspect to my mind, but we can't wait around forever for him to answer his phone. I just need to figure out how to get Jez's username and password for the chatroom.'

'Trying to deliberately lure someone might lead to trouble,' Miss Givens said.

'He can't hurt me over the Internet.' Arran noticed her troubled expression and added, 'I just want to talk to him and find out what happened on their date.'

'What about going to the police with what you've found?'

'It's nothing more than hot air and speculation. They would laugh me right out of the station. Again. For them to take us seriously and start a proper inquiry, we need to take them hard evidence.'

Arran climbed the stairs to Jez's bedroom and sprawled out on the bed, staring at the ceiling. Ten minutes later, he raced over to the laptop and found the ManConnector site. He clicked on *Registration*. Having put in Jez's name and email, he pressed *Enter*. A message came up, asking if he'd forgotten his password. He clicked on the *Forgotten your password* button, which was answered with a message telling him it would be sent direct to his email address. A couple of minutes later and Arran had the key to unlocking Jez's ManConnector account.

Cockyboy.

Typical Jez. Arran couldn't wait to try it, even though he was due in for his shift at Bananas. On signing in, Jez's username came up as Jerry. Looking over the navigation bar on the website, he narrowed the selection to London, clicked on *Find Guys* and started to trawl through the messages of those currently using the site. Still early in the day, not many men were online, although the number counter was rising all the time. Arran quickly read the names and messages posted. Nothing caught his attention. He logged out and headed off to work, fired up that he was getting ever closer to finding Jez.

*

Late into the night, Arran went back into the ManConnector chatroom. Many more guys were now online. All during his shift, he'd been trying to think up the kind of message Jez might use. He typed—*Jerry likes it outdoors*—and then worked down the list, reading the other messages. Several pings of the message bell announced a number of men interested in him. He clicked on the *Accept* button to connect with one he thought might have interested Jez. For five droning minutes he listened to the guy telling him what he'd like to do to him before backing out; he wasn't in the mood to be spanked tonight.

Arran felt strange, having to put himself inside Jez's mind and think like him. Stranger still, to know he was trying to connect with someone possibly out to trap and hurt gay men. He pictured Jez at the mercy of some maniac, held against his will and praying his friends wouldn't give up on him. Another picture formed. A dead body. Arran pushed the dark image from his mind. He had to hold on to the belief Jez was alive and in need of help. He would do whatever it took to get him back, even if he had to set himself up to fall into the same trap. But for all he knew, Jez had met a perfectly innocent guy. For some reason, their date hadn't worked out and Jez had gone on to something or someone else. Before he would know for sure, he had to find that guy. His plan was to make himself conspicuous by using Jez's handle and coax his date to come to him. None of the guys Arran connected with held his interest, and the night ended in frustration.

For the next few days Arran spent almost all his spare time on the ManConnector site, trawling through countless man messages and chatting with all manner of men without finding anyone who triggered his suspicion. During coffee breaks, he tried to contact Darius again. Unsuccessfully. Despondency was setting in when the message—*Cockyboy's in the building*—appeared. Arran bolted upright, his mind racing.

Cockyboy. Jez's password.

How could that be? Was this Jez on the site? There was only one way to find out. He went to connect with Cockyboy.

The message had disappeared.

Arran's fingers flew over the keyboard as he scrolled up and down the messages in a desperate attempt to find Cockyboy.

He'd gone.

Arran's mind was reeling. What the hell had happened? Had Jez gone into a personal chatroom with someone else? Had he logged off? Did he not want to be found? None of this made sense. Arran slammed his hand down on the table, cursing his bad timing. He stayed online, waiting and praying and cursing for Cockyboy to return. Didn't happen.

Infuriated with himself, Arran logged off and went to bed. He closed his eyes but couldn't sleep. Too many crazy thoughts were swirling around in his head. He focused on the main one. Jez was alive.

FORTY SEVEN

Svetlana had instructed Pyotr to find a target for the next honeytrap. Despite hours of dedication to the task, all he had to show for his trouble were glazed eyes, sore fingers and a numb bum. The guys he'd met were only interested in one thing. Sex. Getting naked and jerking off to sex stories or meeting up for sex right away. They weren't interested in swapping bios. The lonelyhearts who usually fit the gang's profile were laying low.

Then Pyotr's eyes zoomed in on one particular message. He rubbed them, disbelieving what he saw. Not possible. His hand shot out and cut the connection. He looked around in a panic. Nikolay and Pavel were gone. He didn't know what to do. As far as he knew this had never happened before.

Pyotr found Nikolay and Svetlana in the living room and interrupted their talk. His words came out in a jumble and they couldn't make sense of what he was saying and told him to take a deep breath and then to start at the beginning. After telling them what had happened, he finished by asking whether it might just be a strange coincidence.

'It could,' Nikolay said, 'or it could be that someone knows something and is baiting us.'

Svetlana's eyes widened. 'A reverse honeytrap, you mean?'

Pyotr was alarmed their security might be at threat. 'What should I do?' he asked them, panicked that he was at the centre of this trap. Since delivering a successful honeytrap, his standing within the gang had shot up, the men treating him with more respect, like an equal, rather than the baby of the group. He didn't want to lose his position and didn't want to be the one who let the side down. He felt sick.

Svetlana took Pyotr by the arm, punctuating her words with tight squeezes. 'Connect with the guy. Find out who he is. Suss out whether he's a threat to us or not. And Nikolay, stay on hand for Pyotr. Just in case ...'

Pyotr went for a long smoke and several vodkas before returning to the computer. He logged back on to the ManConnector site, his fingers steadier now. He searched up and down the list of messages but couldn't find the dreaded one. The guy had gone. Lucky for him, this time.

Alex was dozing in his sleeping bag when Pyotr came racing into the living room, babbling away like a halfwit. His frantic discussion with Nikolay and Svetlana poured icy water over Alex, waking him up. He kept his eyes closed, not wanting to give away the increasing alarm he was feeling at what he was hearing. Whoever was using the guy's handle must have been close to him. Who else would have access to his personal information? As soon as Alex asked himself that question, the answer hit him like Maxim's fist.

He knew the person stumbling his way into becoming the next victim of a honeytrap.

FORTY EIGHT

The coffee was making Gregor's heart race. Lately he'd felt as though he was constantly in fight or flight mode and didn't need further chemical stimulation. The visit to Borzov's had set him on edge. He couldn't make it through the night without waking in a sweat. Nightmares about Borzov catching him spying and attacking him. Others about a stalker giving him a heart attack. He'd sworn off further visits to the house, not cut out for shadowing shady characters at night. The decision left him with an uneasy conscience. Jez and Alex were still missing, all their friends were worried sick and the police didn't want to know. Someone had to do something. But what? He got up from the table and threw the remainder of the coffee down the sink, washed and tidied his mug, and left the staff room.

Heading back to the massage cubicle, Gregor caught himself looking around for Borzov. It was instinctive. A sign that he couldn't abandon his friends. Not when they needed his help. Borzov knew something about Alex, and Gregor had to find out what. The problem was how, when he was out of his depth? He made the decision to keep an eye on Borzov from a safe distance. That way he could still find out who he associated with and, if he was lucky, overhear a few snippets of conversation. Gregor made rounds of the baths at regular intervals throughout the day without sighting Borzov. He steeled himself to return to Borzov's house that night. This time he kept strictly to the shadows and didn't loiter too long. Nothing happened. No one looked out of the window or came out of the house. He returned home feeling a mixture of frustration and relief.

The next morning, Gregor rose early and headed over to Borzov's before anyone had time to leave for work. He waited at the end of the street, by the church, frozen stiff by the time the door opened and half a dozen men came out dressed in heavy work gear and carrying toolbags. One of them was Borzov. They headed down the street towards Gregor. With no time to get away, he shrank back against the massive door of the church. As the men passed by he turned away, as if lighting up a cigarette. He wasn't sure if

Borzov looked his way or not. The group carried on to the bus stop in the main road. Gregor waited until the bus had gone before heading off to the baths.

The sighting of Borzov only confirmed to Gregor that he was still on the scene. Everything else about him and his housemates, the work overalls and tool bags, was in keeping with them being regular workmen. Though, looks could be deceiving and so it was still possible they were involved in criminal activities. Construction workers had highly mobile jobs that would allow them to move drugs or people or both. But whoever the men really were, their connection to Alex remained a puzzle. They just didn't seem the type of people he would hang around with.

Having seen Borzov leave for work, it didn't seem likely he would appear at the baths until the afternoon. Gregor left making his rounds until then. He hoped Borzov would show. Getting close to him here would be a lot easier and safer than out on the streets or in a pub. After Gregor had finished his shift, he made one last circuit of the baths. No Borzov. That meant making another risky outing that night.

*

Alex was still awake when another grey and gloomy dawn appeared. Soon after, the men around him stirred, getting up, drinking coffee and smoking their first of the day before making their preparations for work. Alex closed his eyes and pretended to be asleep. All night he'd been unable to settle, going over and over what he'd heard, trying to put a different spin on it and always coming back to the same conclusion—Arran and the others had somehow found out about the online honeytrap.

It was the only conclusion that made sense. He hoped he was wrong, for their sakes. At least it appeared they were still trying to find out who was behind the honeytrap, so they couldn't know much, if anything, about the gang. The scary part was that now the gang had rumbled them, they had no idea of the dangerous game they were playing. The gang was taking seriously the threat to its security and would crush anyone in its way. It wasn't too late for Alex to warn his friends not to go ahead with their plans, if he could only find a way to escape. It wouldn't be easy. This threat against the gang had the men on high alert. Exhausted from a long night of thinking, he fell asleep.

Alex awoke to a quiet house. He felt guilty about having fallen asleep when Arran was in danger and needed him. He had to find a way to leave. It was now mid-morning and most of the men had left for work. Others remained behind to guard him. One guy was over in the corner, messing about on his phone. Another one would be hovering near the kitchen. A third would be upstairs. There was nowhere he could go without one of them following him. Going outside wasn't allowed, not even into the back garden. His phone had been taken and no one left theirs unguarded, so he couldn't ring Arran. At least he'd had the foresight to wipe Arran and the others from his contacts and calls history, or the game would have been up.

Alex climbed out of his sleeping bag and went to the bathroom. After taking a hot shower, he made a coffee and picked at a slice of toast. Despite his captors ignoring him, he could feel their eyes on him. Watching. They had treated him coolly since his return, distrust and dislike showing in their eyes. Distrust because of his running off, and dislike because they had to babysit him. He was considered a nuisance that they could do without. His reaction was to act normally. At some point they would become bored and let their guard drop. That was when he'd act. He picked up a book and pretended to read. The simplest plan would be to rush for the door. This would have to be done in the evening, when the key was left in the lock for people coming and going. During the day, it was removed.

The day passed like sitting through a subtitled film. In the afternoon, stiff from sitting around, he began to exercise, ticking off set after set of fifty press-ups and sit-ups. It made him long for Arran and their times out, running and biking. It made him sad to think that those days might be over for good. Even if he stopped Arran from making the biggest mistake of his life in taking on the gang, he probably wouldn't want Alex back. Not when he learned that he'd been one of them. Not when he learned what he'd done for them.

By late afternoon trickles of men began arriving back from work. Alex didn't stop his workout, pushing his muscles until they screamed, the pain filling his mind and making it impossible to think of anything else. Sweat poured out of him. He went over to the window to cool off and pressed his head and hands to the cold glass. He ached to be with Arran and his friends. Somehow he had to get them to take him back. They were good people and would understand his predicament. They'd see that he'd had no choice. They had to. Without them he had nothing. Boy Lane was a short walk away but might as well have been a thousand miles.

A guy packaged up in winter gear walked up the street, keeping to the shadows. Although it was dark outside, his height and build and the way he moved seemed familiar. For all the world it could have been Gregor. A few minutes later, he came strolling back. Alex couldn't risk banging on the window and moved his hand in a slow wave to attract his attention. The guy stopped and looked over. A big smile came to Alex's face. Everything would be fine now. Arran would be safe.

Oh, no, what was happening?

The guy was leaving. Alex's smile faded away. He couldn't have been Gregor. It had been silly to think his friends knew enough about the gang to have traced it here. What could he have done anyway? If he'd come to the house and confronted them, they wouldn't have let him leave. Both of them would have been kept prisoner. They might even have beaten the truth out of Gregor. That they knew each other because they were both homosexuals. If Gregor had come to the door, he could have sentenced them both to death.

Someone left the house. Alex couldn't make out who it was. The dark shape headed in the same direction as Gregor. Had to be a coincidence.

Frustrated at being kept a prisoner and made bold by the thoughts of his friends, Alex walked out of the room as if to go to the bathroom and made straight for the front door. He had to get out of this house and warn them. Right now, before they made a big mistake. As he turned the key in the lock, a familiar voice came from behind him.

'Going somewhere?'

*

After he'd eaten, Gregor headed out. On the stairs he miscounted and trod on the ninth. The creaking summoned Miss Givens. She popped her head out of the living room to ask if he was going to the Sanctum again.

Great! She thinks I'm an alcoholic.

Perhaps he should let the others know what he was doing. He would when he had something to tell. Passing by the bars, he was sorely tempted to go in for some Dutch courage. He resisted and increased his pace toward Borzov's.

The curtains at the house were open. Someone was standing at the main downstairs window. Blurry. He couldn't make out whether they were just standing close to the window or if they were looking out. Fearful of lingering too long, he carried on walking to the end of the street. On the return leg, he paused in the shadows to take a longer look. Still unable to make out the face, he carried on walking. Behind him, a door opened and closed. He daren't risk a look to see who it was. Seconds later, a bulky figure passed him on the other side of the street. Gregor froze at the sight of Borzov. He reminded himself that this was what he'd been waiting for and set off to follow. On reaching the Church at the end of the street, Gregor searched up and down the main road for Borzov. There was no sign of him; he'd disappeared. Gregor's one chance. Gone. He was useless at this game.

Gregor moved off in the direction of the shops and pubs. He was alongside the big roofed gate of the church when a match struck and flared into life. Borzov's face was lit up and his eyes were on him. Gregor stopped walking, uncertain of what to do.

Borzov's rumbling voice came from a dark place. 'So it is you, the guy from the baths. I just happened to catch you from the bedroom window, strolling by the house. What are you doing here?'

Gregor's eyes darted around, scanning for Borzov's mates, certain they would be close by, waiting to jump him again.

'Don't worry, I'm alone.' Borzov lit his cigarette and threw the match onto the damp ground, where it sizzled out. 'I just want to talk.'

Against his better judgement Gregor stepped into the gate, driven on by what might be his only chance to find out the connection between Borzov and Alex. From now on Borzov would be on his guard. 'I know it was you who beat me up and warned me off, but I still need to find Alexei. How do you know him?'

Borzov didn't react to Gregor's accusation. 'What do you want with Alexei?'

Caught off-guard, Gregor had to come up with an excuse. 'He owes me money.'

Borzov stared at Gregor, searching his face. 'I've been asking around about you, Gregor Gregorovich.'

Gregor went rigid. If Borzov had been digging around in his personal life, what had he found out?

'They tell me you're an ordinary guy, who works hard and keeps his nose clean. Is that true?'

Gregor struggled to keep the trembling out of his voice. 'I just want my money back.'

Borzov didn't appear to be listening. 'They also tell me you're a quiet guy, who keeps to himself and avoids trouble. That's why I was so surprised to catch you casing—'

'I wasn't casing your house. I just want to find Alexei.'

Borzov threw down his cigarette and drove his fist into Gregor's stomach. Gregor bent in two, struggling to get air into his lungs. Borzov punched him on the side of the head, then grabbed him in a headlock. 'Forget the money and forget Alexei.' He flung Gregor to the ground and delivered a couple of swift kicks to his ribs before walking away.

Gregor, writhing in pain on the damp ground, heard Borzov say, 'I know where to find you, Gregorovich. This is your final warning.'

*

Alex cringed and let go of the key. Maxim was standing at the door of the bathroom, a wet towel clung to him. Of all people, it had to be Maxim who had caught him trying to leave. He tried to sound casual. 'I've got a bit of a headache. I was heading out into the garden for some air. That's okay, isn't it?'

Maxim shook his head and waved him inside the living room. 'Get yourself in there. Now.'

The men in the living room looked up to see what was going on. Maxim told them of Alexei's attempt to leave and berated them for not keeping a closer watch on him. As Maxim walked away, he cuffed Alex hard on the side of the head. 'You're going nowhere until you prove to us you can be a good little boy again.'

The other men looked at Alex with undisguised hostility on their faces. He laid down on his sleeping bag, well away from the group. Inside, he was kicking himself at having blown his chance of escaping. He'd made his situation ten times worse. From now on everyone would be watching him like a hawk and time was not on his side to warn Arran. It was on him if Arran did something rash. Alex felt sick.

With nothing else to do, he undressed, stacking his clothes and trainers beside him. He bedded down, facing the wall. The other guys carried on smoking and chatting for what seemed like forever before making their own preparations for bed. Alex closed his eyes and tried to still his mind using the meditation techniques he'd picked up from Mr Cheung. Even then he couldn't stop anxious thoughts hacking through into his consciousness. He'd left Arran and the others to avoid putting them in danger from the gang. Somehow that had happened. If only he'd made good on his efforts to stop the gang, they wouldn't be in this mess. Arran might even have forgiven him and taken him back by now. Life could have been good again.

Although Alex gave the impression of sleep, it was the furthest thing from his mind. Tonight he would make another move to escape. He'd failed once; he couldn't afford to fail again. Arran's life depended on him.

FORTY NINE

Arran was desperate for Cockyboy to reappear on the ManConnector website. The neverending wait was killing him. Where the hell was he? He again put out the same message—*Jerry likes it outdoors*—and clicked on the *Find Men* tab. The counter clocked 373 men currently active on the site. He scanned down the messages—more were being added all the time.

Jerry likes it outdoors
Twink wants to play
Bad boy needs spanking
Mr Footlike needs jam
Regular Joe seeks same

Nothing grabbed Arran's interest, though the pinging of the message bell sounded other men's interest in him. Not a chatroom guy, it surprised Arran how many men used this method to find other men and how direct they were with their requests. None of them struck him as Jez's type. He declined all invitations to chat and carried on reading down the list, willing Cockyboy to enter the site.

Finally ...

Cockyboy's out to play
Exotic needs nurturing
Ginger twink
Chav 21
Top 19

Arran let out a sigh of relief and went to message him. At the last second, he pulled his hand away from the keyboard. Did Jez not want to be found? The question had haunted Arran since Cockyboy had last appeared on the site. Jez must have recognised his own handle, so why had he logged off? He should have known that only his friends could have found out such personal information. So why hide from them? What was he playing at? Arran sat back and waited to see if Jez made contact with him. Less than a minute went by before the message bell pinged.

Cockyboy.

Arran felt happier than he had in a long time. The others would be over the moon, especially Miss Givens and Sydnee. He hit the button to connect.

Cockyboy — *Before we get down to it, let's switch on the webcams. I want to see you in the flesh.*

Arran wanted the same thing and agreed. Rocked by what appeared on the screen, Arran sank back in his chair. The young blond guy in a tight white t-shirt wasn't Jez. The guy's cocky grin slipped.

Cockyboy — 'You don't like what you see?'

Arran gathered himself. Cockyboy—Jez's password and this guy's handle. It couldn't be a coincidence. The assumption Jez had been describing himself wasn't true; the name belonged to this guy. Jez had to be taken with him to borrow it. That made him interesting to Arran. He was possibly viewing Jez's date.

Jerry — 'Sorry, you took me by surprise. I was expecting someone ... older. How old are you?'

Cockyboy — 'Old enough. You wouldn't be disappointed, believe me.

Jerry — Tell me a little about yourself.'

Cockyboy — 'I'm 18, from Prague. Came to London to work and for a bit of fun. I live with other straight Czech guys, so I can't get out by myself to gay bars. It's easier for me to meet guys online and then if the glue's there we can arrange to meet. Somewhere private. What are you into?'

Cockyboy was lying. There was no way he was eighteen. Arran could see why Jez would have been attracted to him, if that was the case. He had boyish good looks tempered by a mean look to his expression. His lean, hard body didn't look to have come out of a gym. More like from manual work.

Jerry — 'I'm 18, too. I moved to London several months ago. Work in a bar, so I could hook up with people I meet there but prefer not to mix business and pleasure. And it can be so much more interesting meeting guys online. You never know who your next playmate will be or what they're into. I'm into straight looking and acting guys who like the great outdoors—parks, woods, cemeteries, old buildings. Love the risk of getting caught, a bit of voyeurism ... Hope you're not shy? You?'

Cockyboy — 'You're turning me on and I'm not shy in front of the viewers.'

Jerry — 'Sounds like you've done this sort of stuff before?'

Cockyboy — 'You got me there.'

Jerry — 'Tell me about it.'

Cockyboy — 'You sound a lot like a guy I met up with—smooth young body, real horny, liked it public. I bet he'd be up for a threesome. Interested?'

Arran's heart almost stopped. Cockyboy was baiting him. With Jez. He was on the right track with this one. Him and Jez were mixed up in some way. Question was, how?

Jerry — 'We could have ourselves a party. Where did you meet up?'

Cockyboy — 'South London.'

Jerry — 'Works for me.'

Cockyboy — 'Let's meet real soon. You won't regret it ...'

Arran was convinced Cockyboy knew something about Jez and was prepared to risk himself. At some point it would have to happen. They would have to meet if he wanted to get any real information out of him. Guys went online all the time to hook up and meet for sex straight away. It was expected. He didn't want to refuse, put the guy off and have him disappear again. Arran knew nothing about the real person; he could be anyone. He would never find him. It was madness to meet up with this guy, but he felt compelled to. He owed it to Jez.

Jerry — 'Know of any place to make this happen?'

Cockyboy — 'Leave it to me.'

Jerry — 'Can make this Friday.'

Cockyboy — 'I have a car. Tell me where you live and I'll pick you up.'

Jerry — 'Vauxhall.'

Cockyboy — 'There's an industrial estate just outside Vauxhall where it would be easy to pick you up in a car. Outside Shah's Clothing Co. Know it?'

Jerry — 'Know it.'

Cockyboy — 'Be there at 8. I'll be driving a black Mercedes.'

Jerry — 'You've got style. What should I call you?'

Cockyboy — 'Pete.'

Jerry — 'Pete, it is.'

Pete grinned. But even the upward curve of his lips failed to soften his flinty features. What did he know about Jez? His ice-chip blue eyes were narrowed and giving nothing away. It had come as a huge shock not to have found Jez. But Pete was the next best thing. And when they met, Arran was determined to make him talk.

FIFTY

Even after the men were snoring up a storm, Alex waited. Three in the morning couldn't come soon enough. That was when they should be in their deepest sleep and when he would make his move. He climbed out of his sleeping bag, picked up his clothes and trainers, and crept out of the room. The door creaked.

Damn.

He held his breath. When no one stirred, he tiptoed to the bathroom and dropped the catch behind him. While it wouldn't keep out anyone determined, it made him feel easier.

So far so good.

All he now had to do was make it down the drainpipe in one piece. He slipped on a tracksuit top and bottoms and knelt down to tie his trainers. Having eased open the window, he moved the many bottles of shower gel, shampoo and deodorant to one side and climbed onto the sill. The drainpipe was behind the window. He stepped onto the ledge and closed it behind him. The bushes rustled in the light wind, four long body lengths below. He tested the drainpipe. It seemed sturdy enough. Having come so far, he didn't want to fall onto hard paving slabs and break his ankle. With so much at stake, he couldn't risk an injury.

Here goes.

Alex took hold of the pipe and began to shin down. His feet scraped the bricks, the scuff sounding like an alarm in the dead of night. He stopped and waited. Nothing happened. No one had heard. He carried on and dropped down the last couple of feet to the ground.

Free at last.

Alex looked up at his ex-prison, dark and silent. Now he would stop Arran from making the biggest mistake of his life. This time he wouldn't mess about and go straight to the police and tell them all he knew about the gang's activities. He would make sure they were put out of business once and for all.

Alex turned to head for the front yard, a big smile on his face. A punch came out of the darkness, knocking him to the ground. He scrabbled on hands and knees, desperate to get away from the kicks to his back and ribs. A dead weight landed on his back, pinning him down. His head was pulled back by the hair, and he felt warm breath on his ear.

'I had a feeling you were going to pull a stunt like this tonight.' Maxim's weight pressed along his full length. Alex could feel his excitement. 'Where were you sneaking off to in the middle of the night?'

Overcome with disappointment, Alex couldn't speak. Yet he had to try to talk Maxim around. He might still get away. 'I was going crazy locked up. Let me go. I promise I'll come back.'

Maxim scoffed. 'Liar! I don't know what you're up to, but I don't trust you.'

'Please, Maxim,' Alex pleaded, 'all I need is some exercise and fresh air. I'll be back before you know it. No one would—'

'You know,' Maxim said, chuckling in his ear, 'no one would be any the wiser if I finished you off, right here, right now. It would be so easy.' Alex gasped as Maxim gripped him, a finger stroking up and down his throat. 'I could tell the others you'd broken your neck, falling from the bathroom window when trying to escape. They'd believe me. You would be buried underground like the homos you seem so concerned about.' Maxim tightened his grip.

Alex could barely speak. 'You're not bright enough to carry it off,' he croaked. 'Svetlana would see through you and then you'd pay.'

This earned Alex a punch to the ribs. 'Your sister won't always be around to protect you. Then we'll have some fun together, you and me.'

Maxim's idea of fun chilled Alex. Maxim pulled him up from the damp ground and half dragged him back into the house. He bundled him into the under stairs cupboard and locked it.

Alex smashed his fist on the floor. He'd failed again. Now Arran would be at the mercy of the gang, and there was nothing he could do. Arran would die and it was all Alex's fault.

FIFTY ONE

The deep rumbling voice turned Gregor's legs to water and sent him tearing down behind one of the massive pillars supporting the domed roof of the poolroom. Having finished his final massage of the day, he'd been taking a last turn around the baths before heading home when he'd heard Borzov. That voice would haunt him for the rest of his days.

Borzov was with two other guys in one of the smaller pools. They had their backs to Gregor. Although he had a clear view, their voices were muffled. He had to get closer if he wanted to hear what they were saying. A handful of men were dotted around but over on the far side, away from where Gregor was hiding. Concealed by the subdued lighting and foliage, he edged forward, crawling on hands and knees to the next pillar. He parted the ferns to clear his view. Borzov and his mates were laughing about something. Gregor strained forward and caught the word *homo*. One of the men stretched out his legs and started kicking his feet around in the water. Gregor groaned with frustration. Juvenile moron! Over the splashing, Gregor could only hear snatches of what was said.

... another queer ...

The rest was lost as the men started jeering at what Borzov was saying. Gregor strained his neck to hear him.

... trap ...

Gregor stiffened. This was what he'd been waiting for, some idea of what Borzov was involved in and it sounded anything but good.

... pervert a lesson ...

A creak sounded behind Gregor. The door. Footsteps approached. He had no time to react.

'Gregor, what are you doing down there?'

At the sound of Yuri's voice, Gregor scrambled backwards on his hands and knees to escape the line of sight of Borzov. He bumped into Yuri and hurried to his feet. Behind him, water crashed down onto the marble floor. Gregor looked around to see Borzov climbing out of the pool, waving his arms and shouting to Yuri. 'Hey, what's going on? Was he spying on us?'

Gregor grabbed Yuri and urged him towards the exit. 'Please don't let them near me. I think they're the ones.'

Yuri's eyes widened. 'The ones who attacked you?'

Gregor chanced a look behind. Borzov was marching their way. 'I'm not sure, I think so. Please help me.'

'Get out of here,' Yuri said. 'Don't worry, I'll fend them off.'

Gregor ran for the exit door, wrenched it open and made for the staff changing room. He opened his locker, grabbed his coat and headed for the exit. He had to get away from the baths before Borzov or one of his mates had the chance to catch him. He opened the door to the alleyway and looked out. Dark and deserted. Gregor slammed the door, then pelted towards the lights at the far end. The safety of the shops and people seemed miles away. With his eyes locked forward, he pounded through puddles of greasy rainwater, struggling to keep from slipping.

A black shape appeared at the end of the alley, blocking his way. Gregor faltered, skidded and pitched forward into the darkness.

'Oh, hell!'

Dropping his coat, he thrust out his arms. Unable to judge the ground, he crash-landed, the air rushing from his lungs. He skidded forward on hands and knees, leaving skin behind. The sight of the black figure hurtling down the alley towards him had Gregor scrambling to his feet. Gulping for air, he pressed his back to the wall. Blocked from going forward, too afraid to go back, and panicked by the thought of another beating, Gregor started yelling. 'No closer. Stay away from me. Help! Someone help me!'

The black figure didn't stop. It crept ever closer. Frozen against the wall and fearing the worst, Gregor braced himself for the attack. The figure was almost upon him.

'Gregor! Gregor! It's all right, it's me ... Valeriy.'

The figure edged towards Gregor with its arms held out in front. 'Here, let me help you.'

Gregor peered through the gloom. It was Valeriy. He snatched up his coat and ran, past the bus stop outside the baths and towards the next one. A bus was at the stop, preparing to leave. Waving his hands, he ran towards it and leapt through the closing doors. The driver told him to get his breath back before coming to pay.

Gregor collapsed into the nearest vacant seat, his lungs bursting and water pooling at his feet. He didn't care what the other passengers thought. He was safe. The drumming inside was his heart and lungs competing for the right to burst out of his chest first. And his hands and knees were burning like the fires of hell. Another episode like the one tonight would finish him off. It was time to tell the others what he'd been up to.

FIFTY TWO

Arran was too fired up to stand still. Sydnee and Miss Givens were sitting side by side on the sofa. Their eyes were on him. Expectant. It was important, he'd told them. They wouldn't like some of what he had to say. 'Cockyboy is Jez's password for the ManConnector site. It's also the handle for one of the site users. Jez must have a thing for him.'

'What have you been up to?' Sydnee said.

The words came spilling out of Arran. 'The first time I came across Cockyboy, he disappeared in the blink of an eye. At first I thought he was Jez. I was mistaken. But this guy knows something about Jez's disappearance, I'd bet my life on it. Seeing Jez's username on the site must have unsettled him. I waited—'

Sydnee held up her hand. 'Just slow down a little. What were you trying to do?'

Arran dropped into an armchair alongside them. 'Jez had to meet his date somewhere. It seemed likely he'd met him online because he was always on the ManConnector site. The plan was to use Jez's handle and let the same person come to me. It worked.'

'You set yourself up as bait?'

'Exactly.'

'You're mad.'

Arran edged to the front of the chair and leaned forward. 'Last night as soon as Cockyboy came onto the site, he sought me out. Don't you see? He targeted me.'

'We do see,' Sydnee said, with Miss Givens nodding alongside, 'only too clearly. The reason he targeted you is the reason we're worried.'

'Him, coming after me means he knows something.'

'So what did you get from him?'

'You should have seen him. Said his name was Pete, but Cockyboy describes him perfectly. Just the kind of guy Jez would have gone for. But cagey. I'll have more luck getting answers from him face to face.'

Sydnee slapped her thighs. 'Please don't say you've arranged to meet up with this guy.'

'Friday night.'

'Now I know you're crazy.'

'I just want to meet with him and find out what he knows.'

'Why can't you do that on the Internet? Why risk meeting him in person?'

'Because if I start asking awkward questions, he might disappear again and then he'd never be found.'

'If he is targeting men online, you're putting yourself in real danger.'

Arran pushed back into the chair. 'I know this guy knows something about Jez.'

'You said the same thing about Darius. What's happened with him?'

'He never answers his phone. Anyway, the guys at *Tapas* didn't recognise him as the guy who'd been in there with Jez.'

'Sounds like you've given up on him.'

'I hope Jez and Darius are back together and living it up somewhere. But until he answers his phone, we won't know for sure. Meanwhile—'

'I know how hard you're trying,' Sydnee cut in, 'but I have a bad feeling about this. The way the guy zoned in on you. The speed of wanting to meet up in person. Not to mention the anonymity. If you go missing, what could we tell the police? You'd end up being just one more statistic, like all the others.'

'Cockyboy would have had to register on the site. They'd be able to find out who he really was.'

'You don't really believe that. If he were targeting men online, he would have taken steps to protect himself. You should go to the police, tell them your suspicions and let them deal with him.'

'You know as well as I do that unless you give them something solid to work on, they wouldn't want to know. I promise that if I get anything useful from this guy, I will pass it over to them. I just want Jez found and home safe again.'

Sydnee squeezed Arran's knee. 'We know how much you want to help Jez. We all do. But it's risky meeting up with the guy in this way. If you confront him and back him into a corner, there's no predicting how he'll react. He might even be carrying. Then what would you do?'

'I'll be careful, I promise. The first hint of trouble and I'll be out of there.'

'Where are you meeting him?'

Arran cringed as he gave the details of the meet, knowing the reaction it would get. He wasn't disappointed.

'Good grief! Why couldn't you have suggested a nice coffee shop or the Eros statue in Piccadilly Circus at high noon? Why did it have to be some godforsaken backwater at night?'

'I wanted to remind him of Jez by having the same sexual habits. It worked and we're supposed to be meeting for wild sex. I couldn't back out without looking suspicious, so we're stuck with it. Most likely it'll be some cemetery or derelict building around here. We can look these places up beforehand.'

Sydnee got up and started wearing out the carpet. 'You could end up being at the mercy of him miles from anywhere and all by yourself. We wouldn't have a clue where you'd gone.'

'Hopefully, it won't get that far. Not if I can get him talking in the car and find out what he knows. But I can get out of the car at any time if I feel something's not right. In any case, I don't intend meeting him alone.'

Sydnee stopped pacing. 'That's the first sensible thing I've heard tonight.'

'If they're up for it, Gregor and Serge can be my back up and follow us to wherever we go. That way there would be safety in numbers. With three of us, he's unlikely to try any rough stuff.'

'What if he has the same idea and brings his mates along?' Miss Givens said.

'I'll make sure he's alone before getting in the car, and Gregor and Serge can check for anyone trailing us. If the worst comes to the worst, I could jump out when he stops at traffic lights. You two could wait here by the phone for extra back up.'

The front door crashed.

They all turned to see what was happening. Gregor rushed into the room and dropped into an armchair.

'You look like you've been through the mill,' Arran said.

'Not again,' Miss Givens said. 'What's happened this time?'

FIFTY THREE

Gregor shuffled around in the chair, rearranging the cushions and buying time to get his story straight. 'I didn't tell you before because there wasn't anything to tell and I didn't want to get your hopes up.'

'Tell us what?' Arran said.

'I know who attacked me. His name's Borzov and—'

'How do you know?'

Gregor filled them in on what he'd been up to.

'So that's why you've been going out every night,' Miss Givens said, raising her eyes. 'I thought you'd become—'

'I know what you thought,' Gregor said. 'And it's not true.'

'This Borzov lives in Vauxhall?' Arran said.

'A ten minute walk from here. He works in construction and lives with other workers.'

'That would fit with what Alex told me about the people he travelled with to London. I got the impression they'd left and he stayed. I mustn't have heard right. Have you seen Alex?'

'No. But Alex has to have been involved with them. Borzov didn't give anything away, but they're still on the lookout for him. They must have had a falling out.'

'You've spoken with Borzov?'

'He caught me watching his house.'

'Did he hurt you again?'

'Roughed me up a bit and warned me off again. Which only goes to prove he has something to hide.'

'It only goes to prove,' Sydnee said, 'that these men are dangerous and ready to resort to violence to protect whatever it is they're hiding.'

'Whatever they're involved in,' Arran said, 'I still can't make the connections with Jez or the other missing guys.'

'Neither can I,' Gregor admitted. 'But Borzov is connected to Alex, Alex can be connected to Jez, both have disappeared just like the other gay guys, and all are connected to Vauxhall. That's way too many connections for them to be dismissed as mere coincidence. That's why I've kept on trailing Borzov, to find out where he fits into this puzzle. Tonight it paid off.'

'I think we need a drink,' Miss Givens said, heading over to the bottle cabinet.

They sipped at large brandies while Gregor relayed the snatches of overheard conversation.

'What do you think it means?' Arran said.

'Well, when someone tosses out the words *gay* and *pervert*, they are unlikely to be gay friendly. When they go on to talk about a *trap* and a *lesson*, it makes them sound actively homophobic. I know from personal experience that these men are not averse to solving their problems with a little violence.'

'This is all getting more and more disturbing,' Sydnee said. 'Are you saying these men could be setting traps for gay men and then attacking them?'

'That's exactly what I think they're doing.'

'How would they go about setting a trap?'

'I don't know. But we do know about guys going missing, Arran and Jez being abused in the street a couple of times and the attack on Big Girls.'

Arran shook his head. 'Verbal abuse, vandalism and abduction are very different crimes. The first two are low level, random. The guy who abused us was drunk both times. Abducting guys would take planning.'

'Sounds to me like Borzov and his mates are planning something,' Gregor said.

'Do you think Alex could be involved with them in this?'

'Alex is gay. He's not the kind of person to want to hurt others. There's no way he would be involved with crazy homophobes abusing gay people. His connection to Borzov must be in some other way.'

'It's baffling. I can't make sense of any of it.'

'The good news,' Sydnee said, 'is that if Borzov and his mates are the problem, then the guy Arran is meeting on Friday night is likely to be harmless.'

FIFTY FOUR

The drive past Shah's Clothing Company, the starting point for Arran's showdown with Pete, showed nothing out of the ordinary. The warehouses, factories and garages of the industrial area on the outskirts of Vauxhall had closed for the evening and most of the workers had gone. Only stragglers remained, hurrying along the cracked pavements. No one was hanging about.

'The coast looks clear,' Arran said to Gregor. The last thing he must do was get caught in an ambush and give Pete the upper hand. If they were to find Jez, he had to stay cool and keep his wits about him.

Gregor nodded. 'The traffic's light, so there's plenty of time for a couple more drive-bys to make sure.'

They passed by Serge, keeping watch from behind a row of bins. The plan was for Serge to follow Pete's car on his less conspicuous borrowed moped and for Gregor to trail him in Sydnee's bright red Audi convertible.

'Do you think we blend in to the background?' Gregor said, chuckling.

Arran grinned. 'Loud and proud, that's our Sydnee.'

Two more drive-bys yielded nothing new or untoward. Gregor drove a short distance away and parked up. Arran left the car and walked towards the meeting point, keeping his eyes and ears open for signs of trouble. The sound of heavy footsteps behind him made him stiffen. He couldn't get caught out again like he had in Soho. He spun around. Two men passed by, barely glancing at him. Dressed in bulky jackets and hats against the cold, they were ordinary workers heading home. Arran carried on walking.

Calm down. You can do this.

The men soon melted into the dark. When Arran reached Shah's, he checked the time on his phone—five minutes to go. He switched incoming calls to vibrate only. A check up and down the road saw no sign of Pete.

He better not have got cold feet.

Anxious minutes passed before a black Mercedes pulled up with only one guy inside. Here we go. Time for Cockyboy to talk.

Arran climbed into the car with Pete and they took off. In the flesh he had blond good looks and a lean, muscular body. He was still growing. 'Where are we headed to?'

Pete grinned. 'Don't ask me to spoil the surprise. Sit back, relax and get ready for all the excitement you can handle.'

Arran loosened up. Pete seemed as excited as any normal guy would on heading for a night out. Maybe he had the guy figured all wrong. Or maybe the guy was just a good actor. Arran resisted the urge to check behind and make sure Gregor and Serge were on his trail. When he glanced across, Pete still had a grin on his face. Arran chuckled to himself. Sex is off the menu tonight, mate. I want answers and you're going to give them. Jez was counting on him. 'Is the other guy meeting us at the place you've picked?'

Pete nodded. 'He's dead excited.'

Suddenly the car took a hard right and swerved right again. Arran held on as they sped through an archway between closed down work units and screeched to a stop. Away from the street lighting, it was darker. He sensed trouble. A glance at Pete. He could handle him.

Arran's door flew open. Two men hauled him out onto the ground. The speed of the attack sent his head spinning. He hit out with fists and feet at the three men coming at him from different angles. They jumped on him, stamping their feet on his body to keep him down. Arran caught hold of one guy's leg to stop him kicking at his head. Left free, the other two piled in on him. Pinned down, Arran was done.

They hauled him up and into the back of the car. Sore from the beating, Arran's mind reeled at how easily the tables had been turned. He wasn't chuckling now. He should have listened to Miss Givens when she'd warned him that Pete might bring along his mates. At least now Arran knew what they were up against. Three of them were trapping gay men. But what kind of scam were they pulling?

One of the men demanded Arran's wallet. When it was slow in coming, he punched him on the side of the head.

'Okay, take it easy,' Arran said, handing over his wallet.

The man rifled through it, pocketed the cash and took out the newly replaced bank card. 'His name's Arran Rush.'

'So, Arran Rush,' Pete said, 'what were you doing impersonating someone else? Don't you know it's a crime?'

Arran tried to say it was all a big mistake, and he'd thought he was meeting up for a night out. Even before he'd finished speaking, the heavies at his side started laying into him again.

'The truth this time or it will be the worse for you.'

Arran dusted himself down, slapping off the dirt. Disgusted he'd walked right into their trap. All the careful planning had been for nothing. But he still wanted answers about Jez. 'I'm trying to find my housemate who's gone missing. I think you may know something about that. If you have him, where is he? Why are you still holding on to him? Is it money you want?'

'How did you find us?'

'Jez left for a night out with someone and never came back. I got into his laptop, found his addiction to the ManConnector site and thought it likely he'd met the man there. I signed on with Jez's username and let that man come to me. That was you. So how about answering my questions now?'

Pete sniggered. 'Well done Mister Arran Sherlock Holmes. We will reunite you with your friend all in good time. First tell us your bank card PIN number and don't be tempted to give a wrong number. It will be checked and if it is false, you will pay. One way or another you will pay.'

Arran gave up the information, not caring about the money. They had Jez. 'Now you have what you want, take me to Jez.'

'No problem,' Pete said. 'Get down on the floor and keep quiet. We'll only take you to him if you give us no trouble.'

Arran squashed down onto the floor of the car, resisting the urge to complain when the men dumped their feet on his back. Despite getting it all wrong tonight, he'd been right. He'd found the men who'd taken Jez. But once he and Jez were reunited, there was the small matter of getting them out in one piece. He prayed Gregor and Serge were still on his trail. Without them, he was outnumbered and didn't stand a chance.

FIFTY FIVE

A smiling Maxim secured Alex to a pillar, unmoved by his protests at the tightness of the bindings. The massive shell of a room was destined to become a call centre. The rest of the men were preparing for the honeytrap. A couple of oil drums had been wheeled in and set on fire, the flames leaping up into the air and casting out a golden light. The window holes were being boarded up and sandbags stacked around the place to sit on. A mountain of booze was being built in the corner behind Alex. To anyone else's eyes, it looked like preparations for a normal party. He knew different. How could he ever have allowed himself to participate in the kind of sick display due to take place here? He pulled at his restraints, achieving nothing but chafed wrists.

Ever since Alex's failed escape, the gang had taken no chances with him. They'd kept him locked up in the under stairs cupboard, with no idea of what was happening and sick with worry at what Arran might be involving himself in. Tonight when they'd come for him, his heart sank.

The honeytrap was on.

Alex blamed himself for a lot of things and especially for leading the gang to Arran's door. Once in their hands, there would be nothing Alex could do to save him from his fate. Arran would be made to pay for threatening the gang in the most inhumane and degrading ways possible. A helpless Alex would be forced to watch every sick second.

The gang's capacity for evil had grown. Now they were gay hunters in the truest sense—baiting, trapping, punishing and killing gay men. With the taste for blood in their mouths, there was no going back. Their murderous campaign would only be ended if they were caught and imprisoned. Alex smashed the back of his head into the pillar. If only he hadn't acted the big hero and gone straight to the police, the gang would be behind bars now and able to hurt no one. Blinded by the need to make amends for what he'd done and by the blood tie to his sister, he'd made the wrong choices. Only now could he see that when it was too late. Alex had lost his battle with the gang, but it was Arran who would pay. It had to be Arran. After everything Alex had heard, he couldn't imagine who else it could be. He hated to condemn anyone else, but he wished with all his heart that he were wrong.

The music system had been rigged up and was belting out the kind of music the gang loved, the men bouncing around to raw Russian nationalistic and patriotic rock and projecting giant shadows on the walls. With religious fervour they sang the lyrics about their Russian warrior ancestors, sacred blood and pride in the flag. On forays to the booze mountain, their patriotism directed globs of spit at Alex—the traitor, the betrayer, the outsider. With passions running high, sporadic wrestling matches broke out, the men rolling around the concrete floor and testing their strength against one another, their energy bouncing off the walls. The appointed time of the honeytrap was nearing.

Svetlana and Maxim were drinking and fooling around. She had avoided Alex of late, letting Maxim deal with him. Perhaps putting distance between them to make it easier for whatever was planned for him.

Was it also his fate to die tonight?

In a way Alex would be glad if that were true. He and Arran would leave this world together, and he would make up for all the crimes he'd committed against innocent gay men. The idea gave Alex a strange sense of calm.

A can popped open in Alex's face, spraying him with lager. Maxim's little joke. He took a swig before thrusting it into Alex's mouth and forcing him to gulp down the beer. He leaned in so close that Alex thought he was going to lick at the beer dribbling down his chin. Instead, Maxim whispered in his ear. 'This is your big night, Alexei. It will either make or break you. I know which I prefer for you.' Smiling, he swiped the beer off Alex's face with a big pink tongue.

Alex shuddered at the intimacy. He had no clue what Maxim was talking about, but if it made him happy, it could only be bad.

FIFTY SIX

Gregor parked at the side of the road and wound down the window to speak to Serge, who pulled up alongside him on the moped. 'What the heck happened?'

Serge looked pale and his voice sounded strained. 'One minute the car was in sight, then by the time I made it to the junction, it had disappeared. Sorry, I thought I was doing the right thing by keeping my distance. I didn't want to tip the guy off that he was being followed.'

Gregor couldn't believe their plan to keep Arran safe had come undone within minutes. Sydnee and Miss Givens would give them hell. Alex, Jez and now Arran ... gone ... all of them. Life as they knew it was unravelling. Pete's car had to be found before it was too late. 'Don't worry, it's not your fault. Look, I'll carry on in the direction the car took, and you shoot back to check for hidden turnoffs.'

Gregor took off in a hurl of dust, speeding down the road and not caring if there were speed cameras or cops about. Arran was in mortal danger. Gregor leaned over the steering wheel, skinning his eyes for a sign of the big black car Pete was driving. He put his foot down to overtake a removal van that was blocking his line of sight. The driver of an oncoming car blasted him on the horn. Gregor ignored him and sped along to the end of the road and around the bend. Still no sign of the car. It had melted into the dark of the night, taking Arran with it. Slowing down, Gregor indicated right and crossed into the Blind Man pub's car park, where he turned around and headed back. He pulled in to the side of the road, and Serge motored over to meet him.

'Anything?' Serge asked Gregor.

'No, what about you?'

'I thought I'd found them, but—'

'What happened?'

'False alarm. A car came out from the back of those old units over there with three men in it. But no Arran.'

'What was the car like?'

'Just like the one Arran got into, a black Mercedes.'

The hairs on the back of Gregor's neck started to prickle. 'Are you sure of the make?'

'Dead sure. It was right in front of me. Why?'

'Maybe we should check behind those work units in case Arran's been beaten up and dumped there.'

They drove over and headed through the arch leading to the back. It was dark. Gregor switched the headlights to full beam. No sign of Arran. Gregor got out of the car to take a look around and trod on something. He bent down and picked it up. 'They were here. This is Arran's phone. Pete must have drove straight here, where the other two guys were waiting to jump him. Arran must have been locked in the boot.'

Gregor fitted together the pieces of the puzzle. Damn! He kicked the ground, scattering gravel. 'When the car passed by earlier, I thought it looked familiar. Similar to one I saw outside Borzov's house. I should have warned Arran straight away, but I wasn't sure. Those men that walked by must have been spotters, sent to make sure the coast was clear before giving the go-ahead to Pete. I've been such a fool. The trap Borzov and his mates were talking about was the one they were planning for Arran. Pete must be a part of their gang. Arran's in big trouble. We need to find him fast. Did you see which way the car went?'

They checked a rough sketch map of the area they'd put together showing building sites, abandoned buildings and graveyards. Before setting off to check them out, Gregor made a call to Boy Lane. He could feel the distress of Sydnee and Miss Givens coming over the airwaves and felt wretched for having let everyone down, Arran most of all. Sydnee demanded he keep in contact. Then the connection went dead.

FIFTY SEVEN

When the music level was turned down, Alex slumped against the pillar. This was it. The honeytrap had been sprung successfully, passing a death sentence on the poor unsuspecting victim.

A buzz went around the room. Four shadowy figures entered the building at the far reaches before the door shut with a resounding slam. Alex stood on tiptoes, straining to see the identity of the condemned man. Hoping against reason that it wasn't Arran.

The figures were swallowed up by the pack surging forward, surrounding them. Hard cracks punched the air. Thumps and kicks, softening up the prey. Heart wrenching cries came from him. Alex pulled uselessly at his ties, unable to help. And this was only the beginning.

When the beating stopped, the bodies thinned out and Alex caught snatches of wild blond hair. He held his breath as the battered man climbed to his feet.

Please don't let it be him.

Alex strained at his bindings, desperate to see. Then sagged against the pillar, his heart sinking into his boots.

Arran.

The terror and confusion on Arran's face was plain to see. His eyes darted about, as if counting the threats around him. Only now realising that there never had been a gay serial killer. Just one man. But a whole gang of sadists. Tears streaked down his face. It had to have dawned on Arran that this is what had happened to Jez. The tears were for his dead friend. Murdered at the hands of these men surrounding him, cheering wildly at the sight of the homo crying, calling him a sissy and throwing beer cans at him. Arran put up his hands to protect himself. Watching from the shadows, Alex felt impotent. His lover was trapped. Doomed. Maybe they both were.

Several men dragged Arran towards Svetlana, casting him down before her, like a sacrifice. He had a peculiar look on his face, as if trying to recall where he'd seen her before.

'I hear you've been dying to meet us,' Svetlana said.

The men fell about laughing.

'We were happy to grant your wish. In fact, as you've witnessed, we couldn't wait to get our hands on you.'

The men couldn't stop laughing. But Arran was defiant. 'You're nothing but a pack of fucking animals!'

Maxim launched himself at Arran, striking him with wild punches. When he backed off, recognition registered on Arran's face. 'You're that drunk who was always mouthing off.'

Maxim spat in his face. 'I'm going to hurt you so badly for disrespecting me, you filthy piece of homo shit.'

'If you want to get out of here alive, you'd better be nice to us,' Svetlana said. 'You can start by answering our questions. Who knows you're here?'

Arran wiped his face free of Maxim's spit. 'I'd clear out if I were you, the police will be here soon. My friends have been tracking me all the way.'

'He's a liar!' Pyotr shouted. 'We checked at every stage, like we always do. He's trying to bluff his way out.'

'How did you find us?' Svetlana said.

'I followed the stench.'

Arran went down under another beating from Maxim. Meanwhile, Pyotr whispered in Svetlana's ear. She gave Arran a sweet smile. 'It's just you and us, queer boy. So how about we have a little fun?'

'You've had all the fun you're ever going to have with me. Do yourselves a favour and let me go before the police get here and arrest you all.'

Svetlana shook her head. 'We're only just getting started and you're the entertainment. We want to see you dance and take off your clothes.'

Alex watched to see what Arran would do. The gang wanted him naked before them, like an animal. They wanted to humiliate him by getting him to dance around at their bidding. They, the masters. Him, a dog, a sub-human. Filth.

'You're insane if you think I'm going to do that.'

Arran wasn't going to let them have the high ground. Alex was buoyed by his spirit.

'You're the insane one,' Svetlana said. 'You must be crazy to be queer. It's the same thing.'

'I'm not some sick psychopath who goes about abducting and torturing innocent men.'

Alex was fearful for Arran. The fury of the men was bouncing off the walls, shouts and jeers at his insults. He was pushing them to their limits.

'Let's see what kind of a man you are then,' Svetlana taunted him. 'Strip!'

Arran refused. The pack descended on him like rabid dogs, ripping the clothes off his body and leaving him naked and defenceless on the ground, his body marked and smeared red. Maxim kicked him in the ribs, then pulled him upright by his hair. 'Dance, cocksucker!'

Arran glared back at Maxim, not budging. The men had seen and heard enough. A chant started up: *Death to the homo ... Death to the homo ... Death to the homo ...* The vile words rang in Alex's ears. They were going to kill Arran, and there was nothing he could do.

Maxim came over and untied Alex from the post. He sent him sprawling onto the ground at Arran's feet. Arran looked in shock, stunned. Almost imperceptibly Alex shook his head at him as he got to his feet. Arran said nothing.

Svetlana strode forward to stand in front of Alex. 'You have betrayed your family by running out on us. No one trusts you. The only way back is to prove your loyalty. Only then will you be allowed back as one of us.'

'What if I don't?' Alex said.

'You have no choice in the matter. We cannot allow one person to compromise the safety of our family. Even though you're my brother and I have given you everything, I cannot allow you to go free. We can't begin to understand why you've chosen to act against us, but we cannot risk you going to the authorities and betraying us.'

Alex saw the steely look in Svetlana's eyes. Now he knew exactly why she'd been avoiding him. If he didn't pass their test of loyalty, he would die. He reached out a hand to her. 'I'm your brother. Doesn't that mean anything to you?'

Svetlana brushed his hand away. 'You have only yourself to blame. You've brought all of this down on yourself with your bizarre behaviour. But you still have one chance to redeem yourself.'

'You can't seriously—'

'Enough talking! It is time for you to prove yourself.'

Alex could see he had no choice but to obey. He would do whatever they asked, prove his loyalty and gain his freedom. Then he would do what he should have done in the first place and go to the police. End this madness. 'What do I have to do?'

Maxim stepped towards him, a look of grim amusement on his face. 'All you have to do is kill one miserable cocksucker.'

Alex heard Arran gasp at what was being asked of him. Maxim pointed at Arran, his eyes blazing. 'All you have to do is kill him.'

The rush of cold that raced through his body froze Alex. They wanted him to kill his lover in cold blood. But if he didn't ... he would be the one to die. 'How can you expect this of me? I'm no killer.'

'The piece of filth deserves to die,' Maxim shouted. 'Guilty of perversion and unnatural behaviour against nature. Do this and you will be bound to us forever. You will never be able to go to the authorities and betray us. You will be one of us again.'

The men roared their approval. Clenched fists pumped the air. Vodka was thrown onto the fires, the flames leaping up and burning the air. The men were at fever pitch and started up the death chant again: *Death to the homo ... Death to the homo ... Death to the homo ...*

Maxim pulled a knife from his pocket. Alex stumbled back from the six-inch blade flicked out before his face. The silver blade gleamed in the firelight, razor-edged and deadly. The noise in the room crashed to a deathly hush. Alex couldn't take his eyes off the polished weapon in Maxim's hand, the blade catching Arran's reflection. Despite being battered and bloodied, his body remained beautiful and his spirit intact. Alex was thankful Arran had picked up on his cue not to recognise him. If he hadn't, the pack would have torn them both limb from limb in rage. Alex didn't want Arran to die in that way, at the hands of these hate-filled monsters. The gang pressed in all around them, itching for some action.

'The men demand to know your decision,' Maxim roared. 'Tell us!'

Alex eyed the men as he spoke. 'I will do as you ask. I will do my duty and kill for those I love.' He avoided looking at Arran shouting and cursing at him, his words drowned out by the men bellowing their approval.

Maxim stepped in front of Alex, holding out the killing blade. 'You know what you have to do.'

Alex could feel the heat from the men's eyes burning into him, crazy for the final act. The bloodletting. The ritual death of another worthless queer. The ending of the threat against them. With his right hand, Alex took the knife. With his left, he grabbed Maxim by the neck and stuck the knife to his throat. The men threatened to surge forward.

'Any closer and I slit his throat,' Alex said, backing up towards Arran.

'Don't do this, Alexei,' Svetlana warned, in a low menacing voice.

Alex ignored her and motioned towards the door with his head. 'Lead the way, Arran. Let's get out of here.'

'I will kill both of you with my bare hands for this,' Maxim said, through gritted teeth. 'There's nowhere you can run, nowhere you can hide where I won't find you.'

Alex dug the tip of the knife into Maxim's neck, a trail of blood trickling out of the wound. Maxim fell silent. A naked Arran shuffled along in front of them, leading the way out. Alex walked backwards so that he could keep an eye on the men. He concentrated on each and every step.

One trip and it would all be over.

Alex had failed to save Jez. He vowed not to fail Arran. A gust of wind at his back signalled they had reached the door to the outside. Arran held it open while Alex backed through to safety before slamming it shut. He looked around for something to block it with.

Alex continued to back away, keeping a tight hold on Maxim. A rush at his back hit him like a train. Crashing to the ground, the knife flew from his hand.

Maxim rolled free.

Alex lay winded on the ground, not knowing what had happened. Scared that he'd failed again. Terrified that Arran would die at the hands of the pack. Jerked upright, Alex's arms were pinned behind his back. From out of nowhere, Maxim appeared at his side, a glint of metal in his hand. Held tightly, Alex was defenceless.

His eyes caught a flash of silver, striking him.

He felt nothing and thanked his lucky stars the knife had missed him.

Then came wave after wave of pain that took him down. All around he could hear shouting and mayhem. Blackness descended like a curtain. His eyes closed. His last thoughts were of Arran.

FIFTY EIGHT

Arran felt lucky to be alive. The doctor reassured him there was nothing broken and no permanent damage done. He wasn't so sure. He gritted his teeth at the sharpness of the needle threading the skin on his scalp back together. It was nothing compared to the ordeal he'd suffered at the hands of that murderous gang. The physical scars, Arran could live with. The mental scars ran deeper. The depth of their hate was something he couldn't fathom. Bottomless hate that led to abduction, torture and killing. But for Alex, he would have become their next victim.

Alex.

When the doctor finished, Nurse Viola took over to tend to Arran's superficial wounds and clean him up. Her big smiling face was just what he needed right now.

'You've been in the wars,' she said. 'What have you been up to?'

Arran shook his head wearily. 'You wouldn't believe me if I told you.'

The nurse didn't press him to talk. While she moved methodically around his body, examining and cleaning each of his wounds, she spoke about some of the bad cases she'd seen in her time in the emergency unit. As gory as each tale was, she managed to inject some humour into each of them. It was her way of telling Arran that as bad as things seemed right now, they would get better. She made him smile when he thought he might never want to again. After a couple of hours of being patched up, he was free to go. Arran thanked Viola for her care and good humour. 'You should write a book.'

'No one would believe me if I did,' she said, quick as a flash.

When Arran entered the waiting area, Sydnee, Gregor and Serge surrounded him. Straight away he asked for news of Alex. All they knew was that he was in surgery. Arran insisted they go to Surgical to check on him. The Nurse in Charge told them Alex would be on the operating table for some time, then in recovery until he came around, before being transferred to the ward where he would need sleep and rest. She eyed Arran's patched up body and advised him to go home and do the same. She gave him the direct ward phone number to ring for news and check when he could visit. Even

223

so, Arran was reluctant to leave. The others had to usher him out, saying he should do as the nurse suggested, get some rest and come back refreshed the next day.

Back at Boy Lane, Arran squirmed as Miss Givens hugged him for all he was worth. When she finally released him, he settled into an armchair. 'Sorry,' he told them, 'I've put you through hell, rushing in like some big action hero and falling into the gang's trap. If you hadn't found me ...' He shook his head.

'That was down to Gregor and Serge,' Sydnee said. 'They raced around all the likely places until they found the building site where you were being held.'

'It was Sydnee who brought in the police,' Gregor said. 'We're just glad it wasn't too late.'

The silence that descended in the room spoke volumes to Arran. He knew the answer to the question on all their lips: 'Jez is never coming back.'

*

Arran came to the door of Jez's room and rested his hand on the doorknob. Afraid to enter. He tried to conjure up a belief in magic so powerful that when he opened the door Jez would be inside as large as life as ever. And twice as loud. He twisted the knob and opened up.

It wasn't meant to be. The room lay silent. Empty. Except for the bits and bobs of Jez's life left behind ... photos where he was still laughing with his mates ... books of stories he'd buried his head in ... a frayed sweatshirt hugging the bedpost.

Jez wasn't here. He'd gone.

Arran gathered Jez's sweatshirt to him and slumped onto the bed. He breathed in his manly scent, musky and sweet. The only physical connection with him he had left. A bolt of panic swept through Arran. The photos would dim, the books would be given away and Jez's scent would fade. Leaving Arran with nothing.

The thought of Jez being reduced to nothing left Arran numb to his core. Empty.

FIFTY NINE

Alex opened his eyes to find Arran by his bedside. 'How long have you been there?'

'Not long. How are you feeling?'

Alex flicked the drip line attached to his wrist. 'Sore.'

A nurse knock-knocked at the open door, fixed Alex's pillows and straightened the bedclothes. 'We've got to have you looking your best for your visitor,' she said, smiling. She closed the door on her way out.

Alex now had a better view of Arran. 'You don't look so good yourself.'

'Minor packaging damage. But still here to tell the tale, thanks to you.'

'I blacked out. What happened back there?'

Arran drew in a breath and slowly let it out. 'Where to begin? All the plans for my meet up with the guy I'd met online, Pete, unravelled at the start, and I walked straight into the ambush he'd set up for me. Gregor and Serge lost my trail and had to go on a search of all the local derelict and building sites. Meanwhile, Sydnee had informed the police of my abduction. When they saw you backing out of the building with a knife to a guy's throat, they thought you were the bad guy and jumped you. The other guy was freed up, grabbed the knife and stabbed you with it. Who was he?'

'Maxim, a major psychopath. Did they catch him?'

'The police had no idea they were dealing with a gang and only had three officers to spare, due to a bomb alert at Victoria train station. They managed to arrest the girl and two other guys. The rest of the gang scattered. Gregor directed the police to a house in Vauxhall, where they caught up with them.'

Alex closed his eyes and sank back into the pillows. The thought of a vindictive Maxim on the loose would have been enough to finish him off. When he opened them again, Arran was watching him closely. Questions were forming on his lips.

'So who were those people? And how come you were involved with them?'

Alex had dreaded this moment coming for all the time he'd known Arran. Now it had arrived, he hardly dared begin. By the end of his story, Arran would hate him and want nothing more to do with him. But tired of living a lie, Alex related the full story of the gay hunters, leaving nothing out and withstanding the disbelieving and hurt gaze of Arran.

'You're gay! How could you do such things to gay people? It was evil, pure and simple.'

The words spilled out of Alex's mouth in an effort to explain the unexplainable. 'I was young when it started. Back then it seemed like fairly harmless messing about. We'd spot a gay guy in the park, give him a bit of a hard time and that was the end of it. I wasn't even involved. A bystander. Only later, after Svetlana met Nikolay and Pavel, who were good with computers, was the online honeytrap born. They wanted someone young and tempting to gays and said I was the one. They gave me no choice. After our parents died, the only person I had in the world was my sister. She looked after me and told me what to do. If you'd said then that I was gay, I wouldn't have believed you.'

'That doesn't excuse what you did.'

'You've heard what Gregor and Serge say about Russia, yet you still have no real idea of just what a hopeless situation it is there for gay people. When the government and the judges and the police and the Church and the people all tell you homosexuality is wrong, you believe it. Somewhere inside, I denied I was gay and tried to make it true. I was also tied by blood to my sister, and the gang was our family. I was trapped.'

'Pretty fucked up family,' Arran said.

'Everything changed for me when I came here. You don't appreciate how lucky gay people are in Britain, free to live their own life. For the first time I could see a future for myself. After one boy was killed, the scales fell from my eyes. Finally, I could see that what the gang was doing was totally wrong. I wanted out and ran away, which is when I met you. You and your friends gave me new hope and changed my attitudes. I wanted to be just like you. I tried to forget everything that had happened in the past, put it behind me and move on. But I couldn't. The night before I left, we were in Flesh, talking about the missing guys and what their loved ones would be going through. I felt terrible. Then I saw the boy who'd died, his face on one of the missing posters on the wall. The horror of him dying in front of me came back to haunt me. I knew then that I couldn't pretend the past had never happened and had to put a stop to what the gang was doing. I disappeared to keep you safe from them, never thinking you would find me, even if you'd come looking. I trailed gang members and found out they'd set up another honeytrap. I wanted to be sure of what they were doing before I called the police, so that they would catch them in the act. But the gang found me first, prowling around the site. They took me inside and beat me for running off.' Alex started to cry. 'That's when I saw him, lying on the ground. Dead. It was Jez. I was too late to save him. I'm so sorry. I tried, I really did.'

Arran's voice was steel. 'How do I know you didn't get to know us in order to set us up? Did you set Jez up in a honeytrap?'

'No! I swear that's not true. Jez was my friend. I could never have hurt him. You were all my friends. That's why I couldn't go on deceiving you. I wanted to make amends so that I could come back and be with you, openly and honestly.' Alex was dying inside. This was every bit as horrible as he'd imagined. Arran was visibly struggling to believe any of what he said. His confusion was understandable. It was hard for Alex to make sense of what he'd done, too. 'I'm so sorry for everything. I love you.'

'I thought I loved you too,' Arran said. 'I pictured us setting up a gym together, buying our own place, maybe even ...' He shook his head. 'Now I realise you weren't the person you pretended to be and don't feel I even know you, much less understand what you did. I should go.' He got up from the chair, went over and opened the door.

'Will I see you again?'

'I need you to give me some time. There's too much to take in. I'm going to stop talking now and go before I say things I can never take back.' He walked out, closing the door behind him.

Alex wished Maxim had succeeded in killing him and taken all the guilt and pain away. With Arran gone from his life, he had nothing left to live for.

SIXTY

Arran let the curtain fall on the sunshine outside. The weather was all wrong when everyone was dressed in black, ready to say goodbye to Jez for the final time. The undertaker had told them the trend at funerals these days was for bright attire to celebrate the life of the deceased. It didn't seem right when Jez had been murdered.

A knock at the door disturbed the hush in the room. The undertaker informed them the cars had arrived to take them to the service. Arran, Sydnee and Miss Givens rode up front, with Gregor, Serge and Jon Jacks travelling in the second car. As the hearse carrying Jez's body led the procession down Boy Lane and along the streets of Vauxhall to the crematorium, Arran saw Jez giving him the guided tour on his first day, his arm around him, their heads up close. His body relived the charge of that first meeting. Never again would they walk these streets together. He was gone. The finality of Jez's death ... They had never even had the chance to say goodbye.

Because Jez hadn't been attached to any religious group, the service was non-denominational. The coffin was taken into the crematorium building, with his friends following on behind. The place was packed, sitting and standing—colleagues and friends from Flesh and the Sanctum, Goyo and his staff from *Tapas*, and other friends, like Andrew, beside a tall, dark headed man. The coffin came to rest in front of a large picture of Jez, which had captured his colour and vitality so fully that he seemed there beside them.

Arran was relieved it wasn't him as Sydnee strode to the front of the gathering. She talked for a long time, telling everyone Jez's story. The shocked looks, murmurs and gasps were from people who'd thought they'd known him but now realised they hadn't. Arran knew exactly how they felt. Sydnee went on to describe how Jez had turned his life around to become the person everyone was more familiar with—the happy-go-lucky guy with the big smile and even bigger heart, who gave a helping hand to newcomers on the gay scene. Arran counted himself in that number. He clenched his fists.

What a mindless waste of a good man.

The gang weren't talking. The police had said they were relying on Alex to tell them where to search for bodies. Jez's body had been recovered from under a partially constructed building. Unbelievably, the contractors had not been pleased to have to demolish it. Arran had saved Miss Givens and Sydnee an ordeal by volunteering to make the body identification for the police. The experience was one he wished he could forget. His body had been pulled from storage and set up in a small side room at the morgue. An attendant pulled back a cover to reveal his head and upper torso. Arran wasn't ready for the sight of what was left of Jez. But for the unruly hair and the outline of his face, he was barely recognisable. Jez had been so full of life it didn't seem possible that anything could have extinguished his flame. Arran had to see his friend's cold body to believe it. He kept to himself his pain at the damage to Jez's body, not wanting to share with his friends the full horror of what he'd seen. It would have broken their hearts to know Jez had died slowly and in unbearable agony.

It broke his.

How the Russian gang could have murdered such a beautiful human being in such an inhuman manner was beyond his understanding. When their trial came around, Arran hoped they would be put away for a very long time. He spared a thought for the families of the other victims murdered by the gang, who would be going through similar ordeals. The screen doors opened. When they closed again, Jez was gone forever. Leaving behind Arran in a world he was struggling to make sense of.

The mourners filed out into the courtyard. Arran noticed a figure standing away from everyone else. He walked over to Alex and stood beside him. It was their first meeting since they'd talked at the hospital. Even though the police had said Alex was helping them all he could, Arran hadn't been able to reach out to him. The sorry figure he cut called out to be hugged. Arran shoved his hands into his pockets, unable to bring himself to touch him.

'I had to come to say goodbye to Jez,' Alex said. 'He was a friend to me, too. I also wanted to be here for you, knowing how hard it would be for you today. I've done that now, so I won't stay any longer. I'll be around if ever you want to talk.'

With that said, Alex walked away. And Arran let him.

Miss Givens opened up 19 Boy Lane to Jez's friends and colleagues to drop by for a drink in his name. Arran saw the tall, dark headed man from the service making a beeline for him.

'I'm Darius,' he said.

'Arran.'

They shook hands.

'I'm so sorry for not getting back to you. I was in a bad place.'

'You weren't to know.'

'After my latest boyfriend finished with me, I had to get away to think about where my life was going. I didn't like myself very much, which is where I think a lot of my anger issues stemmed from. I've said things in the past I'm not proud of, including making threats. All just hurt pride and bluster.'

'How are things now?'

'Better. Though today, I feel like shit. I had no idea what Jez had gone through as a kid. Never once did he mention what had happened to him.'

'I don't think he talked about it,' Arran said. 'The only time he ever did was to Sydnee. I only found out myself much later, after he'd gone missing.'

Tears welled up in Darius's eyes. 'Sorry, I have to go.'

*

After everyone had drifted away, Miss Givens took a phone call and then led Arran, Sydnee, Gregor and Serge to the community garden along the way from Boy Lane. Two men were unloading a brand new bench from a pristine white van. They carried it into the garden and bolted it to the floor. The shiny new plaque had written on it:

Jez Truman
Our beautiful friend
1999 - 2020

All Jez's family had contributed to the cost of the funeral and commemorative bench. The bench was Arran's idea, so that they would have some place to go where they could remember Jez and feel his presence. Arran had put in the money he'd saved towards a fitness instructor training course. Squeezed together on the bench, they told Jez stories until the sun set over Vauxhall.

SIXTY ONE

Arran had an ulterior motive in asking Sydnee out for a drink to the Sanctum. He wanted to speak to her about Alex. 'I'm not sure if I love him or hate him.'

'That's understandable after what has happened. What has he had to say for himself?'

'He finds it hard to believe he was ever involved with the gang and all their evil doing. Talked about how much he'd deceived himself and lived in total denial about being gay.'

Sydnee nodded. 'I can understand that. Over the years I've come across people who deny it for their entire lives. Even some Far Right thugs have been outed for leading a double life, beating up gays by day and sleeping with them by night. So I'd say that anything's possible.'

Arran refreshed their glasses with beer from a pitcher. 'What about the lies and deception with us? I don't feel as if I ever really knew him.'

'When a person is stuck in a particular environment, like Russia is for gay people right now, it probably seems as if that is all the choice there is in life. Coming to London must have been a real eye-opener for Alex. For the first time he could envisage a future, living openly as a gay man. Then he met you. From some of the things you've said, it seems he not only wanted to be with you but also wanted to be like you. To bring up the past would have caused him pain, and he would have risked losing you. Most people choose the path of least resistance to happiness. In that respect they're not so hard to understand.'

'Are you saying I can believe him?'

'I'm saying that the Alex you knew is the Alex he wanted you to know and the Alex he wants to be.'

'So give him another chance?'

'Do you love him?'

'I thought I did. I still do. I'm just not sure I can forget everything he's done. I'm really mixed up right now.'

'Give yourself time. If Alex really loves you, he'll understand and wait until you're ready.'

Arran looked into Sydnee's eyes. 'Can you forgive him?'

'I don't believe Alex is a bad person. He was under the influence of his sister and her cronies from a young age, got caught up in some bad shit and did things he shouldn't have done. I'm sure he knows that. Being around you was good for him. He's accepted his sexuality, which as lots of us know can be no mean feat in itself and learned a totally new way of living. That's why he wants to hold on to you. He's a changed man.'

'What about Jez?'

'Miss Givens was beside herself with guilt, believing she'd cursed Jez at Halloween with the pagan symbols, graveyard cake and RIP biscuits. She sees now it was her grief talking. Although we loved Jez like a son, he was a grown man and made his own choices. No one deserves to die in the way he did, but he was aware he took risks. Even so, he couldn't have foreseen he would run into a bunch of killers. I wish I could have helped him more than I did. But that's all in hindsight. I feel privileged to have known him for the short time I did.'

Arran squeezed Sydnee's hand.

'You've changed,' Sydnee said. 'No longer are you the naïve young boy trailing after Jez. You're a man now, capable of taking tough decisions. I know you'll make the right call. Whatever decision you make, you know Jez would have backed you all the way. So will the rest of us.'

Arran felt a dead weight slip away. 'At least some good has come from a bad situation, with the Russian gay hunters removed from our streets.'

'You should be very proud of yourself,' Sydnee said, gesturing with her hand at all the people around them. 'The bars and businesses are booming again, I'm glad to say. The gay community of Vauxhall owes you a huge debt of thanks.'

Arran corrected her. 'They owe us—you, Miss Givens, Gregor, Serge and me—a huge debt of thanks for bringing those hatemongering killers to justice. We did it together. And I, for one, am so relieved it's finally over.'

SIXTY TWO

Alex could not take on board the words PC Dent was saying to him. One of the gang members had gone missing. Maxim Azarov had eluded detection and capture by the police. 'Maxim is on the loose. Seriously? Is that what you're telling me?'

PC Dent loosened the shirt collar around his neck. 'That would seem to be the case. Having said that, he's had enough time to make plans and get away. He could be anywhere in the world by now. The fact there's no record of him leaving the country doesn't mean much these days. He could have slipped through the net by any number of means. And why would he remain in Britain? He would have to be stupid to do so when he had the opportunity to slip away to freedom. What reason would he have to stay?'

Alex could think of several reasons, with his and Arran's names at the top of the list. He had to warn him and the others.

Nervous about seeing them, he set out from Kennington police station at a steady pace, slowed by the gash across his stomach. Since being released from hospital much of his time had been spent at the station, giving the police all the help they needed to bring a successful case against the gang. The time used up and the worthwhile feeling it gave Alex countered the loneliness. Arran hadn't been in touch.

Alex found everyone gathered in the living room at Boy Lane, the police having just left after breaking the news about Maxim. Sydnee patted the seat next to her, and a grateful Alex sat down.

'Just when we thought this horrendous business was in the past,' Sydnee said, 'this happens and opens up the wounds again.'

Arran shook his head. 'I can't believe it has taken until now for the police to realise that this Maxim is still at large.'

'The gang members have demanded Russian interpreters to make it a slow and laborious process for the detectives interviewing them,' Alex said. 'They know that Maxim is free and are protecting him any way they can. None of them will grass on him. He might be a murdering psychopath, but he's a hero to the gang and they're loyal to him.'

'Do you think he's still in London?'

'I'd bet my life on it. Don't count on him having any remorse for what he's done. He'll be hell-bent on revenge against those he sees as responsible for the gang's capture and won't rest until that is done.'

'He'll want to get even with you and me. Is that what you're saying?'

'I have photos of Maxim that I'll send around. He'll want to finish the plan to get rid of you, and he has scores of reasons for wanting to kill me. But don't any of you let your guard drop for a minute. He hates with a passion, and homosexuals are at the top of his hate list.'

'None of us are safe,' Arran said, 'until every last one of the gay hunters has been caught and put behind bars.'

*

After the group broke up, Alex and Arran were left alone—Alex on the settee and Arran in an armchair.

'How are you?' Arran said.

'Relieved that everything is out in the open. Lies, deception and guilt are heavy baggage to carry around all of the time. But now I'm free of the gang, I at least have the chance of a future. I miss you.'

'The police took our statements and have kept us informed of the case, so I know you've been helping them. Will you face any charges?'

'Svetlana and the men are sticking together and saying as little as possible. I'm the only weak link in the gang's united front. Because the police are relying on me to turn Queen's Evidence, I've been made exempt from prosecution. They've assured me the gang will be going to prison for a long time. When the court cases are over, I will be free to go, although that will take many months. So I'll be sticking around for some time to come. After that I will probably be asked to leave Britain, as I have no right to remain.' He sought out Arran's eyes. 'I miss you.'

'I heard you. I just don't know what to say. It's almost as if you're a stranger to me.'

'Not everything was a lie. When I told you I loved you, that wasn't a lie. Don't you believe in giving people a second chance?'

'Of course I believe in second chances, for little mistakes. What you did … I still can't get my head around it. I can't reconcile that Alex with the one I thought I knew.'

'You don't understand,' Alex said, heat in his voice, 'because you've never faced any real hardship in your life. Your father died, yet you still have a mother and stepfather who love and support you.'

'Whatever my situation, I still wouldn't have done what you did.'

'I hope for your sake you never have to.' Alex took a moment to calm himself, not wanting to widen the rift between them. 'Look, I know how you feel because I feel exactly the same way about myself. I know I'm not a good man and that I've done bad things, but I'm doing everything I can to change. The rest of my life will be spent making up for the hurt I've caused. You make me want to be a better man, and I've learned so much from you. Please don't push me away. Is there any hope for us?'

'I loved you, too. When you were in surgery, you were all I could think about. I prayed for you to come through. Then when I learned of your past, things changed. How could they not? I'm finding it really difficult to make sense of anything right now. I need more time.'

Alex managed a smile. 'Knowing there's some hope for us is enough. Take all the time you need. I really came here because I was worried for you. I couldn't bear it if Maxim hurt you. Don't underestimate him and be on your guard every minute of the day until he's caught.'

'What about you? You'll be his number one target.'

'Don't worry about me. Just keep yourself and the others safe.'

'Where would Maxim go? Who would he turn to?'

'He will have gone to ground within the Russian community in London. There's lots of dodgy types who will keep him hidden, as a favour or for money. He'll be in some hole now, plotting his next steps. How he's going to make us pay.'

'I don't know what will happen with us in the future,' Arran said. 'With Maxim free, normality seems further away than ever. What I do know is that I don't want you to get hurt, either. Why don't you go away, at least until he's caught?'

'You want me to run away?' Alex said, shaking his head. 'I can't do that. I could never abandon you with him on the loose. If anything happened to you, I could never live with myself. I brought this trouble to your door, and it's up to me to deal with it. Whatever happens between Maxim and me is just how it was meant to be.'

SIXTY THREE

Arran hated being handcuffed and kept a prisoner. It was as if he and his friends were being punished all over again. But after all the uncertainty and distress over Jez's disappearance and death, he didn't want to cause Miss Givens and Sydnee any undue worry on his behalf. His rushing headlong into Pete's trap had taught him a serious lesson.

As the police had no clue where Maxim was, he had to be considered still around and still a threat. Normality flew out of the window and security marched in. When Arran and Gregor weren't working, they acted as security guards—checking the lane for presences that didn't belong, accompanying Miss Givens to the shops or bank, calling in on Sydnee at Big Girls ... doing everything possible to keep everyone safe. Previously indifferent tasks—keeping phones charged and turned on, ensuring windows and doors were secured, discovering the identity of visitors at their door before opening up—became obsessive.

Much concern was for Arran and Serge, coming and going from Bananas along the lonely streets of the industrial part of Vauxhall at all times of the day and night. Exactly the sort of place where Maxim would strike. The two made a point of always travelling together.

Talk of Maxim dominated many a discussion, wondering where he was, whether he was still in the country or not, somewhere nearby, keeping tabs on them, building up a picture of their routines and planning when to strike. Did he still look like his picture or had he adopted a disguise? From Alex, they knew he was cunning and capable. They also knew what would happen if Maxim caught any one of them—abuse, torture and death.

Arran mourned the loss of everything he'd previously taken for granted—early morning runs, nights out at the Sanctum, even just the freedom to walk the streets unaccompanied. And it was tiresome to constantly have to look over his shoulder.

The Russian gang hadn't been broken. None of them had given any information to help the police locate Maxim. The brute had simply disappeared. Arran was frustrated by the failings of the police. Each day when he contacted them, they had nothing to report. He suspected that they considered Maxim to have flown these shores and weren't actively searching for him. It was the not knowing that most frustrated Arran and his friends, because whether Maxim was here or gone, his threat stalked them every hour of every day. He had them in lockdown.

*

Arran closed the door behind him and waved to Miss Givens, at the window, checking who was around. It was a habit she'd got into even though nothing untoward had happened. After a couple of quiet weeks, it was assumed Maxim had taken his chance and fled. Life was slowly getting back to normal.

Arran set off for Kennington Park. It was like his first day in Vauxhall all over again. In fact everywhere in Vauxhall triggered a memory. That was part of his problem with Alex. Although he still loved him, he couldn't forget what Alex had done. Young men who should still have been walking these streets were gone, their lives snatched away. If he and Alex were to stay together, it might have to be away from here. The very thought tore Arran in two. From the very first day, he'd loved this place. His life and his friends were here. He wasn't sure he could give everything up, even for Alex. But not moving away meant there might not be an Arran and Alex.

Arran had been stung by what Alex had said of him, that he hadn't faced any real difficulties in his life, which was why he couldn't understand what Alex had been through and what he'd done. At the time he'd been too angry to even consider it. But now ... It must have been tough for Alex, losing both parents at a young age, discovering his sexuality while living with a homophobic sister and gang, having divided loyalties between himself and them, being told by a hostile Russia he wasn't normal, not even a man, and knowing he would have to hide who he was every single day of his life. These were massive burdens. Enough to turn someone into an abuser? A murderer? Harsh on Alex; he hadn't actually murdered anyone. But he'd been there.

Arran couldn't make up his mind about Alex and what to do for the best. Whether to give him another chance or make a clean break. Either way, he would have to come to a decision soon. Whatever he felt about Alex, it wasn't fair to string him along. Jez should have been here. He would have known what to say, how to deal with it, found a laugh in there somewhere. It seemed these days that Arran didn't laugh very much at all. He had nothing to laugh about.

Arran shut down his thoughts and concentrated on running, ticking off lap after lap around the park path. His legs pumped like pistons and sweat poured out of him. After pushing himself to his limits, he found a patch of grass to finish off with some stretches. Finally, he felt alive again. All the days in lockdown had been hell. Life without exercise wasn't worth living. He'd already lost too much from his life, his grandparents, his dad, Jez. Did he really want to lose Alex?

SIXTY FOUR

Arran entered Mr Cheung's neat and orderly home; everything there for a reason and in its place. His mind was just as orderly. He was a man who moved through each day with quiet purpose and dignity. What he said and what he did were in harmony, and he always appeared to be in control of himself and never seemed to get ruffled. Even the way he took tea was ordered, respectful, like a religious ritual. Mr Cheung always acted like someone—God, his mum, his dad—was watching him from above.

Mr Cheung placed a tea tray on a low table. He and Arran knelt facing eachother. Arran took a sip of tea. The papers recently had been full of the Russian gang and the terror they'd unleashed on the gay community of Vauxhall. Some of the articles had mentioned that an Alexei Razin was helping the police with their inquiry. If Mr Cheung had read them, he might have put two and two together.

'I need your help,' Arran said. 'It concerns Alex.'

Mr Cheung nodded his head. He knew.

'The gang started out when Alex was much younger, not much more than a kid. His sister ran the gang and he tagged along. They'd look for gay men on the streets and in the parks, and give them a hard time. It went on from there, got bigger, more organised. When they switched to setting traps online, Alex was given the role of the honeytrap. He was the one who found the victims and led them to the gang for punishment, beatings and robbing them of their money and possessions. The gang came here from Moscow and then the killings started. Only then did Alex leave the gang. Alex is gay. I can't understand how he could have done such things. He said he had no choice. But surely there is always a choice? He has me really conflicted. I don't know what to think.'

Mr Cheung's eyes had a faraway look. After a minute or two he got up and went over to the sideboard. He came back with a photo frame that he passed to Arran. Inside was a cracked black and white photograph. 'This was my family in Hong Kong, in front of our little food stall.' He pointed a wizened finger at one of the figures. 'This one here is me. I was fifteen years old when I joined a Triad gang. Many moons ago I told you how I came to leave Hong Kong, but I didn't tell you the whole story.

'My first weeks with the gang were all good. They're clever like that. They want new members to develop a taste for what they can give—fancier food, better clothes, more money jangling in pockets. Only then do they ask for payment. The leader summoned me. He had a task for me. A test of loyalty. In this way he would bind members to him.'

Arran nodded. 'What was it he wanted you to do?'

'The gang ran a protection racket for businesses in their area. Those that didn't pay faced intimidation and sabotage. The manager of the Black Cat Casino fell foul of the gang. Our leader had found out he'd been skimming the profits and cheating him of his rightful share. He had to be punished. The manager had a daughter ...'

The distant look returned to Mr Cheung's eyes. It was another couple of minutes before he continued his story.

'... The night air was saturated with the sweet fragrances of camellia and magnolia in the manager's garden. Crouched at my back was Kong, another gang member, sent as a witness and to make sure the leader's order was carried out. The muggy air was stifling. Our shirts clung to our backs. The bedroom windows and doors were open in the house. We climbed up the wall and onto the balcony of the daughter's bedroom. The girl awoke with my hand over her mouth, her eyes wide and frightened. I told her not to make a sound while I pulled back the thin bed cover and removed her pyjamas. Her silky skin quivered in the moonlight. I climbed on top of her and—'

'You ... ' Arran couldn't bring himself to say the words out loud. If what he was hearing hadn't come directly out of Mr Cheung's mouth, he would never have believed it. Would have called the story a lie. But Mr Cheung was not a liar.

Mr Cheung bowed his head. 'When I'd finished, Kong dragged me off and took her himself, so excited was he. We left her softly crying, the bedclothes stained with blood. Two days later, she took her own life. She left behind a note. After what had been done to her, she was tainted and worthless to her family. Her name was Ming-hua. She was fourteen years old.'

Arran stared at his mentor, knelt perfectly still, his eyes cast down, one papery hand on the other.

'The full horror of what I'd done hit me. I became very distressed and left the gang, unable to go on intimidating and hurting people. The leader could not allow this to happen and sent men to persuade me otherwise. They beat me to within an inch of my life. My family insisted I leave Hong Kong, and my girlfriend agreed to leave with me. Our families put out the story that I had died of my injuries and that my girlfriend, in her grief, had taken her own life. We left Hong Kong by steamship. The rest you know.'

'How have you lived all this time with the knowledge of what you did?' Arran said.

'One day at a time.'

Arran rocked back on his heels. 'That simple? Didn't you ever consider going to the police and paying for what you did?'

Mr Cheung thrust out his hands. 'You seem to think I haven't paid. I've had to live with the stain of Ming-hua's blood on my hands for a lifetime.'

'I'm sorry, I didn't mean to offend you.'

'My father persuaded me not to go to the police. They were as corrupt as the gangs. This was another place, another time. He told me I'd been greedy for life and stupid, but that I was also young and poor. I would receive only punishment, not justice. He sent me away, trusting me to become a better man. Some might say I chose the easier option, but a man knows in his own heart whether that is true or not.'

Arran left the flat and sat down on the nearest bench. The world seemed darker than ever. Never would he have guessed the burden Mr Cheung carried. All he'd ever known was a kind and giving man. Except, he'd never really known him at all. He'd gone to Mr Cheung for advice and come away even more confused.

SIXTY FIVE

Arran handed lagers and straws to Jonny and Des and moved on to serve the next punter in line. They were elbow to elbow all along the bar, clamouring for his attention. A long night was in the offing without Serge, who was laid up in bed. All through the long winter he'd been fine, but now the weather had picked up, he'd come down with flu. Jason had found a hasty replacement in Alan, a newbie to the bar trade, who was doing his best but was naturally slow. The amount of punters yelling at him didn't help. Arran felt bad he hadn't spoken to him, except to give instructions.

Part of Arran was sickened by the sight in Bananas. It was as if the Russian gang had never happened, as if gay men hadn't lost their lives. The punters had short memories. All they seemed to care about was throwing booze down their throats, finding some man on man action and being whipped up into a frenzy by Denny the DJ. Sydnee had said not to think too badly of them. Now the threat of death hanging over their heads had been lifted, they wanted to get on with the business of living. They weren't being deliberately disrespectful of the dead; they were celebrating life.

Mr Cheung's involvement in the ending of a young girl's life had shocked Arran. He couldn't get the admission out of his mind. His mentor had become a flesh and blood man, with his own tangled history and painful secrets. It was hard to picture the young thug and the old teacher as the same person. They were and they weren't. Mr Cheung had changed. He'd removed himself from a bad situation that may have only got worse and started a new life thousands of miles from home. The move had cost him his family; he'd never seen his parents alive again. He'd channelled the pain he felt inside for good, marrying, starting a business, raising a family and helping people in the community. He taught Tai Chi that helped people master self control, form a healthy mind and boost self esteem. Arran had to respect the way he'd changed his life around. Even though life had placed Mr Cheung in a bad situation and he'd made some bad choices, it didn't make him a bad man in Arran's eyes.

So how could he condemn Alex for trying to do the same?

Arran felt guilty at ignoring Alex when he should have stood by his man. For not considering what he might be going through in coming to terms with his past, as well as shouldering the burden of being the main prosecution witness against the gang. Alex would need him when he had to go to court and face them. Arran made the decision to put things right between them. Mr Cheung, Alex, Jez, Sydnee, Miss Givens and Gregor had all faced hardship and battles, taking decisions from impossible choices. That was what had forged them into the characters they were. That was why he loved them. He did love Alex. For the first time, Arran could see a way forward. He and Alex would face the future together.

Glass smashed around Arran's feet. The punters called for the juggler to be sacked. Above the cheering, Alan mouthed that he was sorry. Arran shrugged and pointed him in the direction of a brush and shovel.

By the end of the night, dirty glasses were strewn everywhere. The two of them trudged around collecting them, putting them through the glass washer and stacking them on the shelves. When they'd got on top of the clean up, Arran let the shattered looking Alan slip away home.

Arran left Bananas at way past his normal knocking off time. He pulled up the zipper of his jacket and hurried through the dark streets, keen for his bed. After a good night's sleep, he would find Alex and make everything right between them. They belonged together. A great weight slipped off his shoulders, and the world appeared a touch brighter.

*

Alex was worried. Every other night, Arran had finished work by this time. The last punter had left over an hour ago. Unless Arran had left early, Alex couldn't have missed him. That still didn't explain why Serge hadn't appeared. He would wait another fifteen minutes and then go to Bananas and find out what was happening. Arran wouldn't be best pleased to find out he'd been shadowing him, but being found out was better than this not knowing.

With three minutes to go, Arran appeared. He emerged alone from the passageway that led to the bar. Serge mustn't have turned up. That explained the late finish. He'd had to work the bar single-handed. No wonder he looked exhausted.

Alex allowed the distance between them to grow before following him. Keeping to the shadows, he crept along the deserted streets, watching his back. For a time they'd been inseparable. Now, this was the only way he got to see Arran. He hadn't been in touch. The separation was testing, but he intended to honour his promise to give Arran time. All he could do was hope for a second chance. Life without Arran would be unbearable.

Alex pushed such thoughts to the back of his mind. For the present he was only concerned with keeping Arran safe. Too late he heard a rush of air. Something solid connected with his head, leaving him with the heart wrenching feeling that he'd failed again. Right before the blackness claimed him.

SIXTY SIX

Alex opened his eyes and wished he hadn't. He had a thundering headache. Through half closed eyes he took in the unfamiliar surroundings. He was lying on a bed of old cushions and blankets. What was that smell? Grease or oil. Car tyres and old bits of machinery were strewn about. This place had to be an abandoned garage or workshop. He went to move an arm. Found he couldn't. His arms were tied, and his feet. Struggling against the constraints, he twisted to the side and found a smiling Maxim.

'At last you're awake, Alexei. I was worried I'd hit you too hard. But I'm relieved to say you're back with me now. It would have been a tragedy if I'd spoiled the fun I have planned for us. Remember that time you tried to escape from the house?' Maxim laughed.

Alex shivered.

'I promised you then we would have a little fun together.'

Alex felt himself pale. Maxim's idea of fun was other people's suffering. 'What do you want with me? Don't you realise it's over? The game's up. The gang is finished and will be put away for a long time.'

Maxim's face creased with anger. 'That's your fucking fault! All of this is your fault. And you're going to pay for what you've done to us.'

'What are you going to do with me?'

'You'll find out,' Maxim said, the laughter returning to his face. 'Don't look so worried, I know you'll enjoy it. Because from what I hear, you've switched sides. You're a bum boy now.'

Alex thrashed about on the makeshift bed. 'You're crazy! You should have left here when you had the chance. Don't make it worse for yourself by doing anything to me. The police will find you, lock you up and you'll die in prison as someone else's bum boy.'

Maxim silenced Alex with a backhander. 'The funny thing is that we knew about you, Alexei. Deep down, we knew. Behind Svetlana's back, the men said things about you. How you were a little too sensitive to be a normal man. How you took to being the honeytrap a little too well, as if you knew instinctively what to do. How you had no stomach for the fight against the queers.'

Alex's only defence was to deny everything. 'You don't know what you're talking about.'

'You were never really a part of the gang, were you? You hid behind your sister's skirt and she protected you, kept you safe. But she's not here now and I am. I knew there was something not quite right about you. Now I know why. You're as queer as all the other homos we put down. Well, lucky you, I'm going to send you to join them.'

'Don't be stupid,' Alex cried out. 'You may get away with manslaughter for the other deaths and be out in a few years. But you murder me in cold blood, and you're going away forever.'

'I'm not going inside for a single day. Not for them and not for you. But before I send you on your way, I'm going to give you what you really want. I'm going to give you a real man. Me.'

'What?' Alex scoffed.

Maxim grinned and winked. 'Don't think I didn't notice all those times you were looking at me. How you were always there when I came out of the bathroom in just a wet towel, your eyes glued to the outline of my cock. How your hands were everywhere during our wrestling matches, feeling me up, getting excited. I bet you lay awake at night listening to me bed your sister and wishing it were you. Well, I'm going to give you your wish. Your dying wish. This will be the last thing you remember on earth, so I'll make it the best. You can ride the memory all the way down to Hell.'

Alex pulled against his bindings. They wouldn't budge. He had to be somewhere in the industrial district of Vauxhall. The area would be deserted now, so calling for help would be useless. He couldn't even count on someone coming looking for him when no one knew he was here. Arran had been oblivious to what had gone on behind his back as he'd hurried home from Bananas. At least he was safe. For now. But after Alex had gone. What then? Would Maxim go after Arran? There was nothing Alex could do. Even if he escaped his ties, there was no way he would overcome Maxim. This abandoned place, filled with unwanted bits and pieces, would be where it ended for him. Overhead was a grimy skylight. It was still dark outside. By the time it was light, he would be dead. 'You really are crazy if you think for one minute I ever lusted after you. I am gay and proud of it. I know gay people who are twice the man you'll ever be.'

'If you're talking about your boyfriend,' Maxim said, 'then don't worry. He's invited to the party, too.'

'What are you talking about?' Alex said, a feeling of dread rising from the pit of his stomach.

'I'm talking about the guy you've been following day after day. Your boyfriend, Arran Rush. I know all about him and where to find him. I knew if I waited with him that he would lead me to you. Which is exactly what happened. All I then had to do was pick my moment.'

'Leave Arran alone,' Alex shouted, his worst fears realised. 'He's done nothing to you. You've brought all of this on yourself.'

Maxim leaned towards Alex, his hand ready to deliver another backhander. Alex fell silent. 'How touching of you to defend him. But he's unfinished business for me and should count himself lucky he got a stay of execution to continue with his sick perverted life. But not for much longer. Tonight I will deal with him right after I've finished with you. In fact he'll have received your text by now, sent from your phone just as you were waking up. You told him you had a clue as to the whereabouts of bad boy Maxim and needed his help. Even if he's a little suspicious, he won't be able to resist your plea. I mean, you're the honeytrap—blond, handsome, Russian. And, in need. He'll come running. When he does, I'll be waiting for him. With you two queers roasting in Hell, the police case will fall apart and the gang freed for lack of evidence. And witnesses. But enough talk, he should be here in half an hour, which gives us just enough time to have that fun I promised you.'

Maxim dropped to his knees and crawled towards Alex, a lecherous grin on his face. His powerful muscles glided beneath a white t-shirt and grey sweatpants. Despite the chill, Alex began to sweat. He stiffened as Maxim eased out his body to lay alongside him and combed his hair with his fingers. 'Are you thinking back to all those times when you were looking at me? Wanting me? Did you wish my towel had slipped down to reveal all of me? Did you imagine what I looked like naked? I could feel your excitement when we wrestled. Well, tonight's your lucky night.'

Maxim reached over to the side of the makeshift bed. When he returned, his hand held a pair of rusty scissors. Alex squirmed to get away from him, his frantic efforts making his scar throb like mad.

He really was going to die.

'Don't make any sudden movement,' Maxim said. 'We wouldn't want a fatal accident now, would we? Not yet, anyway.' He chuckled as he cut away Alex's sweatshirt, exposing bare skin. Stroking Alex's chest with his fingers, he whispered in his ear. 'As it's just the two of us here, I don't mind telling you how I've dreamed about what it would be like to take you both, one after the other, sister then brother.'

Alex whimpered.

Maxim snaked an arm around Alex's neck. 'Is that excitement for me I hear? Patience, brother.'

Alex couldn't speak, consumed by thoughts of Arran. Alex had allowed himself to become a honeytrap for the man he loved. Of all the mistakes he'd made in his life, this was the biggest and would cost both of them their lives. Wracked by guilt, he no longer cared what happened to him. This was poetic justice. His punishment for leading others to their persecution and death. And just like them, he would be tossed into a dark hole, covered over and left to rot. Gone and forgotten. In wanting redemption for his sins, he'd never seriously imagined he would have to pay the ultimate price. His life.

Maxim flipped Alex over onto his stomach. Alex writhed around, not making it easy for him. Maxim used his body to press him down into the soiled blankets. Alex tasted the ingrained sweat. He felt Maxim's excitement, rubbing against him. His terror rose on feeling Maxim's fingertips creeping around his neck, stroking him. His lips brushed Alex's ear.

'You're such a dirty dog, Alexei, for making me do this to you. A dirty, rotten, treacherous dog. And bad dogs have to be put down. It's a kindness.'

Alex couldn't move. This was it for him. The end. He wanted it to come quickly. It even felt sensuous, the way Maxim's fingers gently caressed his skin, tightening and easing ... tightening and easing ... The caresses made his head feel light. Sending him floating away ... to a warm place ... where see through blue water was lapping onto silky sands ... A golden place where he would wait for Arran ...

Suddenly it vanished. He now found himself in a dark place. A great weight was pressing down on him. He couldn't see, couldn't hear.

He was dead.

Then the weight fell away and light entered. He started choking and crying. Despite what Maxim had said and done, he was going to let him live. Alex rolled onto his back and saw Arran. Not understanding, he turned and found the staring eyes of Maxim. Blood was pouring out of a wound to his skull. He wasn't breathing.

Maxim was dead.

The nightmare was over.

Alex had survived. Saved by Arran.

After Arran had cut away his bindings, Alex reached out a hand to him. There was no hesitation. Arran grabbed Alex and held him. Above them the first rays of light of a new day were scratching their way through the grimy skylight.

Author's Note

September 2020

In 2013, the Russian legislative assembly voted in a new law 'for the purpose of protecting children from information advocating for a denial of traditional family values', also known as the gay propoganda law and the anti-gay law. In effect, it gives the green light to the persecution of homosexuals. Since then, gangs have formed that roam the streets and parks in search of gays to abuse, beat and rob. Some gangs target gays online, arrange meets, and abduct them. They are taken to run down apartments where they are violently assaulted. In the UK, a 2014 Channel 4 Dispatches documentary, Hunted, provides a filmed report of the activities of the Russian anti-gay gangs. Svetlana's gang, in this novel, is based on such gangs that hunt gays for sport.

Although the gay village of Voho is real, sadly many of the places where the characters work and play are not. Boy Lane, the industrial area, Sydnee's boutique, the Sanctum, and Flesh are all made up. Bananas is based on a bar I used to frequent in Leeds, Yorkshire way back in the Nineties. Above it was a nightclub called Rockshots. Both are sadly missed.

The Russian Baths is remembered from one I visited in Budapest. The saunas are arranged with differing temperatures, and the pool room does have a vast shallow domed roof with pinpricks of light shining down from outside. It was one of the most relaxing experiences of my life. Almost spiritual.

Don't miss out!

Visit the website below and you can sign up to receive emails whenever MARK HOUSTON publishes a new book. There's no charge and no obligation.

https://books2read.com/r/B-A-FOLL-ZGRIB

BOOKS 2 READ

Connecting independent readers to independent writers.

www.ingramcontent.com/pod-product-compliance
Lightning Source LLC
Chambersburg PA
CBHW050026180626
46810CB00002B/597